Emma knew she had behaved like a wanton. What would he think of her?

She turned to flee the room, but Hugo was before her.

"There is nothing to fear. Pray believe me that I would never hurt you. You have no need to run from me."

Emma turned away. She was afraid of what she might see in his eyes.

"I will go," Hugo said quietly. He sounded strained. "I had hoped you would come to accept me, but I can understand how difficult it must be for a beautiful young woman like you, forcibly married to such a wreck of a husband. Perhaps, in time—"

Guilt engulfed her. "You are wrong, Hugo," she said in a low voice. "I am not afraid of you. And you are not—" In a whisper she continued, "But I *am* afraid of the way you make me feel."

* * *

Marrying the Major
Harlequin Historical #689—January 2004

**Harlequin Historicals is delighted
to introduce Mills & Boon author
JOANNA MAITLAND**

Marrying THE MAJOR

JOANNA MAITLAND

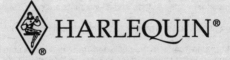

HARLEQUIN®

TORONTO • NEW YORK • LONDON
AMSTERDAM • PARIS • SYDNEY • HAMBURG
STOCKHOLM • ATHENS • TOKYO • MILAN • MADRID
PRAGUE • WARSAW • BUDAPEST • AUCKLAND

ISBN 0-373-29289-9

MARRYING THE MAJOR

Copyright © 2002 by Joanna Maitland

First North American Publication 2004

Printed in U.S.A.

Available from Harlequin Historicals and
JOANNA MAITLAND

Marrying the Major #689

Prologue

1805

Emma Fitzwilliam settled herself high in the branches of her favourite oak, glancing only a little ruefully at yet another tear in her cotton pinafore. She was not usually so clumsy. She would be well scolded for that when she returned to the house, but her punishment would be much worse if they discovered she still climbed trees. Her old governess was still trying vainly to make a lady of her. And Papa—dearest Papa—had lately said one or two things to suggest he was less than totally happy with the way she behaved.

Dearest Papa. For him, if he asked, she would *try* to become a lady, but it would be terribly difficult—and terribly boring. Ladies had to walk sedately instead of romping around the estate, they were never allowed out without an escort, they certainly could not go swimming in the lake, or fishing, or climbing trees—and they weren't even supposed to laugh out loud. Emma frowned at that last thought. Gentlemen were allowed to laugh—and frequently did—but ladies were supposed to smile demurely or, at most, give a melodious tinkle to signify amusement. It wasn't fair. Nor would it be fair to make her spend all her time at ladylike pursuits. Emma could play and sing pretty well, and even set a neat stitch, but she could not imagine doing so *all* the time, with only slow, boring walks for exercise, accompanied by a stony-faced groom. Ugh.

She wriggled about until she could reach into her pocket for her book and her apple. Then she settled down to read, munching blissfully. This was one of the pleasures of *not* being a lady—and she would not give it up.

'Young Lord Hardinge and his friend have called to see Miss Emma, sir,' intoned the butler gravely from the study doorway, 'but…no one is quite sure where she is. Shall I—?'

'Show them both in here, Godfrey,' said Sir Edward Fitzwilliam, rising from his deep wing-chair with a welcoming smile already on his cheery features. 'No doubt my daughter will appear soon enough. She seems to have some kind of sixth sense about welcome visitors—and unwelcome ones, too.' He laughed at his own wit, wondering, none the less, how it was that his mischievous daughter was never to be found except when it suited her. For Richard Hardinge, who was like a big brother to her, she probably would appear. She had been trailing him for years, after all, and Richard had never once rejected her, no matter how demanding she had become. Soon, it would all have to stop. Emma was fast maturing into a young lady—and young ladies did not cavort around the estate with male friends, no matter how trustworthy they might be, nor how indulgent her father. No—soon it would be necessary to find a proper female companion for his only daughter, to give her the polish that a young lady required, the polish that her dear mama would have provided if only she had lived.

Sir Edward sighed slightly at the sad memory, but assumed a polite smile when the door opened again to admit his two guests. The young men were remarkably alike, both tall and dark-haired, with open features and merry eyes. They seemed to have been laughing at some shared joke.

Richard Hardinge bowed politely to his host. 'I collect we have lost her again, sir,' he said with an ironic shake of the head. 'And Hugo was so anxious to make his farewells in due form, too.' Richard grinned at Hugo, who seemed to be unmoved by his friend's sly jibe.

'I suggest you both sit down,' said Sir Edward placidly, nodding in the direction of the old-fashioned sofa on the opposite side of the huge fireplace. 'She will appear, sooner or later.' He turned to Hugo Stratton. 'But I'm sorry to learn that you are leaving, my boy. I had understood from Lady Hardinge that you were to remain at Harding for a month or so yet.'

'That was so, sir,' said Hugo. 'Lady Hardinge was kind enough to invite me to stay for the summer—

until my commission came through. The thing is…well, sir, the fact is that my regiment is ordered to Deal next week—the rumour is that we are preparing for embarkation for north Germany—and unless I join them now, I'll have to wait for months, besides missing the chance of a crack at Boney.' His grey eyes were shining with enthusiasm as he spoke. 'I really do have to go, you see, sir. I'm leaving for home this afternoon.'

Sir Edward nodded sagely. He had seen enough of Hugo Stratton these past few weeks to recognise the makings of a good officer in him, in spite of his youth. 'I understand your haste, my boy. I was much the same at your age. In the circumstances, it's good of you to make the time to call on Emma. You must have a host of more important things on your mind.'

Hugo was still young enough to be able to blush. He stammered a little. 'After all your kind hospitality, sir, it is…the least I could do.'

'Think nothing of it,' said Sir Edward, 'nothing at all.' He rose and paced to the window, pulling back the heavy velvet curtains to gaze out on the deserted terrace and the sweeping lawns beyond. 'Drat the girl,' he said quietly to himself, 'where on earth is she?' He turned back to his guests, smiling apologetically. 'I can understand that time is pressing for you, so I will not attempt to detain you. Since Emma has not condescended to put in an appearance, she will have to make do with second-hand farewells. I will tell her you called, and why. Perhaps now she'll learn not to disappear quite so often.'

Hugo and Richard had risen politely with their

host. Hugo took a step forward. 'I still have half an hour, sir. May we not go and look for Miss Emma? She's bound to be in the garden somewhere—and Richard probably knows where to look. He should, after running tame round your estate for so many years.' This time, it was Hugo's turn to grin at his friend's discomfiture.

Sir Edward smiled indulgently at them. 'Very well, if you wish. But do not, on any account, allow that little minx's pranks to delay you beyond your time.'

The two young men were already making their way into the garden. Watching them, Sir Edward gave a weary shake of his head, 'Heaven help me. Whatever shall I do with such a hoyden?'

Emma was so deeply immersed in the fantastic adventures of the heroine of her novel that it took several minutes before the voices penetrated her concentration. Goodness—they were standing almost directly beneath her. She offered a quick prayer that they would not look up and sat as if frozen.

'Well, she's clearly not here,' said one voice with just a thread of irritation in it.

Emma immediately recognised Richard's voice—and the annoyance. They had been fast friends almost since she was in leading strings but, of late, he was a little less indulgent than before. Her father said that Richard was now too grown-up to bother with a grubby little hoyden, that once he finished university he would have no time at all for Emma. But Richard wouldn't do that, would he?

Emma opened her mouth to call down to Richard,

but thought better of it. Someone else was with him…

'When she doesn't want to be found,' said the second voice, 'she seems to disappear into thin air. I'd have expected you to go straight to her hiding-place, Richard. After all the time you've spent on this estate, you should know every nook and cranny.'

Emma smiled slightly at the second voice. It was Richard's friend Hugo Stratton, and he sounded more amused than annoyed. Hugo was not like Richard—except a little in looks, perhaps. Hugo did not treat Emma like a grubby little sister, to be teased and provoked. Hugo treated her almost like a lady.

Almost, she repeated to herself. For Hugo Stratton had a wicked sense of humour. He was quite capable of behaving like a perfect gentleman while secretly laughing at everyone around him. Only the decided glint in his eye betrayed his unholy glee—and Emma had quickly learned to look for that, before anything else.

But now, from her vantage point, all she could make out was the top of his head.

The tree shook suddenly, as if some giant had leaned heavily against it. It was only the wind, but Emma clutched at her book, loose in her lap, to prevent it from falling. She was too late to retrieve the apple core, though, which rolled down through the branches. Mercifully, it stopped, caught on a tiny twig a few feet below Emma's perch.

'I thought I did know all Emma's hiding-places,' said Richard's voice thoughtfully, 'but clearly not. The little brat has obviously been keeping something from me. And if we don't find her soon, she won't have a chance to see you before you go—and then she'll be fizzing mad.'

'Why should she be?' Hugo sounded puzzled. 'She hardly knows me.'

'With Emma, that's not the point. She may be only thirteen, but she believes she has a divine right to know everything about everyone round here—and to put in her two penn'orth. If you leave without saying goodbye, she'll ring a peal over me for ignoring her.'

'But she's only a child—'

'Only sometimes, Hugo. Sometimes, she sounds exactly like a Society lady. It's uncanny—especially since she still looks like a child, all dirt and scratches and tangles.'

'Maybe she's growing up,' said Hugo quietly.

'Now, that *would* be a pity,' replied Richard. 'We've had such fun together. She's a great sport, you know. Never complains about cuts and bruises, or getting wet and muddy when we go fishing. I can't imagine her as a young lady, all prim and proper and simpering—and clean!' He laughed aloud at that.

Emma did not pause to wonder why Hugo was leaving, for she was almost overcome by righteous anger at Richard's words. She was not *always* a grubby urchin as he seemed to believe and—

And then her eyes became riveted on the apple core. The tree was moving again, almost as if it were responding to Richard's laughter. The apple core had become half-dislodged and it was starting to slip…

She held her breath. For a long moment, there was silence.

'I wish I were going with you, Hugo,' said Richard, sounding suddenly very serious. 'But with m'father the way he is...'

'I know.' Hugo sounded sympathetic. 'But even if Lord Hardinge were not ailing, you still wouldn't be permitted to go, you know. There are times when I'm really glad I'm only a younger son. And this is one of them. My mother's brother has told me what great fun he had when he first joined the regiment. The older officers played all sorts of tricks on him of course—it's a bit like school, in that sense—but he had such adventures...'

'Yes, I know. You told me, remember?' Richard was more than a little envious of his friend's good fortune. Emma could hear it in his voice. As an only son, he would never be allowed to join the army.

'Where on earth can she be?' said Richard with a sudden burst of fury. 'You go and look in the orchard, Hugo. I'll search down by the river, but that's it. If we don't find her in the next ten minutes, we'll have to go. You can't afford to be late.' He thumped the tree in exasperation. 'Blast the brat. Why can she never behave?'

The apple core jumped just a fraction, hung suspended in mid-air for what seemed like seconds, and then disappeared down through the leaves.

Emma swallowed a gasp. Then, with a tiny shrug of her shoulders, she leaned towards the gap in the branches. She might as well give in gracefully. They were bound to find her now.

But Richard had gone, striding angrily across the lawn in the direction of the river.

Down below her, a sudden shout of laughter was quickly stifled. Hugo's voice, rippling with amusement, said quite clearly, 'Now, that *is* strange. My education must have been sadly at fault. I'd have sworn that this was an oak tree, but it's obviously an apple. Unless this is an oak-apple… Yes, that must be it. And the teeth-marks must have been made by a…a squirrel, I suppose. Very large squirrels they have on this estate. Next time, I'll bring my gun…'

Emma could have sworn she saw a flash of white teeth through the leaves. The next moment, Hugo was sprinting across the grass to the orchard, without once looking back.

She stuffed her book into her pocket and began to climb down, automatically finding the well-known footholds. Little brat, was she? Never clean? Well, she would show Richard Hardinge.

She raced across the lawn to the side door, raging inwardly all the while. With Nurse's help, she would be clean and ladylike in a trice—well, ten minutes, at most. She would appear as a prim, proper—and demure—young lady. She'd show him…*them*.

No. That wasn't fair. Hugo Stratton had not called her a grimy brat. Hugo had known perfectly well where she was, but he had just laughed—and flashed that wonderful smile…

Chapter One

1816

Emma Fitzwilliam slowed her chestnut mare to a relatively sedate trot just before she came in sight of the lodge gates. It was bad enough that she had ridden out without her groom. No need to make matters worse by galloping into the Harding estate like a mannerless hoyden.

She patted her blonde hair into place. Time to assume the role of the perfect lady—the role that she had long since learnt to don as easily as a pair of fine silk stockings.

Emma was longing to see Richard and his wife again. It was only a few months since the Earl and Countess Hardinge had left England for the Continent but, to Emma, it seemed like years. Surprisingly, given that Richard had been her childhood friend, it was his wife, nicknamed Jamie, whom Emma had really missed. The two women had become as close as sisters since Jamie's marriage. Letters had been exchanged, naturally, but that always meant delay; communications with France remained, at best, uncertain, even though the war had been over for nearly a year and Napoleon was now safely installed on St Helena.

There was nothing like a long, comfortable coze—and that was precisely why Emma had come.

She urged her mare to slightly greater speed.

As she rounded the corner of the house, Emma saw a little group of figures sitting on the lawn under the ancestral oak. She started towards them, but then paused, for Jamie was not there. Two men were sitting on a rug with a very small child, much hampered by his petticoats. Goodness, how Dickon had grown. Emma barely recognised her little godson. He must be nigh on a year old by now.

Dickon's anxious nursemaid was hovering as close as she dared, watching lest the clumsy males should mishandle her charge. Not much chance of that in Richard's case, Emma thought, for he doted on Dickon and spent much more time with his little son than most fathers did. The other gentleman, however, seemed not to have noticed the child. He was half-turned away, apparently gazing into the middle distance.

Emma screwed up her eyes against the glare to get a good view of the second man. She did not know him, she was sure, though she could see little more than his profile. He was dark, like Richard, but his lined face looked older and much more serious—rather austere, in fact, in Emma's opinion. She hoped, secretly, that she would not have to meet him. It would spoil the happiness of her day to meet a man who preached at her.

At that moment, little Dickon started to toddle towards the newcomer, holding out his arms and grinning toothily. His inarticulate squeals of joy at his own prowess carried across the lawn. The nursemaid started forward, arms outstretched to catch her darling before he fell. Richard—apparently unconcerned—smiled benignly. Dickon took two more steps, rocking unsteadily from one side to the other. His precarious balance was obviously beginning to desert him; his infectious grin was turning into the quivering lip that promised a wail of disappointment.

And then the stranger turned back towards the child, bending forward to catch him and lift him high in the air. In a matter of moments, Dickon was convulsed in shrieks of delighted laughter.

When, at last, the man moved to return the child to his father, Emma caught sight of his profile once more.

She could scarce believe what she saw. Why, he was almost like a different person. Playing with Richard's child had transformed the unknown from a harsh, forbidding man into someone much younger, someone whose face was alight with laughter and a flashing smile…and all because of one tiny child.

Emma suddenly felt as if she were eavesdropping on the visitor's innermost thoughts. Instinctively, she urged her mare towards the house.

The door opened well before she reached it. The butler stood waiting for her, his normally impassive countenance wreathed in smiles for the young lady who had been running around the Harding estate almost since she had learned to walk. 'Good day to you, Miss Emma. Her ladyship will be delighted to learn that you have called, I am sure. If you will just step into the blue saloon—'

'Oh, I don't think her ladyship would have us bother with such formality, do you, Digby?' Emma bestowed a dazzling smile on the butler. 'I'm sure I don't need to be announced.' Laying her whip and gloves on the hall table and lifting the generous skirts of her blue velvet habit with both hands, Emma started to run lightly up the stairs. 'I assume Lady Hardinge is in her sitting room?'

'Why, yes, ma'am,' the butler called up to the disappearing figure, 'but her ladyship is—'

Emma was not paying attention. She was much too keen to see her dearest friend again.

She knocked quickly and entered the Countess's sitting room without waiting for an invitation.

Lady Hardinge was seated on the low chaise longue by the bay window, looking out across the lawn towards the oak tree. 'Emma!' she cried delightedly. She started to rise from her place, leaning heavily on the back to push herself up. After a second or two, she abandoned the effort and sank back into the cushions. 'Forgive me, Emma. It is rather difficult to rise from this seat. You see—'

Emma flew across the room to embrace her friend. They hugged for a long time. Eventually, Emma stood back and said, in a voice of concern, 'Are you unwell, Jamie, that you cannot…?' Her words trailed into nothing as her eyes came to rest on Jamie's middle. 'Oh. I see,' she said, a little uncertainly, mentally calculating the months since she had last seen her friend. 'You did not tell me you were increasing before you left.' Emma regretted the words as soon as they were spoken. They sounded like an accusation.

'No,' agreed Jamie with a somewhat tired smile. 'I didn't—' she reached for Emma's hand '—because I wasn't.'

Emma looked at Jamie in disbelief. Surely she was at least six months gone?

'The midwife in Brussels said it was twins,' Jamie explained, 'and, judging by how tired I feel—never mind the size of me—I think she must be right.'

'Twins?' Emma sat down quickly on the footstool by the chaise longue. 'But—'

Jamie patted Emma's hand reassuringly. 'I know it sounds rather frightening, but I've had time to get used to it now. And it's not my first, remember...'

Emma forced herself to return her friend's smile. 'Congratulations, Jamie. I should have said so at once, but I was so...you looked so...'

Jamie laughed. 'Richard was at a loss for words, too, when I told him. I don't think I've ever seen him look so...so stricken. I told him there was nothing to worry about. I'm as strong as a horse. And I say the same to you, Emma. Don't worry. Please.'

Emma squeezed Jamie's hand. 'I promise I'll try not to. When is it...when are they due?'

'Ah, now, that is more difficult. In the autumn, I think, but the midwife said twins are always early, often by several weeks. So, I don't really know. Probably not before October.'

Emma's eyes opened wide. Jamie had sounded almost nonchalant. 'I see,' Emma said noncommittally. To be honest, she was not sure she really wanted to see at all. Marriage was bound to involve babies, of course, but it was such a dangerous business, besides being plaguey uncomfortable in the months before. Only a very special man would make it worth the pain and risk, in Emma's view. Jamie and Richard were a special case—they adored each other. But to marry a man one did not love...

Emma suddenly realised she had heard not a word of what her friend was saying. She shook her head to clear her thoughts. 'Forgive me, Jamie,' she said. 'I was wool-gathering. What were you saying?'

Jamie looked indulgently at her friend. 'I was telling you about our trip. There is so much devastation, Emma, you would be horrified to see it. Houses and villages in ruins, people in rags and starving. And everywhere, mutilated men begging for a crust. We helped where we could but... Honestly, Emma, I wept sometimes at what I saw. Oh, I know we had to defeat that tyrant, but the cost was so much more than any of us could have imagined.'

Emma nodded. 'Yes,' she said seriously. 'The beggars are in England now, too, and it seems that very few of us are grateful for their sacrifice. Papa said he saw several of them being driven out of town only last week. He has taken one of them on as a stable hand, but he was unable to do much for the others, unfortunately. The money he gave them will not last all that long.'

Jamie was silent for a space, thinking. 'Your father

is a good man,' she said at last. 'He cares for the weak.' She looked up suddenly, her eyes alight. 'We, too, have an extra hand in the stables now, a man to whom we owe a debt we can never repay. He helped save the life of Richard's dearest friend. Richard was sure he was dead on the battlefield. I never told you—for Richard asked me not to speak of it—but we went to Brussels in hopes of finding the grave. Instead, we found… Well, suffice it to say that Richard is over the moon at what has happened. He says that just finding Hugo alive is more than he had dared to hope for. Against that, it matters not a whit that—'

'Hugo? Hugo Stratton?' cried Emma, jumping up from her stool and knocking it over in her haste to reach the door.

'Why, yes,' replied Jamie, puzzled. 'You don't know him, do you? He's down in the garden with Richard and Dickon, but— Emma, wait!' Jamie was again trying to lever her ungainly bulk out of the chaise longue. By the time she had regained her feet, Emma was gone.

Emma raced across the lawn, berating herself at every step. How could she have failed to recognise Hugo Stratton, the man whose wickedly smiling face had haunted her girlish dreams for months on end? The identity of the stranger had burst upon Emma like an exploding star the moment Jamie had mentioned his name…

The little group was still sitting under the oak tree. Emma smiled to herself, deliberately slowing her pace to a more ladylike walk. How apt that they should meet again under an oak, even if not the same one. Emma had climbed Richard's oak, too, many and many a time when they were children. She knew it almost as well as she knew her own.

And much better than she knew Hugo Stratton.

What on earth was she going to say to him?

Emma gulped. Would he recognise her? She was a fine lady now, nothing like the grubby little brat he had generously allowed to tease him. She had been a mere child when Hugo left to join the army. To be honest, there was absolutely no reason why he should remember her at all, especially after all he had been through. And yet…

As Emma neared the little group, she saw that Dickon was now sound asleep in his father's arms. Richard looked proud and happy—and just a mite self-satisfied, too. Hugo was talking quietly to Richard, his back towards Emma. It seemed that neither was aware of her approach.

She hesitated. Then, noticing the enquiring look thrown at her by the nursemaid, she lifted her head a notch and marched across the lawn, arms swinging, skirts trailing unheeded on the warm grass.

'Why, Richard…' she began.

Richard, Earl Hardinge, rose to his feet in a single athletic movement, the child in his arms cradled snugly all the while. He smiled broadly, nodding sideways towards the nursemaid to come and relieve him of his son. He did not speak until he had carefully transferred his burden to her waiting arms. Even then, he still whispered.

'Emma. How wonderful to see you so soon. I had planned to call tomorrow…'

Richard's words were cut off as Emma threw her arms round his neck and kissed him heartily on the cheek. 'I could not wait to see you both…no, all three of you.' As Emma spoke, she became conscious that she had not included Hugo in that number—and that Hugo had not risen to meet her. Intrigued, she turned around.

Hugo was struggling to stand up, pushing an ebony cane into the soft turf in an effort to gain a purchase for his weak legs. His head was still bent, but Emma could see from the heightened colour on his neck how much the effort was costing him. How awful for him. He had been gravely wounded, clearly—Richard had thought him dead—and he was still not fully recovered. The explanation was simple enough—and obvious now she stopped to think about it. Probably it would be best to pretend that nothing was amiss.

Emma fixed her friendliest smile on her lips and waited for Hugo to regain his balance. When, at last, he seemed to have overcome his weakness, she began, cheerily, 'You may not remember me, Hugo, but I certainly remember the last time we met. I owe you a debt of gratitude for not betraying my presence to a certain mutual friend of ours—' she turned back to grin conspiratorially at Richard '—a friend who fails to understand the significance of apple cores.'

'I remember you very well indeed, Miss Fitzwilliam, and I was happy to be of service.'

His tone was flat and formal. And his use of her full name struck Emma almost like a blow. She whirled back round to look at this man who was so quick to reject the easy friendship she was offering.

Emma could not suppress an audible gasp. If only she had been prepared...

Hugo Stratton was nothing like the memory she had treasured. Gone was the handsome, eager young man who had smiled up into her favourite oak tree. Under his obviously new civilian clothes, this Hugo Stratton was thin and pinched, so weak that he could not stand upright without the help of a stick. The profile she had seen earlier was lined, right enough—but the lines were clearly lines of pain, not of joy or laughter. And, on the left profile that had been hidden from her, a thin purple scar ran from forehead to chin, bisecting his eyebrow and his cheek and continuing down below his collar. Heaven alone knew what damage lay below.

He stared her out. And he did not smile.

Emma swallowed hard and bowed her head politely, desperately trying to disguise the horror she instinctively felt. It was a full thirty seconds before she felt able to say, 'How do you do, Mr Stratton?'

Chapter Two

'I am so glad you have met Major Stratton again, Emma, since he will be staying with us for a time—while he recovers his strength.' Jamie was sitting on a high spoon-back chair in the first-floor drawing room, dispensing tea from a fluted silver pot and looking hopefully at her inarticulate guests.

Richard carried a cup to Emma with an encouraging smile. But Emma still could not bring herself to speak again. Out on the lawn, she had wished for the ground to open and swallow her up. Now her feet were resting on a priceless Aubusson carpet, but the feeling was the same. She stared at the delicate pattern, willing it to slide back beneath her chair.

The strained silence continued while Richard ferried tea to his friend, who was seated rather awkwardly on the sofa with his cane propped up beside him. His left leg did not seem to bend very well at the knee.

'Hugo—' began Richard.

'Major Stratton—' said Jamie at the same moment. Richard and Jamie broke off and grinned at each other, quite unabashed. Richard made a very grand bow, indicating that his wife should go first.

'Ignore him, both of you,' Jamie said. 'He's play-acting. Fancies himself to be dressed in a wasp-waisted satin coat and buckled shoes with red heels, making a leg like the veriest macaroni.'

Richard contrived to look pained. 'Nothing of the sort, wife,' he said. 'I was merely conceding the precedence that you have so often informed me is your due.'

His face was such a mixture of innocence and mischief that Emma found herself laughing along with Jamie.

But Hugo did not join in, Emma noticed. He seemed to have withdrawn into himself. And his tea sat untouched by his hand.

Emma decided then that it was up to her to make the attempt to draw him out. After all, her total want of manners had been the cause of severe embarrassment to Hugo. She must stop thinking about how badly *she* felt. Hugo's position was surely far, far worse.

'I am sure you will make excellent progress here, Major Stratton,' Emma said, trying to infuse her voice with as much warmth as she could. 'I know at first hand what attentive hosts Richard and Jamie can be. And the estate is a delight in summer.'

Hugo turned his head to look directly at Emma. There seemed to be a challenge in that look. It seemed, somehow, familiar. Now that she was beginning to see beyond his terrible scars, she could at last recognise something of the young man she had re-

membered so vividly. His hair was still glossy and
dark, his eyes still gleamed like polished steel, and
his generous mouth still looked as if it might smile
at any moment. But it did not. And his eyes remained
hard as they swept over Emma's figure. Emma detected not the slightest sign of approval of what he
saw. Probably he favoured taller women…or bru-
nettes.

'I am sure you are right, Miss Fitzwilliam,' replied
Hugo at last, 'especially about Lady Hardinge's hospitality, for which I am most grateful. As to the estate, I shall do my best, but as I am unable to ride or
to walk very far, I doubt I shall see all that much of
it.'

Emma was suddenly quite sure that Hugo was relishing her discomfiture. Embarrassment vanished, to
be replaced by an unwonted surge of anger. How
dared he? He obviously thought his wounds gave him
licence to behave outrageously. Well—she would
show him.

Emma smiled dangerously. 'I am sure that, with
time and Lady Hardinge's care, you will soon regain
your strength, Major. I pray it may be so. And, in the
meantime, you may fish and shoot to your heart's
content, may you not?'

'No.' He dropped his gaze so that Emma could no
longer see the expression in his eyes. 'I'm afraid not,
Miss Fitzwilliam. My left arm is much too weak for
either.'

'But I saw you throwing Dickon up in the air—'
Emma blurted out the words without stopping to
think. How tactless she was suddenly becoming.

'Dickon is not exactly a heavyweight, you know,' Hugo explained patiently. 'And besides, my good arm took most of the strain.'

Emma looked away. She could think of nothing to say to cover yet another appalling *faux pas*. She ought to apologise—but that would probably just make matters worse. What on earth had happened to the Emma who was held up to débutantes as a pattern-card of feminine grace and good manners? Emma cringed inwardly. Somehow, Hugo Stratton was making her forget all the lessons she had ever learned about how to be a lady in polite Society.

The chiming of the long-case clock in the hall broke the renewed silence.

'Good gracious,' said Emma, 'how late it is. I must go.' She rose quickly from her seat. 'I'm afraid I was so excited about seeing you all, that I failed to tell anyone where I was going. Papa will be worrying by now. I only hope he hasn't sent out a search party.' With an apologetic smile, she started for the door. 'Oh, pray, do not get up,' she said hastily, as both Jamie and Hugo struggled to rise. 'I know my way very well.'

Richard was only just in time to open the door for her.

By the time Richard returned from escorting Emma to the stables, Hugo was alone in the drawing room, leaning against the folded wooden shutter for support as he gazed out across the park.

'Miss Fitzwilliam has an excellent seat,' Hugo said as Richard joined him at the long window.

'Mmm,' agreed Richard. 'Almost as good as Jamie's. Where is my wife, by the way?'

'Lady Hardinge went upstairs to rest. She was rather tired by all the excitement, she said.' Hugo could not drag his eyes from Emma's retreating figure. The urchin had become a real beauty. Her manners were not exactly faultless, but her behaviour was certainly a remarkable improvement on the impossible child he remembered. Besides, she had been doing her best to conceal how repulsive she found him—which could not have been easy. He should not judge her.

Richard put a hand on his friend's shoulder. 'What say we adjourn to the library, Hugo? It's more comfortable down there, and there's some decent madeira.'

Hugo half-turned from the window. Emma was just passing out of sight into the trees. 'I'd rather not, if you don't mind,' he said softly, with a note of apology in his voice. 'It will soon be time to go upstairs to change for dinner, and—'

'And your host has the manners of a boor to wish to condemn you to incessant stair-climbing. I'm sorry I was so thoughtless, Hugo.' He crossed to the bell-pull. 'I'll have the madeira brought up here.'

Hugo looked at his friend and smiled warmly. He owed Richard so very much—and Lady Hardinge, too. Who else would have taken in the wreck of a man that he had become?

'How long is it since you last saw Emma?' said Richard, dropping on to the sofa and stretching out his long legs.

Hugo limped slowly across the room to join his friend, noting that Richard now knew better than to make any attempt to help him. 'More than ten years.' He lowered himself awkwardly on to the spoon-back chair that Lady Hardinge had vacated, grateful for its relatively high seat. 'In fact, it was the day I left Harding to join my regiment. I could never forget that. I was so excited—so certain of adventure, and glory, and...' Hugo's words trailed off into heavy silence.

Nothing more was said until the butler had received his orders and returned with the tray of refreshments.

Pouring out the madeira, Richard showed a renewed determination to be cheerful. 'So, what do you think of Emma now? You have to admit, she's changed.'

Hugo nodded. 'She didn't have the look of a beauty then, certainly.'

Richard laughed. 'How could you tell, under all that dirt?'

Hugo raised an eyebrow. 'Your memory is at fault, old friend. By the time we actually saw her that day, she was really quite clean. And remarkably well behaved, considering she'd been skulking up trees.'

'Had she?' Richard drank his madeira thoughtfully. 'You may be right about that day. I'm afraid I don't actually remember it very well at all. Emma's been around for so long that all my early memories of her tend to merge. She was always there, always ready for anything, and always dirty. Until her father took her in hand and insisted she learn to be a lady.

By the time of her come-out, she was totally transformed. A blonde beauty—with faultless manners for every occasion. I was quite sorry, in a way. I was very fond of her mischievous spirit. I miss it.'

Hugo said nothing. Richard spoke as if Emma had been moulded into a completely different person, a sort of beautiful automaton. What made him think that Emma's mischievous spirit had been extinguished? Surely, having known her so long, he could see that Emma was still the same person under her conventional façade? Wasn't it obvious?

'In one way, though, she is still the same girl,' Richard continued after a moment. 'Can't tell you how many offers she's had, but she's refused them all. She's already mistress of her own household, of course, and a considerable heiress to boot, so she can afford to be choosy—though I fancy Sir Edward is beginning to worry that he'll never see his grandchildren. He still dotes on her. And she knows exactly how to wind him round her little finger—just as she does with almost every man she meets. She may have perfect manners—but I warn you that she's highly accomplished at getting her own way.'

'Sir Edward may have hoped that *you* would offer for his daughter,' said Hugo. 'After all—'

'I did think of it at one time,' interrupted Richard, looking slightly embarrassed. 'But then I met Jamie...'

Hugo nodded. Marriage to Emma Fitzwilliam would have been a business arrangement, a marriage of convenience, whereas Richard's marriage to Jamie was a union of two souls. Hugo took a deep breath and closed his eyes in sudden pain. He envied Richard his happiness. There was no point in denying that, not to himself. Once, he too might have hoped to marry for love—but now he would never marry at all. Love—and children—were not for him. No woman would have a disfigured cripple—especially one whose honour was as scarred as his body. The best he could hope for would be a comfortable home and kindly servants to wait on him. At least he had wealth enough to secure that, and his own independence. He would make a life for himself, somehow, however much the world might shun him. He would learn to survive alone.

Emma was sure Hugo was watching her from the house, but she refused to turn in her saddle or to increase her pace. He would not be allowed to see how much their meeting had unnerved her.

'Just a few yards more, Juno,' she said, stroking her mare's glossy neck, 'and we'll be hidden by the trees. Then we'll take the shortcut home across the fields. I think we could both do with a good gallop.'

The chestnut's ears twitched in response, as if she understood.

Emma continued to stroke the mare's neck absently, allowing the horse to make her own way along the familiar route from Harding to Longacres. There was something niggling in the back of Emma's mind, a fleeting memory about Hugo Stratton, but she could not catch it. Like a soap bubble in the bath, it floated out of reach every time she tried to grab for it.

'Oh, fiddlesticks,' groaned Emma, deliberately swallowing the curse that had risen automatically to her lips. 'I've let him see enough bad manners for one day. I'd better practise being a lady for the rest of it. Once I reach home, at least…' She dug her heel into Juno's flank. 'Come on then, Juno,' she urged. 'Let's show them what you can do.'

The chestnut flew across the grass as though the devil were at her heels. By the time they reached the stable yard, Juno was in a lather—and Emma was gasping for breath. But at least they had lost no more time.

'Where on earth have you been, Miss Emma?' cried the grizzled old groom, dashing out of the stables to grab Juno's bridle. 'Your father's worrying fit to burst. He—'

Emma slid from the saddle and stopped the old man's tirade with an apologetic smile and a touch on his arm. 'One of the keepers told me Lord Hardinge was back from London—so I called in at the house. It was on my way—more or less,' she added, hoping she was not blushing. 'But I stayed too long. Is Papa very worried?'

'Well—he hasn't started scouring the woods yet, Miss Emma, though I dare say he might have done, in another hour or so. If only you wouldn't ride out alone, Miss Emma…'

Emma grinned. 'Look after Juno for me, please,' she said. 'I'd better present myself for inspection, to prove I'm all in one piece.' Looping the tail of her habit over her arm, Emma hurried up to the house and her father's study.

'Emma!' he cried, the moment she appeared in the doorway.

Emma could hear the note of concern in his voice. Oh, dear. First, she had upset Hugo, and now her father.

She ran to him, wrapped her arms tightly round his neck and kissed his cheek. 'Forgive me, Papa, for being so thoughtless. I went to visit Richard and… and I'm afraid I lost track of time. I'm sorry you were worried.'

Her father cleared his throat rather loudly. 'Emma, if you would only take a groom with you, I'd have no cause to worry. Why don't you—?'

Emma fixed her wide blue gaze on her father's face. 'Oh, Papa, must I? Don't you think I can ride well enough to be trusted out on my own?'

'It's not that—and you know it,' he responded gruffly, removing each of her arms in turn. 'The very best of riders can be caught out. That includes you, Emma.'

He was right. Even Juno had been spooked on occasion by a strange noise or a sudden movement.

Emma kissed her father a second time. 'I'll try to be good, Papa, I promise,' she said. His answering smile told her she had won him round yet again. He was easily satisfied.

'Well,' he said, settling himself back in his favourite chair, 'tell me about Richard. Is he well? And little Dickon? Did you see Lady Hardinge, too? I dare swear she is worn out, after all that travelling.'

'They are all very well, Papa. And Dickon has grown so much that you will not recognise him. He is starting to walk, too. Jamie is…' Emma hesitated. 'Jamie is…increasing again. The midwife says it will be twins.' Her words all came out in a rush.

'Twins?' echoed Sir Edward. 'Oh, my… Oh, dear…'

Emma could see that he was thinking back to the loss of his own wife, when Emma was born. Emma sat down beside him and patted his hand. 'Don't worry, Papa. Jamie says she's as strong as a horse. And it's not as if it's her first…' Emma's voice tailed off once more. What a stupid thing to say, reminding her father that first babies—like Emma—were by far the most dangerous. What was the matter with her today? Her brain seemed to be scrambled.

'You'll never guess who is staying at Harding, Papa.' Emma changed the subject with exaggerated cheerfulness.

Sir Edward smiled a little wanly. 'Tell me,' he said.

'Hugo Stratton. *Major* Hugo Stratton. Do you remember him?'

Sir Edward nodded. 'Yes, I do. A Major, eh? Well, I'm not at all surprised. I thought he had the makings of a good officer, even then. Let me see—how many years is it since he joined the colours? Eight?'

'Nearly eleven, Papa,' said Emma.

'Really? Strange that he hasn't made Colonel, then,' said Sir Edward, half to himself. 'Though he'd have to compete with all those fellows buying their promotions, I suppose. There aren't that many field promotions, even in wartime. And a majority is still something to be proud of.'

'Papa, I don't understand. What is wrong with being a Major?'

'Nothing, my dear, nothing. I'm sure Major Stratton has had a distinguished career. He's sold out now, I suppose?'

'I…I don't know, Papa. He…he has been badly wounded. I'm not sure how, or when. He walks with a limp and has to use a cane. And he…his face is horribly scarred, Papa.' Her father's shock was evident. 'Oh, I'm sure it will look better in time but, at the moment…'

Suddenly, Emma's eyes filled with tears. 'Oh, Papa, I've done such a dreadful thing. I didn't know, you see. And when I saw Hugo, I got such a shock that I…I embarrassed him terribly, staring at his scars. I couldn't tear my eyes away. And Hugo was insulted. He could hardly bring himself to speak to me. Oh, Papa, I'm so ashamed. What shall I do?'

Sir Edward patted her shoulder consolingly. 'You must apologise,' he said quietly.

'I tried to, but I couldn't get the words out, not when he was staring me out with those hard grey eyes of his. And now, it's too late to say anything. That would only make matters worse.'

He offered her his handkerchief. 'You may be right, my dear.' He paused to pull at his ear lobe, as he always did when he was worrying about something. 'Well, if you cannot tell him you are sorry, you must show him, go out of your way to help him to…to come to terms with his injuries. Can you do that, do you think?'

Emma nodded dumbly and wiped her eyes, feeling

more ashamed than ever. She never lost control. She had always prided herself on that. And she *never* allowed herself to cry—especially not in front of her papa. He liked her to be gay, and cheerful, and...and strong-minded. As she would be again.

Even with Major Hugo Stratton.

Chapter Three

'No. I could not accept.'

Jamie cast an imploring look towards her husband. She had clearly exhausted her own arguments and was desperate for him to intervene.

'Hugo, please reconsider,' Richard said seriously. 'The Fitzwilliams are our oldest friends. They will be very hurt if you refuse.'

'I have absolutely no intention of providing a raree-show for Miss Fitzwilliam and her dinner guests, Richard. Acceptance is out of the question. Now, if you will excuse me…' Hugo limped towards the door. 'My apologies to you, ma'am,' he said as he opened it, 'if my refusal creates difficulties for you with your friends. But my mind is made up. I will not attend.' He closed the door quietly behind him.

'Oh, dear.' Jamie's shoulders had slumped. 'How will we ever persuade him to return to Society if he will not attend even a small dinner amongst friends?'

Richard shook his head sadly. He hated to see his wife so upset. 'I don't know, my love. I really don't. I'd ask Emma to talk to him—but, after yesterday's

encounter, he seems to wish to avoid her completely.'
He started to pace. 'I had better ride over to Longacres to warn Emma, though, before she receives
Hugo's note. If she learns of his refusal by letter, we
really will be in the suds.'

'Tell her how hard we tried, Richard,' said Jamie,
a little wearily.

'I will—but she will know that without my telling
her. Remember, she knows *you*.' Richard bent to
place a gentle, lingering kiss on his wife's lips.
'Don't worry, my love. Even if we can't resolve this
now, it will soon blow over. And Hugo is bound to
become less sensitive—eventually.'

That thought remained with Richard throughout
his ride across his own estate to Sir Edward's. Hugo
was as stubborn as a mule—and stiff-necked besides,
as well as proud, touchy, exasperating... Richard
could have continued with his list for some time, but
he did not. Hugo was a good man, and a good friend,
who had suffered a great deal during his years as a
soldier. With time, his testiness would mellow—
probably.

'Richard!'

Emma was almost upon him before Richard realised that she was there. Damn! He hadn't yet worked
out how he was going to explain to her about Hugo's
refusal.

Emma was too full of her own laudable aims to
notice that there was anything amiss with Richard.
'You weren't coming to visit me, were you, Richard?' she asked brightly. 'No need, for I am before

you. And since I have already covered a much greater distance than you, it would be ungentlemanly in you to expect me to retrace my steps—' she smiled like the cheeky child she had once been '—would it not?'

Richard's answering smile was a little forced, Emma thought. Perhaps he had been coming to remonstrate with her in private about her unacceptable treatment of Hugo. He had cause, but she would not permit any man to lecture her. 'To tell you the truth, Richard,' began Emma, more seriously now, and determined to make a clean breast of her failings, 'I was hoping for a chance to talk to Hugo, to apologise for my behaviour yesterday—' that was not quite true, she realised '—or, at least, to try to show him that I mean us to be friends again. It was just that I…I was unprepared for the change in him. I—'

'Jamie did try to warn you, Emma.' Emma recognised Richard's 'big brother' voice. 'If you hadn't rushed out so quickly—'

'I know. And I'm sorry, Richard. Truly.' Emma tried to look contrite, but she knew she was not making a very good fist of it. She was going to make amends. Surely that was enough? 'However, once Hugo has been introduced to all his old friends, he will have no more cause for concern. I shall visit all the guests before the dinner party to warn them so that—'

'Hugo refuses to attend, Emma.'

'No! He wouldn't! He—'

'He's adamant, Emma. That's what I was coming to tell you.' Richard was looking away suddenly, unable to meet Emma's eye. 'He…he thinks you invited him in order to use him as a sort of…' He cleared his throat rather too noisily. 'He hates to be stared at,' he finished at last.

Emma was shocked, then disbelieving, then angry when the import of Richard's words sank in. She urged her mare into a trot. 'So that's what he thinks of me,' she said hotly. 'Well, let's see if he has the gall to say so to my face. How dare he assume—?'

'Emma.' Richard caught up with her and laid a hand on her arm. 'Emma, calm down. Please. If you fly up into the boughs with Hugo, he'll probably pack his bags and leave. And considering the trouble we had in persuading him to come here in the first place—' Richard broke off suddenly. From the look on his face, Emma fancied her friend had said more than he intended.

Emma slowed Juno to a gentle walk, forcing Richard to do the same. 'Richard,' she said earnestly, 'I don't really understand what is going on. I know I behaved unpardonably yesterday; and I do want to set matters right. That was why I persuaded Papa to hold a little dinner party for Hugo. I thought he… Well, no matter what I thought. Obviously, I was wrong. From what you say, it seems as if it's more than just… Oh, I know the scars are dreadful, but surely they will fade?'

Richard hesitated for several moments. 'Hugo has changed a great deal, Emma. It's more than just his wounds, I think, but he will not speak of his experiences, even to me, his oldest friend. Jamie had the devil's own job persuading him to come to Harding at all. He was set to bury himself on a rundown manor miles from anywhere.'

'Oh.' Emma did not know what to say. Nothing in her upbringing had prepared her to deal with a man like Hugo Stratton.

'Perhaps it would be best if you didn't come to Harding for a day or two, Emma. Give Hugo time to come down from his high horse.'

'Of course, I...' As she spoke the words politeness demanded, Emma knew instinctively that they were wrong. 'No,' she said flatly. 'I shan't give him time to persuade himself that I am a heartless trophy-hunter. I was *not* planning to put him on display, as he seems to think, and I intend to make him admit as much.' She shook her head in frustration. 'Devil take the man,' she said fiercely. 'Can't he see that I'm trying to help him?'

Emma's resolution had all but deserted her by the time she finally caught sight of Hugo among the trees. He had walked much further from the house than she had expected. Judging from his painfully slow pace, it must have taken a very long time to come this far.

Emma swung the tail of her claret-coloured velvet habit over her arm and hurried down the woodland path to intercept him. She knew she was looking her best in her new habit and jaunty little hat, and she was determined not to make a mull of this second meeting.

'Major Stratton.' She smiled encouragingly at Hugo's tense figure. He had stopped at the sight of her. She stepped forward to meet him, holding out her gloved hand. 'Good morning to you,' she said, refusing to be daunted by his hard gaze and willing her hand not to shake.

Eventually, Hugo transferred his cane to his left hand and quickly shook Emma's hand. 'Good morning, ma'am,' he replied.

Emma could detect no trace of warmth in his deep voice, nor any hint that he wished to prolong their encounter. But she would not cry off now. 'I see that I was wrong to take you at your word yesterday, sir,' she began in as light-hearted a tone as she could muster.

He threw her a sharp glance from beneath frowning brows before busying himself once more with his walking cane.

'You told me you could not walk very far, did you not? But I find you a considerable distance from the house. I collect you have been bamming me, sir.' She looked straight at him then, letting him see the smiling challenge in her eyes.

He returned her gaze frankly for what seemed an age, but she could read nothing of his thoughts.

'Even cripples may improve, ma'am,' he said quite softly. 'The more I walk, the more I shall be able to walk. Would you have me lie down and moulder away?'

'No, certainly not. How could you think it?'

The tiniest smile crossed Hugo's lips as she spoke.

Emma's temper snapped like the dry twigs beneath her boots. 'Oh, you are quite impossible, Hugo Stratton, all thin skin and stiff-necked pride. You imagine

that everyone is relishing your misfortunes or repelled by your scars. You believe that I invited you
to my father's house in order to provide cheap entertainment for my other guests. You think—' She
shook her head so sharply that the long red feather
on her hat whipped at her cheek. 'Whatever you
think, you are wrong,' she continued quietly as he
made to speak. 'When I was a child, you were my
friend. I wanted us to continue to be friends—so
much so that, as soon as I realised who was sitting
with Richard and Dickon, I dashed out to meet you
without listening to what Jamie was trying to tell me.
So—yes—I was shocked when I saw you. And I...I
wish to apologise for my rudeness. I hope you will
forgive me.'

Was there a slight softening in Hugo's stern features? Emma ventured a small smile. 'I hope we can
still be friends.'

Hugo sighed softly. 'I am no longer the boy you
knew, Miss Fitzwilliam,' he said at last.

'No,' replied Emma, 'but I do not believe that it
changes matters.'

Hugo raised his good eyebrow. 'Indeed?'

There was something about that quirked eyebrow... Years before, it had always been accompanied by a gleam of hidden laughter...

'Major Stratton—' Emma stared at Hugo through
narrowed eyes '—I declare you are laughing at me.'

Clearly, she must be wrong, for there was not the
slightest trace of amusement in his face as he took a
menacing step towards her. Emma retreated auto-

matically, but the heel of her riding boot caught on her trailing hem, throwing her off balance.

A strong right arm saved her. In that same moment, Emma heard Hugo's cane clatter against the granite rocks alongside the path.

Emma found she was gasping for breath, like a winded fighter. The arm supporting her felt immensely strong, much too strong for Hugo's emaciated frame. It felt warm, too, and somehow gentle. How strange that—

'Are you all right, ma'am?'

Hugo's question brought Emma back to earth. At last, that cold, hard edge had gone from his voice.

Emma used her free hand to pull her trailing skirt from under her heel. The skin of her other arm was beginning to heat within Hugo's sustaining grasp. The glowing warmth was like nothing she had ever experienced before.

'Miss Fitzwilliam?'

Emma blushed rosily. What was she thinking of? 'Thank you, Major,' she said. 'Your prompt action prevented me from becoming an undignified heap on this path. I am most grateful.' She smiled up at him through her lashes, forcing herself to maintain the expression even when he withdrew his hand from her arm. 'If you will permit me to say so, sir, you are much stronger than you look,' she added saucily.

Hugo grinned briefly and, Emma fancied, somewhat ruefully. 'Needs must when the devil drives, ma'am,' he said. 'With only one good arm, I could not have lifted you from the ground, you know. So I had no choice but to stop you while I still could.'

Emma stared at him in frank amazement. Was he actually laughing at himself? This time she could not be mistaken, surely?

She stooped quickly to retrieve his cane—and to hide her whirling thoughts from his penetrating eyes. She could not begin to understand him. Her childhood friend was still there—somewhere—but, overlaid on the young Hugo there was the oddest chameleon of a man...

'Your cane, Major.' Straight-faced, she handed it to him.

'Thank you, ma'am,' he said politely. There was a moment or two of awkward silence between them. Then Hugo surprised her yet again by saying, 'I was about to return to the house, as it happens. If it would not be too tedious for you, I would welcome your company for a space.'

Emma nodded in astonished agreement. What had come over him? He sounded—

'I am only sorry,' Hugo continued in the same polite tones, 'that I cannot offer you my arm.' He flourished his cane with his right hand as he spoke.

Emma smiled to herself but said nothing. For twenty minutes, they walked slowly along the path in companionable silence. The pine needles and the previous season's dry leaves crunched beneath their feet. A faint scent of crushed pine rose up around them. A woodpecker was drumming in the distance.

By the time Emma had worked out what she needed to say, they had reached the edge of the wood. From there, the long path led straight up to

the stables and the house. They were now in full view
of anyone watching from the windows.

Emma stopped under the last oak tree, waiting for
Hugo to turn back to her. She smiled at him in wide-
eyed innocence, hoping for even the slightest hint of
a response. With most men, she knew exactly what
reaction to expect, but Hugo was totally unpredictable.

At last, his gaze seemed to soften the merest fraction.

'Major,' she said gently, 'I do hope you will accept
our dinner invitation.' He started to frown, but she
hurried on. 'It is to be a very small affair, you know,
just ourselves and the Hardinges...and a few old
friends. You remember the Rector and Mrs Greenwood, I'm sure, and Mrs Halliday? I know they
would all like to meet you again.' She dropped her
gaze and let her voice sink a little more. 'I promise
you that all of them are much better-mannered than
I. You will not be embarrassed.'

Emma could feel the heat of a flush on her face
and neck. She did not dare to raise her eyes.

'How can I possibly refuse?' said Hugo quietly.

Emma looked up at last to see that he was limping
slowly back to the house. She had won.

But she had guaranteed Hugo would not be embarrassed in her house. Could she ensure that her
promise was kept?

Chapter Four

Hugo lay back on his pillows and gazed out through the open bed-curtains at the first faint glimmerings of the dawn. Years of living in the Peninsula had taught him to love the huge expanse of the night sky and the unchanging patterns of the stars. He would never again permit drawn curtains to shut them out—or to shut him in.

Gingerly, he raised his injured left arm so that he could clasp his hands behind his head. That simple movement, never before achieved, gave him profound satisfaction. Yes, he was making progress—a little progress.

He focused on the day ahead—and on the evening. He was a fool to have accepted her invitation. It would mean nothing but embarrassment for him; and the usual expressions of pity and horror at his injuries. But she had been so apologetic about their disastrous first meeting. And, for just a single moment, she had made him feel like a whole man again.

Hugo groaned aloud. It would not do to remember Emma too clearly. Her figure-hugging riding habit would have fired any man's blood; and that long feather had reached down from her saucy little hat, caressing the soft bloom of her cheek like a lover's hand. He had known that she was working her wiles on him—but, even as he recognised how artfully she was using her huge blue eyes, he had found himself unable to resist them.

The hoyden child had become a siren woman.

Hugo closed his eyes once more, trying to shut out Emma's persistent image. It would not do for him to think too kindly of her. She was a spoilt, flirtatious little minx—in some respects she had not changed one jot—and she obviously enjoyed making a May game of every man she met. How many offers had she rejected out of hand? Richard had not said precisely, but there had certainly been quite a number. And, in spite of such behaviour, she was still the toast of London Society, with every eligible male dangling after her.

Hugo's weak arm was now very stiff. He straightened it with difficulty, and some pain, which reminded him that he, at least, was far from eligible.

Hugo leant back in his chair, his right hand playing idly with his glass of port. So far, at least, the Longacres dinner party had passed off much better than he had dared to hope. None of the guests had stared; and no one had embarrassed him in any way, not even by offering to help him on the stairs. Clearly, Emma had been as good as her word. Hugo felt himself warming to her even more. She might be a little spoilt—just a very little, he had now decided—but she could be thoughtful, and kind. She was upstairs now with the ladies, where she would be dispensing coffee with that radiant smile of hers, and ensuring that every one of her guests felt she had been singled out for special attention.

Exactly as he had felt, when he arrived with the Hardinges.

Naturally, Emma's first priority had been Lady Hardinge, but she had welcomed Hugo with gentle words, and with warmth in her eyes and in the clasp of her hand. He had had leisure, then, to admire her from a distance while she settled Lady Hardinge into a comfortable chair in the saloon, putting extra cushions in the small of her back. It was no wonder that Emma had become the toast of London Society, he had concluded; her radiant golden beauty would have ensured her success, even if she had been penniless. Tonight, she was glowing in a simple gown of cream silk, with a posy of forget-me-nots at her bosom, their clear blue serving only to point up the intense colour of Emma's eyes. Hugo found himself envying the man who would win her.

'Don't you agree, Hugo?'

Richard was speaking. But what had he said? Hugo raised his glass and sipped, savouring the rich sweetness for a moment. Then he smiled a little ruefully. 'Forgive me, Richard. I was miles away. What did you say?'

Richard shook his head. 'I never had you down for a dreamer, Hugo—except about adventures, of course.'

'That was a long time ago, I fear,' Hugo responded

neutrally. These last few days, Richard had begun to make oblique references to their shared past and to Hugo's years of soldiering. It was necessary, Hugo knew, and he was grateful to Richard for his tact.

'As it happens,' Richard continued with barely a pause, 'we were talking of the Derby. Sir Edward's Golden Star is being heavily backed at Tatt's. Is that not so, sir?' He turned to his host at the head of the table.

Sir Edward paused in the act of refilling his own glass. 'I'm afraid so,' he smiled. 'Odds are terrible. I wouldn't hazard your blunt on him now, Major, even if he is the favourite. There's no such thing as a certain winner for the Derby, as I know to my cost. You'd get better odds on one of the others. Try Grafton's nag. After all, his horse won last year. Can't remember what this one's called…something foreign, I fancy.'

'Alien,' put in the Rector from further down the table. Beyond him, young Mr Mountjoy nodded eagerly.

Hugo suppressed a chuckle at the thought of such precise knowledge coming from a gentleman in clerical bands. The Reverend Greenwood had been an avid man of the turf in his youth and made no secret of his continuing interest, even though he had long ago ceased to place bets himself. 'Thank you, sir,' said Hugo. 'And is he worth a wager, in your opinion?'

'Possibly,' said the Rector doubtfully, 'though I prefer Nectar myself. But if Golden Star is on form, he'll show them all a clean pair of heels, you mark my words. I suppose Alien might be good for a place, though.'

'Thank you, sir,' said Hugo again. 'I think I'll save my blunt for better odds.'

'You're probably very wise, Major,' said Sir Edward, nodding. 'But I hope you'll join our party to Epsom, none the less. It promises to be a very jolly affair. Richard is coming, are you not, Richard?'

Richard looked suddenly somewhat disconcerted. 'Well, sir,' he began, 'I'm not exactly certain. I…Jamie's condition…'

Sir Edward reddened visibly and cleared his throat. 'Beg pardon, Richard,' he said gruffly. 'I'm afraid I—' He rose abruptly from his chair, without draining his glass. 'I fear we are neglecting the ladies. Shall we adjourn to the drawing room, gentlemen?'

Hugo allowed all his companions to move out ahead of him, so that he would be the last to mount the stairs.

Emma was deep in conversation with Mr Mountjoy when Hugo gained the drawing room. As houseguests of the Rector, the young man and his sister had had to be invited, even though they were not close friends of the Fitzwilliams. Hugo could see that the brother appeared to be much taken with Emma—for, although he was conversing with animation, his eyes held the slightly dazed look that tended to afflict very young men on first meeting a ravishing beauty. Hugo himself had been the same—a lifetime ago.

Miss Mountjoy rose from the pianoforte and

crossed the room to join her brother. 'Oh, Miss Fitz-william,' she began impulsively, 'this is such a lovely room—just made for dancing. Might we not make up a set? It would be such fun.'

For a moment, Emma seemed to be at a loss for words. Hugo thought he could see the beginnings of a flush on her neck.

Mr Mountjoy beamed at his sister's suggestion. 'Why, that would be wholly delightful,' he said. 'I should be honoured if you would consent to partner me, ma'am.'

Emma's flush was mounting. Hugo wondered how she would respond to her young guests' highly improper proposal without embarrassing them. Lady Hardinge could not dance, given her condition. The Rector's wife and Mrs Halliday would probably view such an impromptu affair with stern misgivings. That left only Miss Mountjoy herself—and Emma.

'Well…' began Emma doubtfully.

Lady Hardinge intervened. 'I'm afraid I am not able to dance myself,' she said with a mischievous twinkle in her eye, 'but I would gladly play for those who can.'

That settled it, for no one would gainsay the Countess. Hugo saw that Emma was both relieved and sorry. However, she said nothing more on the question, merely turning her attention to ensuring the servants set about rolling back the Turkey carpet.

Hugo tried to avoid Miss Mountjoy's hopeful glances. In spite of her youth—and his disfigure-ment—she had clearly marked him down as the only bachelor in the room. She was pretty enough, but incredibly gauche—seemingly she did not begin to grasp that country dances were quite beyond Hugo's capabilities at present.

Richard came again to the rescue. 'My wife may have excused herself from dancing,' he said brightly, 'but that is no reason why I should deny myself the pleasure. Will you honour me, Miss Mountjoy?'

The sudden glow on the girl's features suggested that she had never before been led into the dance by a peer of the realm.

Two couples looking somewhat sparse, Sir Edward offered his hand to his old friend, Mrs Halliday. Then Lady Hardinge struck up the opening chord and, in no time, the set was forming and re-forming.

Hugo crossed to the instrument to offer to turn for her ladyship.

As he bent forward, she said softly, 'I hope you will forgive me, Major—but Miss Mountjoy does not really know how to go on. She is so very young...' Her voice trailed off.

'So young that you stepped in to save her blushes—as Richard saved mine,' said Hugo warmly. 'You are, both of you, most thoughtful, ma'am. Miss Mountjoy may be too unschooled in the ways of the world to collect what was done for her, but I certainly am not. Thank you.'

'Major Stratton—now you attempt to put *me* to the blush,' said Lady Hardinge with mock severity, 'besides distracting me from my task. Emma will upbraid me roundly if I fail to keep time.'

Hugo smiled down at her, even though she was looking at her music rather than at him. Her playing was expert—not a note out of place. He was lucky to have such friends.

At the end of the set, Miss Mountjoy came rushing back to the pair at the pianoforte. 'Oh, Lady Hardinge, that was such fun. Thank you so much. You played quite beautifully.'

Her brother appeared at her elbow, echoing her thanks. 'Could you be persuaded to just one more set, ma'am?' he continued. 'This is terrifically good sport.'

Lady Hardinge nodded and began to leaf through the music on the instrument.

Mr Mountjoy was clearly remembering his manners, at last. 'But I must not monopolise our hostess,' he said, looking towards Emma and then back to Hugo. 'If you wish to stand up with one of the ladies, sir, I should gladly take over your duty here.'

Hugo swallowed the biting snub that rose temptingly to his lips. The young puppy meant well enough. And his sister was still looking hopeful, unfortunately. 'Thank you, but no,' Hugo said. 'I do not dance this evening.'

Mr Mountjoy bowed and withdrew, looking relieved.

Lady Hardinge, having selected her music, was about to begin to play once more. 'Major,' she said in an undertone, 'I really do not need a page-turner, you know.'

Hugo laughed quietly. 'Thank you, ma'am. I shall take that as my *congé*,' he said. With a polite bow, he made his way to the door as quickly as he could without drawing attention to his departure. He would go down to the terrace, just for a quarter of an hour or so, to smoke a cigar in private. All the ladies were occupied. He would not be missed.

Emma was not best pleased to be dancing a second set with Mr Mountjoy. She told herself it was because a hostess should not allow herself to be monopolised by a single guest—but out of the corner of her eye, she found she was watching Hugo's every move. She felt very proud of him—even though she knew she had no right to be, for she was nothing to him, not even a friend. She had feared he would snub silly Miss Mountjoy—or her equally silly brother—but he had shown remarkable restraint. Probably he had been used to dealing with rash young subalterns during his army days and knew just how thin-skinned they could be.

Noticing Hugo slip out of the room, Emma remembered that he, too, was thin-skinned. It was not surprising that he wanted to escape from the Mountjoys and the dancing. Emma wondered, while she mechanically executed the steps of the figure, whether Hugo had liked to dance before his injury. All the more distressing for him, if it were so. Poor Hugo.

No, not 'poor Hugo'. She was beginning to feel sorry for him—as he was feeling sorry for himself. But it was wrong to encourage him to withdraw even further into his shell. No matter how dreadful his injuries, he should not hide from the world. No true friend would permit him to do so. It was already obvious that he was making some progress; he climbed the stairs much more easily than before. Surely he could learn to ride again—and to drive and to shoot—if he were but prepared to make the effort? Emma resolved to enlist Richard's help in making Hugo face up to the future. Between them they could help Hugo to become more like the man he had been. Why—he might even be able to dance again, one day.

At that moment, Emma thought she heard the sound of the front door being opened. Hugo could not be leaving, surely? He would not be so impolite. And besides, he could not leave without Jamie and Richard. No. Someone else must have called.

Emma gratefully excused herself to Mr Mountjoy and hurried out on to the landing to see what was happening. Looking over the balusters, she saw that a complete stranger had been admitted. A tall dark man was lounging carelessly against the delicate spindle-legged table in the hallway and lazily twirling an ivory-handled quizzing glass. On his face was an expression of acute boredom.

But he was, without doubt, the most beautiful specimen of manhood that Emma had ever beheld.

Emma stood transfixed on the landing, unable to tear her eyes away from the gentleman's finely chis-elled features. Then, from the vicinity of her father's study, she heard Hugo's voice exclaim in surprise, 'Kit! What on earth are you doing here?'

The newcomer raised a mocking eyebrow, but did not move an inch from where he stood. 'Why, wait-ing for someone to relieve me of my coat,' he replied in an affected drawl. 'What else did you think I might be doing, brother?'

Chapter Five

Emma was still standing as if frozen when her father—probably alerted by her hurried departure from the dance—appeared at her side. He took one look into the hallway below and rushed down the stairs as fast as his bulk and his tight satin breeches would allow.

Sir Edward strode across to the newcomer, hand outstretched. 'Welcome, my boy, welcome,' he boomed, clapping the new arrival on the shoulder. 'What brings you here at this hour? Something important, I'll be bound.' Without giving anyone a chance to reply, Sir Edward turned in the direction of the servants' door. 'Godfrey! Where the devil are you, man? Do you not know we have guests?'

The butler materialised almost immediately on the landing behind Emma and glided down the staircase with no appearance of haste or of concern. He bowed politely to the visitor. 'May I take your coat, sir?'

Emma watched in trancelike immobility as the newcomer allowed himself to be relieved of his caped driving coat and curly-brimmed beaver. He had smiled at Sir Edward's greeting, but the expression of lazy disdain had returned to his handsome face a moment later. It seemed he was too bored to speak— or even to look around him.

Sir Edward did not appear to have noticed anything amiss. 'I am sure you'd like a private word with your brother,' he said, gesturing vaguely in the direction of Hugo who was standing motionless in the shadow of the gallery, leaning on his cane. 'But I hope you will join us upstairs when you're done. We are entertaining a few friends—quite informally, you understand—and the young people are dancing. My Emma would—' He broke off, looking round suddenly. The butler had disappeared as quietly as he had come. 'Where on earth is she?' he said in a burst of irritation.

From her vantage point above them, Emma stirred at last. 'I am here, Papa,' she said, trying vainly to tear her eyes from Hugo's incredible brother.

Three heads turned. Three pairs of eyes looked up at her. The brothers were remarkably alike, even though they did not have the same degree of beauty. Nor did they share the same colouring, Emma noted absently. The younger man's hair was lighter—dark brown, highlighted with glints of red, like finest rosewood. His clear blue eyes were skimming over the female figure above him, making a rapid assessment of her face and form. Emma felt herself beginning to flush under his all too obvious scrutiny. His faintly lifted eyebrow and curling lip did nothing to reduce her embarrassment. She was behaving like a chit just out of the schoolroom, both thunderstruck and tongue-tied at the sight of a handsome male face.

She tossed her head in annoyance. The spell broke. This young man was too well aware of his effect on hapless females, Emma concluded with sudden insight. Let others fall at his elegantly shod feet. She most certainly would not.

Lifting the hem of her cream silk gown with one hand, she laid the other on the polished banister rail and moved serenely down the staircase into the hallway. She knew the newcomer's eyes would fix on that tantalising glimpse of a shapely ankle. And she made a play of dropping her skirts and straightening them demurely before she looked at him. Women, too, could use the tricks of flirtation, she reckoned. She doubted that young Stratton could be more adept than she at the arts of allure.

A movement behind her reminded Emma that they were not alone. There was the click of a cane on the chequered marble before Hugo's voice said politely, 'Miss Fitzwilliam, you will allow me to present my youngest brother, Christopher—usually known as Kit.'

Kit took a small step forward so that he could take Emma's hand. For a moment, she thought he was going to kiss it—that would have been totally in character, she decided uncharitably—but he did not. He simply bowed gracefully and relinquished her hand. There was nothing to cavil at in his company manners. He would be the perfect gentleman—were it not for that calculating look in his eye.

'Your servant, Miss Fitzwilliam,' Kit said.

Emma dropped the tiniest curtsy, but did not bow her head by as much as an inch. 'I am delighted to welcome any relative of Major Stratton's,' she said with a polite smile. 'You already know my father, I take it?'

'Indeed, I do,' replied Kit. 'We have had—'

'Belong to the same clubs, m'dear,' broke in Sir Edward quickly. 'Had one or two encounters over the card table. Young Stratton here seems to have the devil's own luck—playing against me, at least.' Sir Edward laughed good-naturedly. He loved to gamble, Emma knew. And he could afford to lose. But what of Kit Stratton? Could he?

'Where are you staying, Kit? You can't mean to drive on again tonight.' Hugo was smiling indulgently at his younger brother.

Kit smiled back with genuine warmth. 'Don't worry, brother. I shan't be importuning the Hardinges. Arranged to rack up at the White Hart. Got to make an early start in the morning. Things to do, you know.'

The corner of Hugo's mouth quirked in sudden irony but he said only, 'I see. London calls, no doubt. And the urgent business that brings you here in the middle of the night?'

Emma made to move back towards the stairs. She had no desire to eavesdrop on Hugo's family affairs. Her father was obviously of a similar mind, opening the door of his study so that the two guests might converse in private.

Kit still did not move an inch. 'Oh, it's nothing so drastic, Hugo. John asked me to let you know that they're off travelling again—Scotland, this time, I think he said—so the house at Stratton Magna will be shut up for a few months. He didn't want you arriving to find you'd been abandoned. Knows you find travelling difficult.' Kit cast a surreptitious glance at Hugo's weak leg and then quickly looked away.

'Good of him,' Hugo said curtly. 'But he could as easily have written, you know. A crippled leg doesn't affect my ability to read.'

Kit grinned like a naughty schoolboy. 'Oh, very well. If you must know, I offered to come. Wanted to see for myself how you were. Should have known you'd be just as cantankerous as ever.'

Hugo cast his eyes up to the heavens for a second and then turned to Sir Edward. 'It is not surprising if I am, sir. John and I have tried every avenue we could think of over the last few years, but nothing can tame this scapegrace brother of ours. Gambling, drinking—' He stopped abruptly. Such matters should not be mentioned in front of young unmarried ladies.

Emma broke the taut silence by saying politely, 'Will you come and meet our other guests, Mr Stratton? There will be refreshments upstairs, too—if you can spare the time, of course.'

Hugo stifled a laugh. 'I'm sure he can, ma'am, no matter how early his call to London. He never did seem to need much sleep.'

Kit cast a quelling look at his brother, but it produced no response at all, Emma noticed. Hugo was really very good indeed at dealing with provoking young men.

Emma re-entered the drawing room a little behind Kit and her father. She knew that Hugo would hate her to watch his slow progress on the stairs. And yet, she lingered by the door. She was not needed immediately. Her father would make the necessary introductions.

A soft gasp, quickly swallowed, made her turn back to the drawing room. Miss Mountjoy's eyes were as round as guineas as she gazed at the new arrival. Her mouth hung partly open. Emma suppressed a desire to take the girl by the shoulders and shake her. No wonder Kit Stratton had such a disdainful view of womankind if this was the reaction he had learned to expect.

Emma did not wait to witness the introductions. It was all too embarrassing. She moved instead to meet Hugo who had just regained the landing.

'Your brother has certainly made an impression,' she said somewhat tartly.

'It is to be expected,' said Hugo in a flat voice. 'Kit has the happy knack of being welcomed wherever he goes.'

Emma thought Hugo was about to say something more, but he did not. She wondered what was hidden behind his apparently simple words. He had called his brother a 'scapegrace', after all. Was there something to be ashamed of about this beautiful—and undoubtedly somewhat arrogant—young man? She would have to find that out for herself. Of a certainty, Hugo would not tell her.

'I was just about to order the supper brought in, Major. I am sure your brother would welcome some refreshments after his travels. And you, too, perhaps?'

'You are most kind, ma'am,' replied Hugo, stopping in the doorway. Emma, too, paused to survey the scene. Jamie was seated at the instrument once more, choosing her music. Kit Stratton was leading a blushing Miss Mountjoy on to the floor. Emma was relieved to see that Mr Mountjoy was partnering the Rector's wife. If the young man had been forward enough to ask Emma to dance a third time, she would have been forced to snub him. That would have given her no pleasure at all.

The Rector came to claim Emma and lead her into the set. Her father looked on, smiling benignly. He liked nothing better than to see his guests enjoying themselves—even if it was a little improper for them to be dancing in this way.

Hugo crossed to the pianoforte once more. 'May I turn for you, Lady Hardinge?' he asked quietly.

'If you wish,' she replied. 'Your brother's arrival was unexpected, I collect? I hope he has not brought bad news?'

'Have no fears on that score, ma'am. It's only Kit's insatiable curiosity. He always has to know everything about John and me. A problem of being so much younger, I think. He always wanted to do whatever we could do, and long before he was old enough. He's a born rebel, I'm afraid. He was sent down from Oxford because of it. And, of course, he was much indulged, being the child of my parents' old age—besides having the face of an angel.'

Hugo smiled wryly, fearing for a moment that he might have said too much. But the Hardinges, of all people, were to be trusted. He bent to turn the page of music and received a brief nod of thanks. 'I would not have you think unkindly of Kit, ma'am,' he continued earnestly. 'He is a little wild, I admit, but he has a good heart under that splendid exterior. It is only a pity that the ladies cannot see beyond the handsome face.' And that he trades on it with so little compunction, Hugo added to himself. In spite of Kit's comparative youth, he had left a string of broken hearts behind him—never mind the discarded mistresses. Every one of them had thought she would reform him. And every one had failed.

Hugo raised his eyes to watch the dancing. Miss Mountjoy was gazing up at Kit as if she had never beheld anything so beautiful. Hugo shuddered inwardly. Yet another impressionable female...

Emma, now...Emma was clearly made of sterner stuff. Hugo assessed her carefully. Her attention was firmly focused on her conversation with her partner. She was sparing not a single glance for Kit. And earlier, in the entrance hall, she had seemed to have the measure of him. Perhaps...

At that moment, the dance brought Emma round to face Hugo and she looked directly at him. She smiled, fleetingly, before turning back to her partner.

Entranced, Hugo watched her retreating back move down the set. He could see that Kit was watching her closely, too. But Emma was studiously ignoring Kit Stratton. Excellent tactics on her part.

Kit had broken altogether too many hearts, in Hugo's opinion. It would do him the world of good to fall in love a little, especially if his love were not returned in equal measure. Hugo had little experience of Society ladies—he had spent too many years with the army—yet it seemed to him that Emma was just the kind of woman to give Kit the lesson he needed...if she once decided to take any notice of him at all. But why should she?

Hugo allowed himself a little smile. It would not be so surprising, surely, in the down-to-earth world of *ton* matches? Emma, as an heiress, was in need of a husband. Kit was a very attractive man—and better husband material than many a suitor. He might be a scapegrace... No, that was not quite true. Hugo had to admit to himself that, at twenty-two, Kit was already a fair way to becoming an out-and-out rake—though without as much wealth as he would have wished to fund his spendthrift habits. A good marriage might be the making of him. And what woman could resist the challenge of reforming a rake?

Hugo turned back to the music, feeling suddenly guilty. How quickly his mind had moved from love to marriage. It was not his place to arrange Emma's future, even to help tame his incorrigible brother. Kit was still very young, younger than Emma. Flirtation might provide a useful lesson—but marriage would be a disaster. He should not interfere. Let the young people make their own decisions.

A sudden burst of laughter from Kit drew everyone's attention. Most of the dancers were soon laughing heartily, too. Miss Mountjoy looked a trifle embarrassed though she, too, joined in eventually. Emma, however, was looking daggers at Kit.

In that instant, Hugo realised that Emma was aeons older than his frivolous young brother. They would never suit—not for a moment.

A wicked thought arose unbidden. Poor Kit—her wealth would at least have kept him out of the sponging house.

Chapter Six

'You sent for me, Papa?' Emma shut the study door quietly behind her.

Her father rose from his favourite chair, smiling determinedly. He carried a letter in his hand. 'Emma, my dear, how well you look this morning,' he said, admiring the picture she made in her simple sprig-muslin gown. 'No after-effects from last night's entertaining?'

Emma returned his smile. 'No, indeed, Papa. It was most enjoyable. And I am used to dance till dawn when I am in London, you know. Country parties—even our own—are much tamer affairs.'

He pulled at his ear lobe. 'Ah...that was what I wanted to talk to you about, m'dear. Your Aunt Augusta has written.' He waved his letter in Emma's direction. 'She thinks you should return to London. Says you are missing too much of the Season. That, at your age, you—'

Emma was relieved to learn that the letter contained nothing worse. Her father's widowed sister was a busybody of the first order. Having no children of her own, she did her best to arrange Emma's life instead. 'Forgive me for interrupting you, Papa, but I'll wager I can quote my aunt's letter word for word. At my age,' she began, mimicking Mrs Warenne's very proper voice, 'I am like to be left on the shelf if I do not bestir myself to attend every single rout party. New gentleman are constantly appearing in town and it is *so* important to make an impression on them at the very *first* opportunity.' She looked up at her father's face through her long dark lashes. His hand had left his ear and he was trying not to laugh. 'Do I have it right, Papa?'

'Yes—well, it is much along those lines, I admit. But—' he was suddenly serious once more '—Emma, your aunt is only being sensible. You are twenty-three years old and still unmarried.' He must have detected hurt in Emma's eyes, for he hastened to say, 'Oh, I was more than happy to send all those fortune hunters to the rightabout. Not one of them valued you as he ought. But… My dear, I am concerned about your future. I am not as young as I was, you know, and when I am gone, you will be alone here.'

Emma's eyes widened as she took in the import of his words. He shook his head a fraction to forestall the protest that had sprung to her lips. 'I would so much like to see you happily settled, Emma. As would your aunt. And, however much you love the country, my dear, even you have to admit that it is not exactly awash with potential suitors.' He looked sadly down at her, counting off the names on the fingers of his left hand. 'Richard is married. Kit Stratton is a reckless young ne'er-do-well with much too fine a face. And Mountjoy is barely out of leading strings. Apart from the old widowers—who are not for you, I sincerely hope—no other eligible man has put in an appearance in this neighbourhood for years. So…much as you may prefer the country, m'dear, I'm afraid it has to be London.'

Emma was silent for several heartbeats. Then, in a very small voice, quite unlike her usual confident tones, she ventured, 'You did not include Major Stratton in your list, Papa.'

Her father's eyes widened in surprise. 'No, of course I did not,' he said brusquely. 'The Major may be a very fine man. A hero, too, perhaps, I dare say. But he is not…' He put a heavy hand on his daughter's arm and warned sharply, 'Emma, he is scarred and crippled. He may not even be a whole man.' He reddened slightly as he realised what he had said in front of his unmarried daughter, but he was clearly too angry and too concerned to stop. 'He is no fit husband for you, Emma—nor for any other young lady. You must not give him another thought. Indeed, I doubt he is marriageable at all. It is a pity, I admit, but there is nothing to be done.'

Emma was staring at her slippers, trying to make sense of the tumbling, whirling thoughts that her father's words had provoked. She wanted to re-establish her easy friendship with Hugo Stratton, that was all. She had never thought of him as a husband. At least…when she was a child…but those were only a child's romantic daydreams and long ago forgotten. Besides, the man who had returned from the wars was nothing like the fantasy she had fashioned in the schoolroom. Nothing like. With a flash of insight, Emma now saw that Hugo believed himself to be unfit for marriage. He would never propose to any woman of his own free will.

She swallowed hard. Her father must be right. He had her best interests at heart, as always.

She was about to say that she would do as he asked, when another picture of Hugo rose in her mind, a picture so vivid that he might have been before her—Hugo's laughing eyes as they had once been. Could they not be so again? There had been a moment during that walk in the wood at Harding when he had been so close to his former self... Must he remain a bitter recluse just because he had been wounded in the service of his country? It seemed so very unfair.

'Emma?' Her father was now beginning to sound more impatient than angry.

Emma smiled sweetly up at him, waiting until the last remnants of his anger had melted away. 'No doubt Aunt Augusta is right, Papa. London in the Season is the place for suitors—and fortune hunters, too, alas. I will go back and join the throng. Will that content you, Papa?'

'Aye,' he smiled. 'You were ever a sensible lass, Emma. You know it is for the best.' He sounded relieved.

Emma's smile dimmed. 'Oh, Papa—but what about the Derby? You said you planned to go. But if I am in London with Aunt Augusta... Surely you would not deny me the chance to see Golden Star run? You always said you named him for me.' Her face was set in a picture of childlike innocence as she gazed hopefully up at him.

He plucked at his ear. 'Well...' he said, looking again at the letter in his hand. 'I suppose it might be possible to make up a party, if your aunt agreed. I'd have to take a house nearby, of course. Too far to go otherwise. Might be a goodish notion, though,' he mused abstractedly. 'We could all see the race then. And your Aunt Augusta could ensure that a few eligible young people were invited to join us at the same time.'

Emma groaned inwardly at the thought of a houseful of young ladies, all carefully schooled by their matchmaking mamas, and Aunt Augusta's choice of eligible gentlemen. But, at least, it would be a change from the interminable London round. After so many full Seasons, that was beginning to pall.

Her papa seemed to have convinced himself. 'Yes,' he said, 'I'll write to your aunt today. And I may tell her that you will be returning to London immediately, Emma?' His raised eyebrows demanded a precise answer.

'In a day or two, Papa,' Emma said. 'I should like to spend a little time with Jamie before I go.' Her eyes lit up with sudden mischief. 'If I try really hard, I might even persuade her to join your Surrey house party, Papa. Would that not be delightful? It was so clever of you to think of it.'

Papa—who had a very soft spot for the lovely Countess—agreed that his daughter might remain in the country for a few days more, in hopes of adding the Hardinges to his guest list.

Emma kissed his cheek. 'Thank you, Papa,' she beamed. 'I had better ride over to Harding at once to begin to work on her, do you not think? And, before you mention it, I *will* take a groom. I am resolved to prevent you from worrying about me any more.'

Sir Edward sighed contentedly and patted her arm. 'Thank you, m'dear. You are a good girl.'

Emma left the room before he could remember that any visit to Harding must provide yet another opportunity to meet the unmarriageable Major.

'Good morning, Miss Emma.' The butler beamed at her. 'You will be pleased to know that my lord has driven over to the Dower House to visit his lady mother.'

Emma's spirits lifted at the news. The Dowager Countess had been almost like a mother to Emma for as long as she could remember. Emma resolved to ride on to the Dower House as soon as she left Jamie. It would be a happy duty to welcome Richard's mother back home.

'That is splendid news, Digby,' Emma said. 'I will go to pay my respects to her ladyship this very day.' She picked up her trailing skirts, turning to make for the stairs and Jamie's sitting room.

Behind her, Digby coughed discreetly. 'I believe her ladyship is in the conservatory, Miss Emma.'

'Oh.' Emma turned quickly on her heel. 'Yes, of course. It is such a lovely spot when the sun is shining. Don't trouble to announce me, Digby. I know my way very well.'

Emma walked briskly along the corridor to the conservatory at the end of the house, where Richard had created a luxurious oasis for his wife's enjoyment. Jamie's green fingers had ensured that all kinds of exotic plants now flourished there. And it had given her an opportunity to indulge her passion for gardening in even the most inclement winter weather. Emma knew her friend would probably be surrounded by cuttings and compost. Even heavily pregnant, Jamie was rarely to be found simply enjoying the delights of her private paradise.

The door opened silently on well-oiled hinges. The warm, moist air settled around Emma like a fine velvet cloak and the sweet scent of newly turned soil filled her nostrils. She breathed deeply, savouring the moment. For Emma, this place was a peaceful haven, a refuge from all the artifice of Society life.

The conservatory seemed to be empty. Jamie's workbench was strewn with soil and potting implements, but she was nowhere to be seen. Emma was just turning to leave when she heard a muffled noise. It sounded like a groan.

Someone was there. And something was wrong.

Emma pushed her way through the lush greenery to the far side of the conservatory. Jamie was there, sure enough, sitting awkwardly on the edge of a small wooden bench.

But Jamie was not alone. Hugo Stratton loomed over her, his hands clasping her face and his eyes gazing down into hers. As Emma watched in shocked astonishment, Hugo lowered his head to Jamie's.

Emma whirled and fled from the scene, unwilling to believe the evidence of her own eyes. How could he? Jamie was the wife of his best friend…and pregnant, besides. It was wicked. It was dishonourable.

And Jamie…Jamie had not seemed to be resisting Hugo's advances…

Emma choked back a sob. Her heart was beating as rapidly as if she had fled from a charging bull. Her knees seemed to have turned to water. She had to lean her forehead and breast against the cool paintwork of the corridor to stop her legs from buckling beneath her.

Jamie—and Hugo!

It was indecent.

It was utterly beyond her comprehension.

'Emma?'

Jamie had appeared in the conservatory doorway. Her cheeks looked remarkably flushed, and she was holding a handkerchief to her eye as if she had been crying.

Perhaps she had not welcomed Hugo's kisses after all?

'I thought I heard someone in the conservatory… Why—are you quite well, Emma? You look as if you are about to faint.'

Emma shook her head dumbly. Her throat was so dry that she could not utter a sound. She forced her lips into a somewhat shaky smile.

'Go and sit down in the conservatory, my dear, and I will send some water to you immediately.' Jamie sounded concerned now. 'Forgive me for not staying with you, but I must get Annie to help me bathe my eye. I stupidly allowed some soil dust to get into it. Major Stratton assured me he had removed every speck, but the desire to rub and rub is overwhelming. If I cannot do something about it, I swear I shall scream.' With an apologetic smile, Jamie hurried away to find her faithful abigail, Annie Smithers.

Emma took a deep breath and swallowed hard. It had all been perfectly innocent.

Or had it?

Emma forced her legs to carry her calmly back to the conservatory. However much she wished to avoid setting eyes on Hugo Stratton, she had no choice. The servants would certainly expect to find her there. And there was no knowing what the Major—or Jamie— would read into her actions if she left without a word.

She must behave as if she had seen nothing at all. A short, polite conversation was what the situation required...followed by a speedy retreat.

Emma had her fingers on the handle of the door when the butler arrived, carrying a carafe of water and a glass on a tray. 'Thank you, Digby,' Emma said, smiling. 'I am much better now, but I would welcome a glass of water and a moment of quiet repose. Perhaps you had better announce me after all. But have Juno brought round in ten minutes, if you please. I cannot stay longer.'

Hugo looked up in surprise when Emma was announced. For once, he had been sitting in a comfortable chair, Emma noticed, but the lower seat made it a struggle to rise, especially as he seemed to be without his cane. The exertion was apparent in his face. If there was guilt there, too, Emma was unable to discern it. She remained standing just inside the door to give him time to collect himself before moving forward to offer her hand. Behind her, the butler quietly withdrew. Emma heard the soft click as the glass-panelled door closed at her back. In any other room, the door would have been left ajar, as convention demanded. Here, their actions could still be observed—yet Emma felt trapped by that tiny sound.

'Good morning to you, Major,' she said in her most cheerful voice. 'I hope I find you well after last night's exertions.'

Hugo bowed, frowning slightly as if he were looking for a hidden—and offensive—meaning behind her words. Emma forced herself to remain polite and in control, though inwardly she bristled. How dare he? *She* had done nothing wrong.

'Your brother will have left for London by now, I collect?' she continued rapidly. 'What a pity he could not stay to be presented to Richard's mother. I am sure Lady Hardinge would have been charmed to make his acquaintance.' Emma stopped short. Why on earth was she gabbling so? She had been so determined to remain calm.

Hugo was looking searchingly at her. She hoped he could not read the suspicions behind her polite façade.

'No doubt,' Hugo replied quietly. 'Kit was ever a charmer.'

Emma's heightened senses were fully alert to every nuance in his voice. If he betrayed himself by so much as a breath, she would know it. But his voice was laced with irony; and she fancied she detected a hint of something deeper, too. It could not be envy, surely? It was true that the contrast between the brothers was now very great, but—

'May I say that you look blooming this morning, ma'am?' Hugo's words interrupted Emma's train of thought. 'Obviously you thrive on company. It was a splendid party. I am sure all your guests enjoyed the entertainment.'

Emma was not deceived. He was obviously determined to put her on the defensive in this encounter by making clear that he disapproved of the dancing—which she knew she should not have permitted at such a gathering. She threw him a challenging look. 'A good host,' she said rather tightly, 'will always have the wishes of his guests at the forefront of his mind. And if those desires should prove to be somewhat…less than conventional, a good host will ensure that nothing occurs to embarrass his guests.'

Emma saw—with a silent crow of triumph—that Major Stratton was trying to suppress the faintest glimmer of a smile. He tilted his head a little to one side as if to examine her better from that angle, though it might have been to hide that unwilling twitch of the lips. 'And you, ma'am, are most certainly a very good host.' His quiet words sounded almost sincere, but there was a gleam of something unfathomable in his grey eyes that warned her not to believe him. He would always find a way to turn her barbs back on her. Besides, he was clearly a practised deceiver.

Emma dropped a tiny curtsy. She must get away from him. 'Thank you, sir,' she said, taking refuge in convention once more. 'You are most kind. But, if you will excuse me, I must be on my way to the Dower House. My horse is at the door.'

Hugo bowed a trifle stiffly. 'I hope you find the Dowager well after her travels. I know Richard is delighted that his mother is returned. He is very much concerned about his wife's health.'

Emma looked up sharply. For the first time, Hugo had said something to reveal his inner thoughts. He appeared to be worried for Richard—and glad that the Dowager had returned to share her son's burden. It made no sense at all. She found herself replying more sharply than she had intended. 'Jamie will not permit herself to be cosseted, Major, even by Richard and his mother. You would understand that, if you knew her history. She is—'

'I do know,' he said softly.

Oh, dear. Jamie and Hugo must be even closer than she had imagined. Not many people were entrusted with the secret of how Jamie had disguised herself as a garden boy to escape from her stepmother's machinations—and how Richard had married her out of hand when he discovered who she really was. Oh, poor, poor Richard.

'Lady Hardinge told me herself,' Hugo said. 'I think,' he continued pensively, 'that she did so to show me that she, too, had episodes in her past that were best not discussed in polite Society. I admire her a very great deal.'

'That—if I may say so, sir—was perfectly obvi-

ous.' Emma's angry outburst echoed in the sudden
stillness. She closed her eyes in despair and bit down
hard on her lower lip, but she knew it was too late.
How could she have allowed herself to say such a
thing?

She turned to leave. She did not dare to look at
him.

'A moment, ma'am.' Hugo's voice was as hard as
granite and as cold as ice.

Emma stopped but did not turn.

'What—precisely—was the meaning of that last
remark?'

She could feel his warm breath on the back of her
neck. He had moved to stand mere inches behind her.
The threat in his voice was unmistakable. She had
two choices—retreat…or attack.

Emma took a single step forward, putting just a
little distance between them, and then spun around to
face him. Her finger pointed accusingly. 'I should
have thought the meaning was obvious, Major,' she
said, pouring out all her pent-up fury. 'It means that
I saw you kissing Richard's wife. Do you dare to
deny it? You are a guest in his house, and you—'

Hugo's face had blanched under his tan. The thin
line of his scar stood out starkly, drawing Emma's
unwilling gaze. Articulating every venomous word as
if he were a judge handing down a sentence of death,
he said, 'I am a guest in Richard's house and a man
of honour, Miss Fitzwilliam.'

Emma stood motionless, staring at him with bitter
contempt. She could not trust herself to speak.

'Your accusation is writ plainly on your face,

ma'am. You believe I would be Lady Hardinge's lover, do you not?'

The silence seemed to stretch endlessly between them.

At last, Hugo broke it. 'You do not have the first idea of love, if you could so mistake my actions,' he said grimly. 'I fear your education is sadly lacking.' He took a step forward to close the space between them and seized Emma roughly by the shoulders, his fingers biting into her flesh as if the barrier of her habit did not exist. 'I'll show you what lovers do,' he said, lowering his mouth to hers.

Emma could not move. She could not think. She could only feel. Hugo's hard, bruising kiss was full of anger, frustration and—Emma somehow understood—dawning desire. For what seemed an eternity, he continued to punish her with his mouth, holding her body prisoner between his hands. Anger appeared to have given them unexpected strength.

At last, the grip of his weakened hand relaxed. The pressure of his mouth on hers seemed somehow gentler, too. His fingers began to stroke slowly over the fine velvet of her sleeve. Emma was sure Hugo's touch was burning through to her naked skin, just as his lips had put their brand on her mouth. No man had ever kissed her with any kind of passion. Fury had caused this, to be sure, not love—and yet Hugo's kiss was wildly exciting. Emma's heart was racing and every inch of her body seemed to be glowing so hot it would melt at any second. It was glorious to be so alive. Emma willingly yielded to the temptations of pure feeling.

When Emma moved her head the tiniest fraction—not to pull away, but to enjoy this wonderful sensation to the full—Hugo reacted instantly to forestall any possible escape. He clamped his right hand to the back of her head, his fingers splayed across her silky hair to hold her steady for his continuing kiss. He started to explore the pleasures of her mouth with his lips and tongue, testing and teasing, while his left hand caressed her arm with never a pause.

Emma was close to fainting from the pleasure of it. She no longer cared who—or where—she was.

Until the loud rattle of the door handle announced that they were no longer alone…

Chapter Seven

Dear God, what had she done?

Emma dared not turn to see who was at the conservatory door. She knew that one glimpse of her flushed face and bruised lips would betray her. It mattered not that she was now alone, or that the lush greenery had probably concealed their embrace from anyone looking in from the corridor. Her behaviour had been scandalous. A lightskirt from Covent Garden would have known better.

It seemed a very long time before the door was opened. And the handle rattled much more than usual. Emma had time to take several deep breaths, and to pray that her flush might be fading.

'Miss Emma.'

Emma was perversely glad to be discovered by the butler who had known her all her life. Jamie would have understood her plight, but what Emma needed at this moment was absolute discretion—not sympathetic questions.

'Miss Emma, her ladyship is in her sitting room upstairs. She asked if you would join her there, instead of riding over to the Dower House. She expects that his lordship will bring his lady mother back with him.'

'Thank you, Digby, I—'

'I shall tell her ladyship that you are still feeling a little faint, shall I? And that you will join her presently?'

'Thank you, Digby. Yes, I shall. Presently.' Keeping her back to him, Emma busied herself with examining a curiously shaped leaf, hoping that she appeared totally engrossed. Her sudden interest in plants might also excuse her rather strained tone of voice…and hide her shaking hands.

She closed her eyes, breathing deeply. Digby was still standing behind her, waiting. Drat the man. Why would he not go? She dare not turn round.

At last he said, sounding remarkably like her father, 'I shall convey your message to her ladyship. Shall I have your mare taken round to the stable, too?'

Emma almost laughed at being so easily caught. Everyone knew that her first concern was always for her horses, yet she had completely forgotten that her beloved mare was standing at the door. Digby, at least, would not be deceived. And she would not act the coward before him any more. She turned slowly, saying, as calmly as she could, 'Thank you, Digby. You think of everything.'

Digby was studying the pattern on the tiled floor. And he managed to make his exit without once looking into her face.

Emma sank into the low chair that Hugo Stratton

had vacated. It all seemed like hours ago. She covered her face with her hands. Her cheeks still felt burning hot…though not nearly as hot as the rest of her body. Hugo's passionate kisses had set her every fibre aglow in a way she had not thought possible. *This* must be why the matchmaking mamas took such care to chaperon their maiden daughters on every occasion…and why the gentlemen were always so eager to tempt the ladies into a shady alcove or a secluded bower. If mere kisses made a woman melt as she had done, what was there still to be discovered in the love between a man and a woman? Surely nothing could be more thrilling than the feelings she had just experienced in Hugo's arms? And yet…

Hugo forced himself to move through the pain. It was the least he deserved. He had told her he was a man of honour. What kind of man of honour would take advantage of an innocent and helpless young woman as he had just done? Never mind that his honour was smirched even before he set eyes on her.

Guilt overpowered him, like water bursting through a dam. Soon it was overflowing.

Why had he done it? Had he absolutely no self-control?

After a pause, his re-awakened conscience supplied the answer. No. These days he had precious little self-control—and none at all where Emma Fitzwilliam was concerned. He had desired her from that first moment, when she stood staring at his scars, her back ramrod straight in her tight riding habit and her eyes like saucers as she took in the horror he pre-

sented. He had wished himself anywhere but there—
exposed—in the middle of the sweeping lawns of an
English country house. The bloody battlefield would
have been preferable to the horror and disgust he had
seen in Emma's eyes.

Or so it had seemed.

Hugo paused in his headlong flight from the conservatory. His only thought had been to protect
Emma's reputation. She must not be found alone with
him, and certainly not in his arms. His desire to protect her must have given a strength to his limbs that
he did not know he possessed, for he was now a good
hundred yards from the house. Somehow, he had
pushed his way out through the plants and halfway
across the garden without even his cane to aid him.

A further sharp pain in his left leg reminded him
of the weakness that was trying to dominate his every
waking hour. This time he refused to acknowledge it.
If concern for Emma's reputation could bring him
this far, then sheer stubborn determination would en-
able him to become a whole man again. He might
never aspire to Emma Fitzwilliam, scarred and dishonoured as he was, but he would not permit her to
pity him. Anything but that.

And yet…and yet, it was not pity that had made
her respond to him as she had. She had resisted at
first, to be sure, but that was hardly surprising, given
the violence of his attack on her. Hot-blooded fury
had governed him at the thought that she believed
him capable of such perfidy…but it had taken mere
seconds for his anger to evaporate. The touch of her
soft lips had been his undoing. He had wanted to hold

her, to caress her, to kiss her until they were both
mindless with passion. Heaven alone knew what he
would have done if they had not been interrupted for,
somehow, he knew that—on this occasion at least—
she would in no wise have been able to resist him.
He should feel nothing but shame.

Hugo struck out for the woods, willing his legs to
obey him. He had behaved like the worst sort of
lecher, the kind of man he had always despised. He
would walk until he could walk no more—and until
long after Emma Fitzwilliam had returned to the
safety of her father's house.

'Oh, dear,' Jamie said. 'It is a splendid idea,
Emma, but—'

'But sadly impractical,' put in the Dowager
briskly, patting Emma's hand fondly to soften her
words. 'We cannot just abandon Major Stratton,
Emma. It would be the height of bad manners—especially as the Major's brother has shut up the family
house. Where would the poor man go?'

Emma bit back the highly improper response that
rose to her lips. She was torn between anger and
guilt, but neither must be permitted to show. 'He may
join the party too, ma'am,' she said quickly, trying
to sound her normal light-hearted self. 'I am sure a
change of air would speed his recovery. Why, he
could even take the waters at Epsom. They are said
to work wonders, I believe.'

'If you can stomach the foul taste.' Richard's voice
emerged from the depths of a chair by the fire.

Everyone laughed. The last vestiges of Emma's

tension dissolved. She would reflect on what had happened—and those intensely strange feelings—later, when she was quite alone.

'I suppose we might succeed in persuading him,' added Richard thoughtfully. 'He was ever one for the turf in his early years. Horse mad. Second only to being army mad, of course. But it will depend on you, my love,' he said, looking at his wife with some concern. 'Do you feel able to contemplate such a trip? The doctor said you needed to take care—'

'The doctor would have me spend the whole of the summer in bed, not moving so much as a finger,' Jamie said with more than a touch of asperity. 'I am not such a poor creature, Richard. I refuse to be treated like an invalid. I am not ill. Besides, I have never been to the Derby. I am sure I should like it extremely.' She turned to Emma. 'You, too, Emma.'

Emma looked at Jamie in surprise. Her friend sounded…different. But the mischief in Jamie's eyes gave her away. She was plotting. If she had her way, the Derby excursion was settled—and Major Hugo Stratton would have no choice in the matter, either. Jamie smiled at Emma in silent understanding. She clearly believed she was forwarding Emma's own plans.

But Emma could not begin to know what she wanted where the maddening Major was concerned. Not here. Not yet. She had to get away from Harding.

'Mama, you will join Emma's party, too, will you not?' Jamie continued bluntly. The Dowager looked a little taken aback, but laughed when Jamie added, 'We cannot allow the Major the slightest hope that he has anywhere else to go, you know. It must be the Derby for us all.'

'I am so glad that is settled,' Emma said, ruthlessly suppressing the wayward emotions that threatened to overpower her. She rose from her place on the sofa beside the Dowager. 'Papa will be so pleased. And now I must go home to finish my preparations. I am returning to London first thing tomorrow.' She did not attempt to hide a little grimace of distaste. 'The Season is—apparently—bereft without me.'

Richard laughed heartily. 'I am sure it is, Emma. All those poor young men…'

Emma allowed herself to give vent to something very close to a snort. 'Poor, indeed,' she said vehemently, preparing to launch into a tirade against the fortune hunters who plagued her at every turn.

'Now, Emma,' said the Dowager gently, 'you really must not blame them. It is not, after all, of their own choosing that they are younger sons, or penniless. What choice do they have? An heiress—especially one as lovely as you—must seem to them like manna from heaven. You should have pity on them.'

'Oh, I do, ma'am, I do,' replied Emma. 'Except when I am constrained to be in their company.'

Richard and Jamie dissolved into laughter. The Dowager, too, smiled broadly. 'Emma,' she said after a moment, 'you are become quite incorrigible. You will allow me to say it is a very good thing that the world at large is not aware of it. What would Mrs Warenne say if she heard you?'

Emma tried to adopt a prim and proper expression. She failed. 'My Aunt Augusta has endless patience with me, ma'am. She presents me with one eligible gentleman after another and is never deterred if they do not come up to scratch or—worse—if I refuse them. And she tries so hard to shield me from undesirables, too.' Emma threw a conspiratorial glance at Jamie. 'Sometimes, I wish she would not,' she added with a flashing smile, 'for at least a few of the rakes are most entertaining. Why is it, Richard, that respectable gentlemen are always so very boring?'

Richard strode across the room to take Emma by the arm. 'I think I must escort you out, madam, before you become even more outrageous. Boring, am I, indeed?'

Emma smiled her farewells to the ladies, shook herself free of Richard's restraining hand, and dropped him an impudent curtsy. 'You are mistaken, my lord,' she said demurely, making for the open door. 'I should never have dreamt of calling *you*…''respectable''.' With a final saucy toss of her head, she whipped through the door, leaving Richard transfixed in the middle of the room and his ladies desperately trying to conceal their mirth.

'Emma…' began Richard menacingly, but he was too late. She closed the door firmly and ran lightly down the stairs, savouring her triumph.

Success, thanks to Jamie. It was quite wonderful— and consolation for the fact that she was bound to return to London and to the stuffy confines of the Season. Now, at least, she had the house party to look forward to. All the Hardinges would be there—and Major Hugo Stratton.

Emma swallowed hard, forcing her mind to con-

centrate on practical matters. Her father would not be
overly pleased that the Major would be one of the
party, but she was sure she could soon bring him
round to the idea, especially as there was nowhere
else for Hugo to go. No. Papa was a kind man. In
the end, he would welcome Major Stratton, along
with all the potential husbands that Aunt Augusta
would marshal for Emma's approval.

Emma offered up a little prayer that Aunt Augusta's young men would not *all* be respectable and
boring. There was nothing more difficult than refusing the suit of a respectable man, especially one who
was conscious of his own worth. She had called
Hugo Stratton thin-skinned, but that was surely preferable to the elephant hide of some of the pompous
windbags who had pursued her, unable to accept that
they might have any shortcomings in the eyes of an
eligible young lady. At least Hugo had the grace to
laugh at some of his own failings…

Chapter Eight

'And I am delighted to say that no one has declined.' Mrs Warenne was in full flow, at the same time dispensing tea to her brother and to Emma. The trio had already made themselves at home in the long, rambling Surrey mansion that Sir Edward had rented. None of the guests would arrive before the morrow and so Emma and her aunt would have plenty of time to organise all the final details for their large party. 'Even Major Stratton's brother has accepted,' Aunt Augusta said with satisfaction.

Emma's hand shook slightly as she took her cup. Kit Stratton one of their house party? She would never have believed that Society matrons would allow their daughters to stay in a house in such company, but, evidently, they had accepted. They would have been reassured by the presence of Aunt Augusta and the Dowager, but still... Perhaps Kit's reputation was not as black as Hugo had painted?

Aunt Augusta's flow continued without pause. 'I thought he would be company for his brother, Emma, since the Major cannot get about as well as the younger men. And Mr Stratton is a charming young man, quite charming. All my friends positively dote on him. He has been invited everywhere since his arrival in London.'

No doubt, Emma thought sourly. What was it that Hugo had said? That Kit had the happy knack of being welcomed everywhere. Yes, that was it. Why, then, did she feel not the least desire to welcome him herself? She could not be sure, but she suspected that she had glimpsed an aspect of his character that he was normally at pains to conceal. The man she had observed from the upstairs landing in her father's house was much too conscious of the perfect image he presented and of the charm he could exude at will. He knew how to manipulate—and he would do it for his own ends, she was sure.

She would be very wary of Kit Stratton.

'Good grief, who on earth is that incredible female?'

All the eyes in the Fitzwilliam barouche followed Kit Stratton's gaze to rest on the elderly lady in the opulent but old-fashioned open carriage. She was dressed in the height of fashion from more than thirty years earlier—powder and patches, a huge feathered hat, and a striped brocade gown over elbow panniers. Richard, sitting calmly beside his wife, laughed softly. 'Oh, don't you know, Kit? That's the Dowager Lady Luce. I thought you, of all people, would know her, considering how much you frequent the gaming tables these days. She—' A discreet cough from Jamie stopped him in mid-sentence.

'Lady Luce was a great beauty in her youth, I believe, Mr Stratton,' said Jamie calmly. 'I understand that she disapproves of modern fashions and modern manners—hence her refusal to adopt either of them. Have you met her son, the present Earl?'

Emma smiled to herself at Jamie's skill in changing the subject to avoid further mention of Kit's disreputable habits. The Dowager Countess Luce was renowned for her passion for gaming. She tended to win—or lose—extremely heavily and was known to be the despair of her son who, as often as not, found himself paying her enormous debts. Kit would certainly not have forgotten any encounter with Lady Luce. Given half a chance, she would win the shirt from his back. And what would Kit Stratton do then?

Jamie's polite conversation continued while Emma's attention wandered. But, after several minutes of inactivity alongside Sir Edward's barouche, Kit's black stallion was beginning to become restive. It was clearly unused to being in such a noisy and unpredictable crowd. Emma decided, uncharitably, that the stallion was a poor choice of mount for such an excursion. Horse and rider might make an admirable picture—especially in the eyes of impressionable young ladies—but the horse was much too highly strung for Epsom. Yet, in spite of herself, Emma found herself admiring Kit's skill, for he controlled the powerful beast without apparent effort.

Emma wondered whether Hugo would soon be riding alongside his brother. He had certainly made remarkable progress during Emma's weeks in London. He had now totally abandoned his cane—and his scars were much less noticeable than before. He had agreed to join the Derby outing with no hesitation at all.

Kit's sidling horse caught Emma's eye once more. She looked away deliberately. It chafed her to remain confined to the barouche, even in company with the Hardinges, but no lady could appear at the Derby on horseback. Convention demanded that, if a lady attended at all, she should sit demurely in her carriage accompanied by her chaperon. Unless the lady was old, and from a rich family, like Lady Luce. Such a woman could do exactly as she pleased. Emma smiled inwardly at the thought. If she remained single, she would—probably—become just as eccentric and demanding as Lady Luce. She might even take up gaming, too. After all, she would be rich enough to afford it…

'Emma?'

'I beg your pardon, Jamie. I'm afraid I was miles away.'

'Your father is returning. Over there.' Jamie pointed across the milling crowd. Sir Edward was struggling to force his way through. 'He looks as if he has lost a guinea and found sixpence.'

'Oh, dear,' Emma said. Her father looked ruffled, and irritated. That did not bode well for Golden Star. Perhaps their horse was injured?

'Is something wrong, Papa?' she said when he reached their carriage at last, puffing a little from his exertions.

'Not exactly,' he said. 'York's here, with his cronies, to see his horse run. He's invited us to join his party. Fellow owners together, he says.'

Emma knew that her father must be in two minds about this invitation. It was a great honour, of course, but Papa thoroughly disapproved of the Duke of York's scandalous and profligate mode of life. Like his brother, the Prince Regent, the Duke had ever an eye to a pretty woman. And, knowing the risks his only daughter could run in such company, Papa would certainly have no desire for any royal eye to rest too long upon Emma.

'I'm sure you will understand, ma'am,' Sir Edward said to Jamie, with a slightly hesitant smile, 'that His Royal Highness was most insistent. The royal party has a marquee near the winning post.'

'What about our other guests, Papa?' Emma was looking round anxiously to see what had become of the other carriages. She could not, as joint hostess, simply abandon her guests, no matter how illustrious the summons. And Aunt Augusta, in the second carriage with Major Stratton and two of the other ladies, was nowhere to be seen.

'I have sent the grooms to find them,' he said. 'I am sure they will appear in due course, if they can make their way through this crush. I did explain to the Duke how we were placed, but he just laughed and said they were all welcome—if they could actually reach his party. He must know that they will never get through the crowd at all if they do not start immediately—as we must. I fear we shall have to leave the barouche here, Lady Hardinge,' he added apologetically. 'Do you feel able to reach York's party on foot?'

Jamie shook her head. 'I do not think I should like to try it with this huge throng of people, sir,' she said. 'Even a royal invitation may be declined by a lady in my…interesting condition. Richard shall make my excuses.' She glanced up at her husband through her dark lashes and then quickly looked away.

Emma knew that Jamie was perfectly capable of making her way across the turf—but had not the least desire for the Duke of York's company. They both knew exactly how difficult it was to avoid the lecherous looks and touching hands of the Regent and his brothers. It was a pity that Emma herself had no excuse to offer.

Richard gave his wife a speaking look. 'As you command, my love,' he said. 'And I am sure that His Royal Highness will allow me to return to your side as soon as I have done so.' Richard jumped lightly down from the carriage and turned to offer his hand to Emma. 'Kit, will you remain here with Jamie until I return? It should not take me many minutes to do the pretty to our revered commander-in-chief.'

Rising from her deep curtsy, Emma listened with admiration to Richard's skilful handling of the Duke of York. Richard made it sound as if Jamie had been most eager to wait on His Royal Highness, and had had to be restrained for her own safety.

'Of course, Hardinge, of course,' replied the Duke genially. 'You had better return to her at once, too.

Can't leave her unattended in a place like this. Have to look after the little woman, eh?'

Richard bowed politely. Emma knew that he was delighted to have won his point so easily, but there was not the slightest sign of triumph on his handsome features. Emma schooled her own into an expression of concern. 'Take care of her, Richard,' she said. He bowed again, and left them. Emma could have sworn that he winked.

The Duke turned back to Emma. 'Delighted you could join us, ma'am. And you, too, Sir Edward,' he added, nodding affably at Emma's father. 'You will both have a much better view from here. And with your colt so heavily fancied, you will want to be in at the death, so to speak.' He laughed at his own wit. His entourage joined in politely.

Emma smiled up at him. 'Yes, indeed. But what of your own horse, sir? Might he not win?'

The Duke turned to one of the officers who accompanied him. 'What are the latest odds on Prince Leopold, Forster?'

'Pretty long, sir,' replied Colonel Forster, stepping forward to join the little group. At first glance, he appeared to be a handsome brown-haired man in his middle forties but, on closer inspection, his face showed the signs of dissipation common among the royal set. 'At least twenty to one, when I last checked. No one is backing him, it appears—apart from yourself, of course, sir.'

Emma found the Colonel's manner more than a little obsequious. And she did not like the way he looked at her. Small wonder, perhaps, given that he was one of the Duke's cronies.

'A lot of the money is chasing Sir Edward's Golden Star,' the Colonel continued. 'At this rate, he'll be the hot favourite by the time they go to post.'

The Duke sighed. 'Lucky dog,' he said enviously. 'Nothing like winning the Derby, Sir Edward. Nothing at all.' He turned to offer his arm to Emma. 'On the turf, at least,' he added with a knowing smile as Emma placed her fingers lightly on his sleeve. 'Shall we stroll down to the rail, ma'am? You will have a better view from there.' He placed his free hand over her gloved fingers and squeezed.

Emma had no choice but to agree—and to resist the urge to pull her hand away.

The crowd fell back respectfully as the royal party moved out. Emma was surprised to see Kit Stratton on foot, struggling to push his way through to them. He must have left his stallion by the carriage. Perhaps he had realised, at last, that such a beast was singularly ill-suited to Epsom on Derby day.

'Sir,' said Sir Edward formally, 'may I present Christopher Stratton, youngest son of the late Sir William Stratton, of Stratton Magna?'

The Duke acknowledged Kit's elegant bow with a nonchalant wave of his hand. 'Knew your father, my boy,' he said.

Kit bowed again. 'Sir, Lord Hardinge has charged me to say that he doubts that any other members of Sir Edward's party will be able to join you here. The carriages are hemmed in by the crowd and the risks of trying to bring the ladies across on foot are now too great, with all the world and his wife trying to get nearer the winning post. Lord Hardinge asked me to present his apologies, sir.'

'Of course, of course,' said the Duke. 'Not to be thought of. Can't take any risks with the ladies.'

Emma thought she detected disappointment in his face but he said nothing more. Recognising that she would now be the only lady present, she resigned herself to being the focus of his attentions until the start of the race, at least. With luck, he would be so intent on watching his horse that he would forget she was there.

Colonel Forster had stationed himself immediately behind the Duke. 'Unusual name, Stratton,' he said musingly, as if to himself, but loud enough to ensure he was heard. 'Had problems with an officer of that name a few years ago, in the Peninsula. Heard he was killed at Waterloo.' He turned to Kit, who was standing a few paces away, alongside Emma's Papa. 'Any relation to Captain Stratton of the 95th?'

Kit coloured slightly and drew himself up extremely straight. He was almost a head taller than the Colonel. Looking down at the older man with obvious distaste, Kit said, 'My second brother, *Major* Hugo Stratton, acquitted himself with great courage on the field at Waterloo, sir, where he was severely wounded. I collect that you yourself were serving in London by then?'

The scathing sarcasm in Kit's voice was unmistakable. His easy charm had completely vanished. Emma was astonished that he should behave in such a manner before royalty—especially the commander-in-chief—and profoundly grateful that Major Stratton himself was escorting Aunt Augusta and was therefore nowhere near the Duke's marquee. There was clearly something very wrong between Colonel Forster and the Stratton brothers.

A sudden commotion by the rail distracted them. A small weatherbeaten man in riding dress was desperately trying to push his way through. At the sight of the Duke's well-known figure, he stopped in his tracks, clearly uncertain as to what he should do.

The Duke of York was well versed in all matters of the turf. He might not have had dealings with Sir Edward Fitzwilliam's trainer, but he knew perfectly well who he was—and that only trouble would have led him to leave his runner at this stage of such a race. 'Chifney, ain't it?' he said, beckoning the man forward. 'Come through, man, come through. You need to speak to Sir Edward, I collect.'

Mr Chifney removed his hat and bowed very low. Emma could see that the back of his neck had gone deep red.

'Your Royal Highness…' Mr Chifney stopped, clearly unsure of how to proceed.

The Duke smiled at Mr Chifney's anxious face. 'Never mind the protocol, man,' he said genially. 'Your errand is obviously urgent, so spit it out. Don't keep Sir Edward on tenterhooks.'

'Thank you, sir,' said Sir Edward quickly. 'What's happened, Chifney? Is something wrong with Golden Star?'

Mr Chifney's reddened features paled. 'Your Royal Highness…sir…' He cleared his throat.

'Golden Star is dead lame, sir.' The words came out in a rush.

'What?' exclaimed Sir Edward. Then, remembering where he was, he added, 'I beg your pardon, sir, but the horse was in top form when I saw him barely an hour ago. I don't see how he can be lame now.'

The Duke looked concerned. 'I sympathise, Sir Edward. Especially as he was like to be the favourite. Perhaps your man will explain how it happened?'

Mr Chifney looked more than a little guilty. 'Of course, Your Royal Highness,' he said before lapsing into silence once more.

'Well?' said the Duke testily.

Mr Chifney looked stricken. 'He…Golden Star… he was kicked by…by one of the other horses. He's dead lame, Your Highness.'

'You told us that before,' said the Duke. 'I am sure that Sir Edward will want to know how it is that such an accident came about. I dare say that someone has been negligent in the care of him.'

Mr Chifney tried to shake his head.

'And which of the other runners was responsible for this injury?' continued the Duke without a pause. 'Must be a bad-tempered brute, that's all I can say.'

Mr Chifney seemed to shrink in his clothes. 'It was…it was Prince Leopold, Your Royal Highness,' he whispered. 'Mr Lake's horse.'

The Duke reddened angrily. 'You mean *my* horse,' he barked. 'You, of all people, know perfectly well that Lake is my master of horse and has entered Prince Leopold on my behalf. And now you tell me that *my* horse has lamed the favourite. Good God!'

Sir Edward intervened, placing his own bulk between the Duke and the miserable trainer. 'I am sure it must have been an accident, sir. We all know how unpredictable these highly strung thoroughbreds can be, especially on a race day. With your permission, I will go and see Golden Star's injury for myself. With proper care, there will be no lasting damage, I am sure.' Sir Edward bowed in response to the Duke's curt nod and made his way to the rail.

Emma saw that a relieved Mr Chifney was backing his way out of the royal presence, bowing so low that his nose was almost touching his knees. Beads of sweat were dripping from the poor man's forehead. With his vision restricted, Mr Chifney almost collided with Kit Stratton, who had retreated to the edge of the group, as far as possible from the Duke and Colonel Forster. Kit's whole body still seemed to be quivering with rage.

Deliberately drawing the Duke's attention back to herself, she said, in the voice of a bewildered innocent, 'Oh, dear. Poor Golden Star. And I had put almost all my pin money on him, too. May I prevail upon you to advise me, sir, on what I should do now?'

The Duke patted her hand consolingly, though he still looked more than a little irritated. 'Well,' he began, 'the favourite is like to be Nectar now, I fancy. He did win the Two Thousand Guineas, after all. One of these gentlemen would be delighted to place your money for you, I am sure.'

Several of the gentlemen made to offer their services, but Colonel Forster was before them all. He immediately took a pace forward and bowed. Emma thought he leered at her, the moment his face was hidden from his royal master.

Emma produced a girlish giggle. 'Oh, no,' she cried blithely. 'I have had enough of favourites. Since your outsider has made such a point of asserting himself, sir—' she looked up at the Duke through her dark lashes, willing the last of his temper to disappear '—I shall put my money on him. Prince Leopold it shall be!'

Chapter Nine

The Duke was clearly finding it difficult to contain his excitement. His hand was squeezing Emma's fingers so tightly that she almost cried out in pain. 'Sir…my hand…' she began, but it had no effect at all. His attention was all on his horse.

'By God, ma'am,' he said vehemently, 'I do believe he could win.' Under his breath, he was muttering encouragement to his horse, but Emma could not make out any of the words. At least the Duke had enough consideration for the presence of a lady to moderate his language just a trifle, she thought waspishly. The moment he relaxed his grip a fraction, she gently eased her hand away, grateful that he seemed to notice nothing.

But then she, too, was caught up in the excitement of the last few furlongs. Though the favourite, Nectar, had led from the start, two other runners were starting to overhaul him in the home straight—and one of them was the Duke's outsider. For more than a furlong, the three horses battled it out. There was nothing to choose between them.

'Come on, Prince Leopold,' Emma breathed, balling her fingers into fists in her excitement. Beside her, the Duke seemed like to burst out of his tight-fitting uniform. His neck was becoming almost purple.

Half a furlong from home, the third horse started to fall back a little, but Nectar and Prince Leopold were neck and neck.

'Use your whip, man,' muttered the Duke testily.

It was as if the jockey had heard his royal master, for he applied his whip with even more vigour than before. Prince Leopold increased his pace a fraction and started to pull away from his rival.

'Nectar must be finished now,' the Duke grunted through clenched teeth. 'Never should have led from the off.'

Fifty yards to go. Twenty…

A great shout went up from the crowd. Prince Leopold had reached the winning post half a length ahead of the favourite. The royal outsider had won the Derby.

The Duke of York's beaming smile encompassed everyone around him. 'Dashed good show, what?' he said. 'Never would have thought he'd show such a turn of speed.' The Duke's entourage crowded round to congratulate him. Emma's father joined in, too, though his disappointment was evident on his face. Someone called for three cheers, which rang out lustily. In the crush, Emma felt sure that a hand brushed across her breast. She whipped round to find Colonel Forster at her side, with a knowing look in his eye. She shuddered in disgust.

Unfortunately for Emma, the Duke had no intention of letting her go immediately. He soon had her hand back on his arm. 'Well, ma'am,' he said, patting her fingers even more forcefully than before, 'I congratulate you on your choice of runner. Splendid judgement, if you will allow me to say so. Much better than all these frippery fellows here. You will have made quite a tidy sum from today's business, I'll warrant. Good odds, eh?'

At the Duke's elbow, Colonel Forster nodded. 'Twenty to one, sir. Shall I collect Miss Fitzwilliam's winnings?'

'Do,' replied the Duke. 'I'm sure Miss Fitzwilliam would be grateful. You will find us all with the winner when you return.'

'Thank you, Colonel,' Emma said. 'You are most kind.' For a while, at least, Emma would be spared the sight of him leering at her, or worse. As soon as she had received her winnings, she could try to make her escape. Kit Stratton was surely broad-shouldered enough to clear a path through the crowd for Emma and her father. And Emma would welcome any opportunity to probe the reasons for that outburst against Colonel Forster. She was even beginning to feel some softening in her feelings towards Kit. He had, she decided, shown admirable readiness to defend his brother.

Glancing quickly at the young man, she saw that his fury had abated only a little. His face was now a picture of anger overlaid with chagrin. Emma decided that it would be wise to remove him from the vicinity of Colonel Forster, lest their quarrel flare up

once more. The Duke had not noticed the earlier al-
tercation—or so it had seemed. But any repetition
could only spell danger for Kit—and perhaps for
Hugo, too.

The Duke patted Emma's hand and invited her to
accompany him to the winner's enclosure. She responded graciously—what choice did she have?—but
her quick mind was already trying to think of ac-
ceptable ways for the Fitzwilliam party to make their
excuses. Since the Duke had never before had a
Derby winner, the celebrations were likely to become
very rowdy, very soon. Emma had no wish to be a
spectator of drunken revels, even royal ones.

'Well!' the Countess said gaily. 'Whoever would
have thought it? Clearly all you betting men under-
estimated the Duke's colt.'

'Mmm,' her husband agreed ruefully. 'His Royal
Highness will be celebrating for a se'enight, I dare
say. I shall take care to keep out of his way. I put
my blunt on the favourite—and look where it got me.
What about you, Hugo?'

Hugo, now sitting opposite the Hardinges, raised a
knowing eyebrow. He had willingly accepted Lady
Hardinge's invitation to join them in the barouche,
since the Hardinges were considerably more conge-
nial than the company in the other carriage. Mrs Warenne's non-stop chatter was more than a little trying.
And the two young ladies in her charge simpered
unbearably, even with him. They would certainly be
much more at home with the dashing blade who had
so readily taken his place. 'I am heartily sorry for Sir

Edward. I might have backed his horse, too, but after
Golden Star was scratched, I decided the game was
not worth the candle. So…I still have my guineas in
my pocket. Unlike you, Richard, it would seem,' he
added with a twitch of the lips.

'Hugo—'

'Major, I congratulate you,' said the Countess.
'Perhaps I might prevail on you to give my husband
lessons in self-restraint? He—'

Richard grinned and laid a gentle hand on his
wife's arm. 'Look,' he said, pointing, 'Kit has finally
escaped from the royal clutches. And now that the
crowd is thinning out a little, he should be able to
reach us without having the coat ripped from his back
in the process.'

Hugo followed Richard's pointing finger. Kit was
shouldering his way through the good-humoured
crowd, his unusual height ensuring that his progress
was easily followed. Behind him, in the space Kit
had cleared, came Emma and her father. Even at a
distance, Hugo could see that Emma was a little
flushed. And her father looked decidedly irritated.
Hugo was not altogether surprised. Sir Edward had
every right to be cross at losing his fancied runner.
And, no doubt, the royal Duke had been up to his
usual tricks. Emma would do much better to keep
away from such a man, however much it might increase her consequence to be seen in his company.

As the little trio made its way slowly towards the
Fitzwilliam barouche, Emma took Kit's arm, forsak-
ing her father's. Moments later, the pair were conversing with real animation. Hugo was mightily sur-

prised. Although Kit was a good fellow at heart, Emma seemed to have taken against him, from the moment they met. Hugo had been at a loss to account for it, since Kit usually had all the ladies almost falling at his feet. But then, Emma was not just any lady...

Hugo climbed awkwardly down from his place in the barouche so that Emma and her father would be able to rejoin the Hardinges. Now that the main event of the day was concluded, the whole Fitzwilliam party would wish to return to the house to enjoy a relaxing dinner. If some of the young men had their way, there would be many tales of wagers won and lost over the port tonight, and much commiseration with Sir Edward over his appalling luck. He was a genial host and would indulge them—for a while— but, even in his disappointment, he would not forget his duties to the ladies of the party. The gentlemen would be delivered to the drawing room in reasonable time, and not too much the worse for wear.

Emma was laughing gently when she reached the barouche. She looked, Hugo decided, absolutely radiant. Her earlier flush—had it been anger?—had subsided into most becoming colour and her golden hair was glinting under an elegant confection of silk and feathers. Most of all, her beautiful eyes were sparkling with mischievous good humour. For the first time in his life, Hugo found himself envying his brother. Kit seemed to have added Emma's name to his long list of conquests.

Kit was forced to relinquish Emma's hand when they reached the barouche, for Hugo had ensured he

was standing ready to hand her up. Touching her
might bring him pain, but he was drawn to her as to
no woman he had ever known. He smiled down into
her beautiful face. 'Allow me, ma'am,' he said quietly, trying to ensure that he sounded as normal as
possible. He might still be haunted by that outrageous
kiss and by the feel of her in his arms, but he was
determined that she would never know. He prayed
that she might have put it from her mind.

Hugo was perversely glad that Emma's gloved
hand barely touched his as she stepped up into the
barouche. She was as light as a piece of thistledown,
he decided, though nothing like as fragile. There was
nothing fragile about a lady who could ride her high-
couraged horses for hour upon hour without the least
sign of fatigue.

Behind him, Kit murmured softly, 'Prettily done
indeed. Couldn't have done it better m'self.' Hugo
could hear the smile in Kit's voice, but it vanished
suddenly as he added, 'A word in your ear,
brother…'

Taking her seat once more, Emma covered her
burning fingers with her free hand. She could not tell
whether she was trying to conceal her shaking or to
preserve the warmth that had suddenly pervaded her
fingers. Good God, she had barely touched him. If
she could have done so without giving offence, she
would have sprung up into the barouche without any
assistance at all. But he was standing there, clearly
waiting for her, and he had looked so…so…

She was at a loss for words. There had been something in his face...but she could not describe it, even to herself—and she certainly did not begin to understand it.

Sir Edward's voice broke into Emma's ravelled thoughts. He was telling Richard about his horse. 'The Duke was bent on making amends for the injury to Golden Star, though it was quite unnecessary. The accident was no one's fault. Prince Leopold is a thoroughly bad-tempered brute, but he won fair and square. I doubt my colt would have had the beating of him, even on his best form.'

Richard nodded absently; something seemed to have distracted him. 'What on earth can Kit have said to Hugo?' Richard nodded in the direction of the two brothers, who had moved out of earshot. 'He's got a face like thunder all of a sudden. He doesn't usually allow young Kit to get under his skin.'

Emma knew that an explanation was due, however awkward it might prove, but she was saved by her father's intervention. 'I doubt that young Kit is the cause, Richard. There's something havey-cavey going on with one of York's hangers-on, a Colonel Forster. Do you know him?' When Richard shook his head, Sir Edward continued, 'Forster made some very disparaging remarks about Major Stratton's time in the Peninsula and Kit naturally took umbrage. Seemed to me that Forster was baiting him deliberately. Don't know if the Duke heard what was said, but if Forster was repeating rumours from Horse Guards, the commander-in-chief is bound to know. Very awkward. Very.' He smiled lovingly at Emma. 'I was glad Emma extricated us so quickly from that little gathering. It could have become quite ugly, especially as the Duke was on the point of breaking out the champagne.'

Richard frowned. At his side, Jamie too wore a worried look. Emma reached out a hand to her. 'Pray, do not be concerned, Jamie. It seemed to me that Colonel Forster was simply trying to make mischief. And I'm certain that His Royal Highness ignored what was said.' Emma was trying to sound more optimistic than she felt. She had failed to glean any information from Kit after they left the royal party. He had been charming, and entertaining…but he would not be drawn on anything to do with his brother.

Jamie gave voice to Emma's thoughts. 'There is something of a mystery here,' she said after a moment, 'but I, for one, refuse to believe anything against Major Stratton. From what I learned in Brussels, he acquitted himself most honourably on the field at Waterloo. And I know him to be a very fine man. Colonel Forster sounds to be exactly the kind of man whom I would not wish to know.'

At dinner a few hours later, Emma was surprised to find that Aunt Augusta had seated her between Kit Stratton and the Honourable James Frobisher, a singularly dull young gentleman who had nothing but aristocratic lineage to recommend him. Emma, a practised hostess, was equally polite and friendly to them both. Watching her while she listened to Mr Frobisher's self-important discourse, no one would have known that she was longing for the moment when she could, with propriety, turn back to Kit. He, at least, was prepared to converse about something other than himself, his prowess on the hunting field, and his family's numberless acres.

Kit had certainly set out to be entertaining. He had also decided, Emma was sure, that the conversation would be steered well away from any discussion of his enigmatic older brother. Faced with Kit's resolution, Emma yielded with good grace, allowing the light-hearted conversation to range as widely as he wished. Since Hugo was seated at the far end of the table, and on the same side, Emma could not judge whether the other guests were succeeding in drawing him out. But she would be able to find that out from her father—later.

'And so we had no choice but to pretend that the handkerchief belonged to his mother,' said Kit, concluding a slightly racy but very amusing anecdote.

Emma laughed, as did all those within earshot. Kit was certainly an entertaining raconteur. She could not help but notice the envious glances cast her way by several of the young ladies present. For appearances' sake, Aunt Augusta had had to invite a number of débutantes to the house-party, as well as potential suitors. It was rather too obvious for Emma's peace of mind that Aunt Augusta's choice had fallen on young ladies who would be cast into the shade by her niece. Two of them were pretty enough, but too silly for words. The other two were really rather plain. And none of them—of course—was as great an heiress as Emma. No wonder they were looking daggers at her. Not only had they been excluded from an invitation to wait on a royal Duke, but the handsomest gentleman in the room was now focusing all his attention on Emma.

Miss Mayhew, who was not only plain but also ill-educated, in Emma's opinion, was making sheep's eyes across the table at Kit Stratton. Emma was glad to see that Kit was pretending not to notice, at least for the moment. His company manners were exactly as they should be. When the party was eventually reunited in the drawing room, however, Miss Mayhew was bound to resume her gauche assault. Although Kit would surely continue to bear it with good grace, it would be most embarrassing for the other guests. Emma resolved to have a word with her aunt. Although Miss Mayhew's mother had insisted on accompanying her daughter to the house-party, she had done nothing at all to restrain her daughter's unbecoming behaviour. It must fall to the senior hostess to drop a word in the girl's ear.

When Mrs Warenne rose to signal the ladies' departure, Mr Frobisher almost knocked over his own chair in his rush to help Emma from hers. His fingers brushed against her bare shoulder—intentionally, Emma was sure. She felt nothing. Mr Frobisher was neither attractive nor repellent. He simply left her totally unmoved…whereas the slightest touch of Hugo Stratton's fingers made her skin prickle and heat, even through several layers of clothing. She tried to remember whether it had been so before that incredible kiss. For the life of her, she could not say. All her encounters with the Major seemed to have merged, somehow; she was no longer sure what she had felt when they first met again. Perhaps that was because they had not touched until that fateful day in Jamie's conservatory? No…that could not be right. They must have shaken hands a score of times. It was a conundrum, to be sure, and Emma knew that it would require cool detachment to puzzle it out.

But, whenever Major Hugo Stratton was concerned, Emma's cool detachment seemed to fly out of the window.

Chapter Ten

'Perhaps you would favour us with some music, Miss Mayhew?' Emma was resolved to be kind to the girl, especially as she was likely to receive a sharp dressing-down from Aunt Augusta, some time later in the evening. 'You have such a sweet singing voice, you know. Some of the gentlemen have remarked upon it, most particularly.' Emma's generous compliment had the advantage of being true.

Miss Mayhew simpered and blushed a little, before making her way to the instrument. She must know that she would appear at her best if she was in the middle of a song when the gentlemen returned to the drawing room. And if she were in any doubt, one look at her smiling, nodding mother, comfortably ensconced on the sofa alongside the Dowager Countess, would have settled the matter.

Miss Mayhew had barely started her song when the door opened to admit the gentlemen. Emma was at first surprised to see that Major Stratton arrived along with the others, but a moment's reflection explained matters. This house, unlike her father's or

Richard's, had all its public rooms on the ground floor, and only bedrooms on the floor above. It might have been expressly designed to accommodate a man who had difficulty climbing stairs. It was even possible to reach the garden directly from the drawing room, via a stone terrace that ran the length of the room. Emma had not yet taken time to explore the gardens, but Jamie had assured her that they were splendid, laid out in the old style with high hedges and secret nooks and crannies, all brimful of beautiful plants.

Emma looked longingly at the French windows. The room was already uncomfortably hot—and the arrival of eight gentlemen would certainly make it even hotter. A few moments in the cool evening air would be delightful…but, as joint hostess, she must not be seduced away from her duties to her guests.

Emma's father was looking quite pleased with himself. Good food and wine had helped him forget his disappointment. Taking his sister to one side, so that only Emma and Jamie could hear, he whispered, 'Here they all are, m'dear. Told you I wouldn't let them linger in the dining room. Now, what about a few tables for cards?'

Aunt Augusta gave him a withering look. 'There's no point in bringing them back early if you're going to allow them to be tied to card tables for the rest of the evening. Really, Edward, you should know better.' Her voice had risen enough to start attracting attention, but she simply turned her back on the other guests and said, in a voice that was almost a whisper,

'The young men must *circulate*, Edward, else what is the point of bringing them here in the first place?'

Emma looked at Jamie and then looked quickly away. It would not do for either of them to laugh. Emma forced herself to give all her attention to Miss Mayhew's performance on the pianoforte.

The song ended. Under cover of the polite applause, Jamie said quietly to Emma's aunt, 'I can quite understand that Sir Edward would welcome a rubber of whist, ma'am. Richard's mama is a fine player, you know. Perhaps Richard and I might make up the four?'

Aunt Augusta was surprised. 'Well, if you are sure, ma'am,' she said, hesitating a little. 'I suppose there is something to be said for indulging my brother's desire for cards—provided the table is set up in some other room. It would not do to distract the young men. It's difficult enough as it is...' She bustled off to collect the Dowager.

Emma's papa was beaming at Jamie. 'By Jove, ma'am, you think of everything.' Jamie merely smiled and led the way out to the library where the little card party would not be disturbed.

Aunt Augusta brought up the rear, fussing as usual. Emma was forcibly reminded of a sheepdog snapping at the heels of its flock. Aunt Augusta was quite determined that all the young male guests should have an opportunity of setting out their stalls before her niece, though Emma was very sure that none of them would suit. She looked around the room. One of the gentlemen would be at her side in just a moment, of that she was quite certain. Please, Lord, let it not be that boring—

'Mr Frobisher.' Emma smiled gamely at her erstwhile dinner partner who had come to station himself between her and the other guests. There was no escape.

'Delightful music, ma'am,' said Mr Frobisher. 'I hope you will favour us with a song or two in the course of the evening.'

Emma nodded politely. If Mr Frobisher was determined to monopolise her, the evening was set to become duller by the minute.

Hugo retreated as far as possible from the instrument the moment Miss Mayhew rose from it. None of the other three débutantes had any musical talent at all, and it pained him to be forced to listen to them. There was a darkish corner at the far end of the long room, by the French windows. From there, he would be able to watch all the younger men circling round Emma like vultures. And, if watching became too much of an ordeal, he would slip out on to the terrace and into the blessed solitude of the garden.

Hugo saw that Kit was being his usual charming self. While the males were buzzing round Emma, the females were using every trick in the book to attract Kit's attention. All except Emma. She was concentrating her full attention on the appalling Frobisher. He had been fawning over the poor girl all night, and now—

Hugo's senses were suddenly on the alert. Frobisher, presumably unable to hold his wine, was starting to paw Emma in a most unseemly fashion.

Before Hugo could get his stiff limbs into motion, his younger brother had taken charge. 'I think you've had your share of our hostess's company, Frobisher,' he said lightly. 'Time to give the other fellows a chance, eh?' He offered his arm. 'Tempt you to a turn about the room, Miss Fitzwilliam? It is a little hot—especially in this stuffy corner.'

Hugo found himself smiling a little ruefully. Kit was really very, very good. Frobisher was looking stunned. Had he understood the import of Kit's words? Probably not—especially if his brain was fuddled with wine.

Emma and Kit made an exceptionally handsome couple promenading round the huge drawing room. And all Emma's earlier hostility to Kit seemed to have disappeared. It was more than mere gratitude for having saved her from Frobisher, Hugo concluded. The pair were laughing together now as if they had been fast friends for years...perhaps more than friends. Trust Kit to succeed with the most desirable woman in the room. He certainly seemed much taken with Emma. It would not be merely her beauty, for Kit had had more than his fair share of Society beauties in his short career on the town. No, Emma was a match for Kit in all sorts of ways. Above all, she equalled Kit in independence of spirit. She cast all the other ladies into the shade.

When all the guests had performed, the lot fell to Emma. Hugo fancied she was trying to resist her aunt's persuasions, but her protest could not last long.

Mrs Warenne was like the hot wind blowing up from Africa—a wise soldier soon learned that there was no alternative but to let it have its way.

Leaning back against the wall in his obscure corner, Hugo let Emma's music fill his mind. It was the first time he had ever heard her sing—and it was beautiful. Her singing voice was lower than he had expected, and full of honeyed warmth. She sang her simple Italian ballad with real feeling, almost caressing each word, as if she herself were that abandoned Italian girl mourning the loss of her love.

The enthusiastic applause was interrupted by the arrival of the tea tray. There would be no encore from Emma, who immediately set herself to pouring refreshments for her guests. Frobisher was among the first to present himself to her and seemed inclined to linger at her side. Watching, Hugo found his hands balling into fists.

'Will you inform the party in the library that tea is being served, please, Godfrey?' Emma said. As usual, her first concern was the comfort of her guests.

'The table has already broken up, Miss Emma,' replied the butler. 'The Countess and the Dowager Countess send their apologies. They wished to retire without intruding on the other guests. Lord Hardinge and Sir Edward have repaired to the billiard room.'

Hugo could see that Emma was disappointed at being deserted by her father. He was not therefore surprised to hear her encouraging Frobisher to join the billiard party. She must be heartily sick of the man after this evening's unsavoury performance. Un-

fortunately for Emma, Frobisher did not seem inclined to take the hint.

Kit intervened once again. Taking Frobisher firmly
by the arm, he said, 'Splendid idea, ma'am. Know
Frobisher is the very devil with the cue.' He took
Frobisher's cup and handed it to Emma, who was
looking warmly up at Kit. 'You're not afraid of a
challenge from me, are you, Frobisher?' Kit continued. The sarcasm in his voice was unmistakable.

Hugo almost felt sorry for Frobisher. The man had
no chance at all against Kit's stronger will. With a
few carefully chosen words, Kit had taken charge and
propelled Frobisher out of the room. Emma would,
undoubtedly, be very grateful. Not that it showed for
even a second though, for no sooner had the door
closed behind the pair than Emma was busying herself in organising further entertainment for her guests.
In a moment, she would notice that Hugo was missing from the main party, and then...

Hugo slid his hand behind the curtain to undo the
window latch so that he could slip out into the garden. He did not want Emma's solicitude. She would
not look up at him as she had looked at his magnificent brother. For tonight, at least, he would rather
she did not look at him at all.

Emma took a deep breath and stepped out on to
the terrace, allowing the heavy drapes to fall back
into place behind her. She needed just a few moments
of solitude and cool air to clear her head, and then
she would return to her guests. No one would notice
her departure, surely? The party in the drawing room

was now totally involved in a childish game of lottery tickets, the young ladies squealing with pleasure every time they won. Even Mrs Mayhew had been persuaded to play, though in rather more restrained fashion. And the billiard room group was bound to be deeply absorbed in their game. She supposed Major Stratton must have gone to join them, too. One moment he was leaning nonchalantly against the far wall, clearly unmoved by Emma's singing, the next he had disappeared. No doubt he preferred the excitement of billiards to the tame entertainments on offer in the drawing room.

His indifference hurt. Emma had to admit that to herself. Knowing he was listening, she had poured all her unvoiced longings into that song, immersing herself in the character of the heartbroken peasant girl. She felt those longings still, as if some part of that character were also her own. Strange, for she had never loved and lost. She had never even loved.

The grey stone balustrading was pleasantly cool under Emma's hands. It felt calming, somehow. Emma took a deep breath of the scented night air. She tried to distinguish the various perfumes, but could not. Jamie, with her vast knowledge of plants, would have known them at once, but she had retired to bed. If Emma wanted to find the source of the elusive fragrances assailing her senses, she would have to go into the garden and seek them out. Why not? It would take but a few moments. The heady perfumes were incredibly seductive, making her whole body feel as if she were relaxing into a warm, soothing bath, yet heightening all her senses at the same time. A most extraordinary combination.

Intrigued, Emma wandered from avenue to avenue, more than half-dreaming now. The scents were becoming stronger at every step, almost intoxicating. At the corner of a secret garden, she paused, wondering. Yes, here! She closed her eyes and executed a lazy pirouette, relishing the feel of fine silken petticoats as her skirts billowed and then settled back against her limbs. It was as if velvet gloves had stroked her bare skin. Velvet gloves worn on gentle hands...

Emma paused to inhale yet more of the voluptuous perfume in the tiny garden. This strange place was meant to be seen by moonlight. Its white trumpet flowers shimmered mysteriously on long stems that were almost invisible. In the centre, a tall arch was dripping with pale roses. At the far end of the path, framed by the arch, was a marble statue of some ancient pagan goddess, beautiful and commanding. The venerable yew hedge, dark and brooding, stood sentry against any intrusion into her hidden grotto. Was this the secret garden of the fairy tales, appearing only once in a lifetime and then only to those in love?

For she *was* in love...in love with Hugo Stratton. It was as if she had always known it.

She picked a stem of the magical white flowers, inhaling deeply of their ravishing scent. For an instant, she felt as if she were hovering somewhere above the ground, looking down at her own body meandering among the flowers. And then she floated softly back to earth.

She reached up to pull down a branch of roses, awed by their pristine perfection. Were they white— or perhaps pale pink? It was of no moment. In the silvery moonlight, they were unbelievably beautiful. She stroked a soft petal, marvelling at its velvet bloom, like a baby's soft cheek.

If Hugo were here—and if he loved her in return— he would pluck these roses and offer them to her as a token. He would tell her that the roses would fade and die, but that his love would last for ever. He would take her in his arms and...

The moon went behind a cloud. Emma sank down on to the old stone seat and closed her eyes. She could still see the magic garden in her mind. She knew she was dreaming, but she was unable to break the powerful spell that seemed to have wound itself around her. It was so enticing... She would let it carry her away...for just a little while. She put her hand on the cool stone, stroking languidly, wondering what it would be like to stroke a man's taut body, to feel his skin under her fingers—

A strong hand covered hers. She opened wide, un- seeing eyes. In barely a heartbeat, she was pulled gently to her feet and into powerful arms. She knew that Hugo had answered her unspoken summons and come to claim her. And now he was going to kiss her, to reawaken those wonderful feelings that had been haunting her, it seemed, for ever.

Shafts of pain were stabbing through Hugo's body, but he could not close his eyes against the sight. The woman he loved was melting into the arms of his rake of a brother! By God, Kit had excelled himself this time! One day the pair were almost at outs, the next they were kissing like some latter-day Romeo and Juliet. Well, Kit Stratton was no Romeo, faithful unto death. Don Juan, more like. She would find that out soon enough. And it would be a fitting reward.

Hugo allowed his fury to overpower him, obscuring the pain. He looked round, vainly, for an escape route from his dark corner. There was only one entrance to this tiny garden. He would be seen. He closed his eyes deliberately then, dwelling on the picture they made, trying to fuel his anger yet more. Not only had she come to an assignation with his brother, she had even arranged matters so that he was forced to provide an audience for her wanton conduct. Damn her! She was—

The stillness was rent by a woman's scream.

'Mr Stratton! Miss Fitzwilliam!' The high-pitched outrage came from a slight figure in white muslin who stood, transfixed, between the dark hedges flanking the entrance to the secret garden. 'Oh, how could you?' The figure turned and fled in the direction of the house.

Kit and Emma had sprung apart at the sound, but there would now be no hiding their guilt at being so discovered. For a second, Hugo felt intense pleasure at the thought of their fate, especially when he detected a hint of self-satisfaction on his brother's insufferably handsome face. They would be well served, the pair of them.

But the look on Emma's face banished all trace of malice from his mind.

She was stricken. She was looking at Kit Stratton as if she had never laid eyes on him before.

She took several steps back from him, like someone retreating from a horrifying apparition. Her hands had gone to her flaming cheeks. Her eyes were wide, fearful, and very dark in the strange half-light.

'Mr Stratton!' Her voice was a low, intense whisper, throbbing with suppressed emotion. 'Oh, how could you?' she said, echoing that earlier heartfelt cry. 'I thought…I thought I was… Oh, dear God, what made you follow me here?' She turned from him to lean her forehead against the rose arch. Her shoulders were shaking.

Kit made to comfort her but she thrust him away. 'Stay away from me,' she hissed, turning back to face him like a spitting snake. 'How dare you touch me? Would you do me even more harm? You have ruined me. Let that be enough for you.'

Kit stood motionless, undecided. Guilt was beginning to show on his features now—at last—but overlaid with a degree of confusion. 'Miss Fitzwilliam, I—'

Emma cut him short. 'There is nothing you can say to me now. Please leave.' As he still hesitated, she drew herself up to her full height, in the proud posture of the garden's marble patroness, and cried, 'For God's sake, go!'

Kit swallowed hard, bowed with considerably less than his usual elegance, and quit the field, totally vanquished.

Emma stood motionless until his figure was completely hidden from view. Then she crumpled, sobbing, on to the cold stone bench.

Chapter Eleven

It was suddenly very cold. Emma wrapped her arms around her bare shoulders, trying to stop the shivering that had taken control of her body. Tears were still running down her cheeks, though much more slowly now. She made no attempt to brush them away. She berated herself with the thought that, if someone should come to find her, she would present the proper picture of abject misery, entirely as expected for a lady whose reputation had been ruined.

How had it happened? And with Kit Stratton, of all people?

Emma did not know. It was something to do with the silence of the moonlit night, the hypnotic scent of the flowers in the magic garden…and her own folly in allowing herself to dream of Hugo Stratton. The arms that had enfolded her had been Hugo's. She had looked up into Hugo's grey eyes, warm with love. And Hugo had kissed her…

But it had not been Hugo—none of it. Surrounded by childish fantasies of her own weaving, she had persuaded herself that she was melting into Hugo's arms, but no amount of dreaming could turn Kit's kiss into Hugo's. Kit's was a practised, seductive kiss. But it was empty, none the less. And then that benighted child had appeared among the yews, screeching like a demented harpy, before Emma had had time to tear herself away from the wrong brother. She could never face either of them again.

'Miss Fitzwilliam. Emma. May I do something for you? Some water, perhaps?'

Hugo Stratton was standing before her, like some dread apparition come to haunt her. Where had he appeared from? Surely no one had come through the gap in the hedge? Dear God! He must have been there all the time. He must have seen—

Emma's tears stopped abruptly, overtaken by a surge of scorching anger that threatened to deprive her of speech. Blazing with fury, she stared up at her tormentor. How dared he look pityingly on her plight, when he was responsible for it? For all of it. Not only had he beguiled her heart, he had sat by, savouring her downfall, as she took the fateful step that would ruin her life. Hugo Stratton was utterly hateful.

'How dare you address me, sir, when you have behaved in such a dishonourable manner? You are not worthy of the rank you bear. And as for your brother…' Emma shook her head in disgust. She could find no words terrible enough to describe Kit Stratton. 'You will have the goodness to leave this place, Major Stratton.' With those cold words, bitterly spoken, Emma turned her back on Hugo Stratton and every vestige of love she had ever felt for him.

* * *

'Emma! Emma, where are you?'

It was Aunt Augusta's voice. Emma rose a little shakily to her feet and swallowed hard. She had hoped for more time. At least her tears had long since dried. No one—not even Aunt Augusta—should see how weak she had been.

'Emma, child, you are frozen.' Aunt Augusta tenderly placed a warm shawl round Emma's shoulders and then pulled her niece into a quick hug. She had never done such a thing before.

'That woman…' she began, with venom, 'that woman has absolutely no breeding. And as for her daughter…'

Emma put her hand on her aunt's arm. 'Tell me what happened, dear Aunt. I must know what they are saying of me before I return to the house.'

'Yes, of course. Yes, indeed.' Aunt Augusta looked flustered, and more than a little embarrassed. It took her some time to marshal her words. 'Miss Mayhew came running back into the drawing room and promptly had a fit of the vapours. As far as anyone could make out, she had come upon you and Mr Stratton alone in the garden, and had seen that he was behaving in a…a libertine fashion—and that you were doing nothing to deter him. Oh, I did my best to throw cold water on her story. After all, she is barely out of the schoolroom. How could she know what she saw? And, in any case, what was she doing alone in the garden at that time of night?

'Unfortunately, everyone in the room had already put the worst possible complexion on her hysterical outburst before I could say a word. If only the Dowager had been there...' Aunt Augusta sighed. 'There was only myself—and Mrs Mayhew, who immediately took it upon herself to pronounce you—' She stopped abruptly.

Even in the half-light in the garden, Emma could see that her aunt was mortified by this part of her tale. 'What did she say of me, Aunt?' she said quietly.

'Her words do not matter. And I would not repeat them. But... My dear, she took great delight in saying that you were ruined. And that her daughter, and the other three young ladies, would leave first thing in the morning, lest they be corrupted by further contact with the Fitzwilliam household.'

It was even worse than Emma had feared. Within twenty-four hours, the story would be repeated all over London. No member of Society would even acknowledge her in future. She was indeed ruined. And it could all be laid at Hugo Stratton's door. Hateful, hateful man.

Only one thing could make matters worse. 'Is Papa very angry?' Emma said in a small voice.

'Yes. I doubt even you can sway him this time, Emma. It matters not what you did—only what the world will say of you. Your father feels it very much. He is in the library.' Aunt Augusta took a deep breath. 'And Mr Stratton is with him there.'

'Mr Stratton? Mr Kit Stratton?' At her aunt's nod, Emma turned quickly away in an attempt to conceal the horror that must be written on her face. If Kit had been summoned to the library, it could mean only that her father was demanding he marry her to save her reputation. Kit would never agree, surely? Would he not laugh it off as just another of his many indiscretions? *His* reputation would not really be damaged by the tale. He would probably continue to be received by the *ton* as if nothing had happened.

But what if he did agree? What if her father presented Kit Stratton to her as a future husband? What would she do? She did not love him. She could not begin to trust him. He would be unfaithful, she was certain. He would take her dowry to fund his gambling. And, once forced into an unwelcome marriage, there was not the slightest reason why he should show her even a modicum of kindness.

Such a future would be bleak indeed. But could she endure the alternative?

Hugo was standing by his bedroom window, fully dressed and staring out at the night sky, when Kit finally made his appearance.

Hugo cast a quick look round at his loose fish of a brother and then went back to gazing out at the stars. Kit's reflection was all too clear—he looked like a man who had had a very bad night at the gaming tables, or with the bottle, or both.

Kit threw himself down into a chair by the empty grate and sank his chin on to his chest. After several moments, he broke the heavy silence. 'Nothing to say to me, then, brother?'

Hugo shook his head. 'I am sure Sir Edward has said all that needs to be said.' He had his temper well in hand, he was almost sure, but it would be best if he said as little as possible. Emma had been a fool—

and Kit even more so. Kit must never find out what Hugo had seen—or how he felt about Emma Fitzwilliam. That knowledge could only make matters even worse.

Kit jumped to his feet again and started to pace. 'You are right there, brother,' he said angrily. 'Oh, how very right. Sir Edward laid all my iniquities before me in the starkest possible terms. How I had taken advantage of an innocent young lady when I was a guest in her father's house. How I had ruined her before the world. And precisely what he thought of my morals.' He laughed harshly. 'I will not bother you with a recital of that, Hugo. Your imagination can furnish all the necessary details, I am sure. However—' He laughed again.

Hugo shuddered. The devil himself might be in his brother at that moment. He sounded half-mad.

'However,' Kit continued with heavy sarcasm, 'the abject state of my morals does not prevent my being a fit husband for his only daughter—and the sooner the better. The announcement of our impending nuptials will be sent to the *Gazette* in the morning. I was only surprised that he didn't roust out the stables to send a messenger on the spot.'

Hugo still said nothing. He could not. He half-turned from the window, but could not bring himself to look his brother in the face. Kit was going to marry Emma! And Kit did not love her in the least. He would make her the worst possible husband. Having been forced into marriage, he could well come to hate his wife, and blame her for what had happened to him. The best she could hope for would be indifference…but Hugo did not expect that of Kit. Not at twenty-two, when he had thought he had years of single self-indulgence in front of him. No, Emma's marriage to Kit could well become a life-long penance.

Kit stopped pacing and stared into the grate for a while. Keeping his back to Hugo, he said, 'You're very quiet, brother. I'm surprised you don't want to know how it came to this pass.'

'Mmm?' Hugo hoped he sounded encouraging. It was the best he could do.

Still without turning round, Kit said in a flat, rather puzzled voice, 'I had gone out into the garden for a smoke. Billiards was downright boring in any case, with Frobisher prosing on all the time. Saw Miss Fitzwilliam—Emma now, I suppose—going into one of the gardens. She… You won't have noticed, Hugo, but this place is full of strange little gardens surrounded by high hedges. Absolutely perfect for a spot of love-making.' Kit gave a snort of anger…or perhaps it was disgust. Hugo could not be sure. He forced himself to remain silent.

'Shouldn't have followed her, I know that now, but I was intrigued. Couldn't believe such a pattern-card of respectability would dream of making an assignation with one of the guests. But she must have done—'

Hugo clenched his jaw to stop the cry of 'liar' that rose to his lips. He had seen her with his own eyes. She had been revelling in the beauty of the garden, nothing more. She would never have consented to the kind of clandestine meeting that Kit had in mind.

'She must have done,' Kit said again. 'She was

sitting alone in that garden, I admit, but her face was such a picture of desire... God knows she's beautiful, but when her face is lit up with passion, she's...she's the most perfect woman I've ever seen.' There was something approaching awe in his voice. 'Whoever she was waiting for, he's a lucky man to inspire such devotion.'

Kit swung round suddenly to face the window. Hugo was grateful that his own face was still in shadow. Kit's face, dimly reflected in the window pane, was a picture of torment, but Hugo was pretty sure that his own would be worse. The vision of Emma in the grip of passion...

Kit laughed, a hollow, hate-filled laugh. 'I should say, rather, that he is *not* a lucky man. For he will not have her now, whoever he is. And if I ever find him out, I'll kill him with my bare hands. *He* is the cause of all this! She thought *I* was her lover...and the moment I touched her, she pretty well threw herself into my arms!'

That was nothing like the scene Hugo had witnessed. He had seen something a great deal more like seduction on Kit's part. Emma had not—

Hugo took a deep breath and tried to bring his rational mind into play. He must try to see things from Kit's point of view, or they would probably come to blows. On the other hand...

He looked towards his brother. 'Really?' he said.

Kit had the grace to look a little shamefaced. 'Well...perhaps not exactly. The truth is, I don't know what happened. One moment I was standing over her, and the next she was in my arms and I was kissing her. I couldn't help it, Hugo.' He sounded positively bewildered now. 'I didn't intend it to happen. On my oath, I didn't.

'And then that poisonous little Mayhew toad appeared, screeching like the devil himself had her by the tail. Must have seen me go into the garden and followed me.' At Hugo's start of surprise, he said venomously, 'She's been trailing after me like a puppy ever since we arrived. God, I wish I'd kicked her away when I had the chance, but you and John had me too well trained. "Young ladies just out of the schoolroom have to be treated gently," you said. "They may appear gauche and stupid, but if they are treated with kindness, they will learn," you said.'

'Kit—'

'I'm sorry, Hugo. That was unfair.' He ran his hands through his hair which was already considerably dishevelled. 'I've made my own bed, and I must lie on it. God, what a coil! I never dreamed I'd be leg-shackled like this!'

Hugo found that he was beginning to feel sorry for Kit, in spite of what he had done to Emma. Brotherly feeling must have something to do with it, but still…very strange.

'If only she'd refuse me,' Kit said despairingly, 'but she won't. Her father will see to that. He's even insisting on a special licence. God, what a coil!'

'You said that before,' said Hugo, not quite managing to conceal his still-simmering anger. 'I take it the announcement will be made in the morning?'

'Yes,' said Kit, 'before the Mayhew party leaves. Sir Edward intends to warn Mrs Mayhew against spreading malicious rumours…since his daughter's engagement is on the point of being announced. He'll take satisfaction in telling her that, I'm sure.'

'True,' said Hugo quietly, 'but he can derive precious little satisfaction from any other aspect of this affair.'

'I have already apologised to him,' Kit replied with dignity, 'and I will apologise to Emma, too, as soon as I have the chance. I will do my best to make her a good husband, I promise you that.'

'I think you should make that promise to Emma, rather than to me. Have you spoken to her?'

'No, not yet. I will, though…soon. Tomorrow, I suppose. Oh, if only Sir Edward were not intent on having us riveted so quickly. We could be engaged, all right and tight, and then, in a few months, when all the gossip had been forgotten, Emma could announce that she had decided we would not suit. And then we should both be free.'

Kit's words took Hugo by surprise for a moment. Kit was right, of course. In his aimless ramblings, he had lit on the only solution to save Emma from a disastrous marriage. But someone would need to persuade Sir Edward…and Emma herself.

Hugo took a step into the middle of the room and looked squarely at his brother. 'If you wish it, Kit, I will put your suggestion to Sir Edward…now.'

'Hugo—' A glimmer of hope flared and then faded from Kit's eyes. 'No, it would never work. The old man is too furious to listen to you or anyone else. He's made up his mind to a wedding next week.'

Hugo took a deep breath. 'If Sir Edward is as determined as you say, then only one person can move him. I will put your plan to Emma herself.'

Chapter Twelve

Emma reached up impatiently to rip back the bed-curtain and let in the early morning light. She had had very little sleep, and she knew she must look hagged. The new day had changed nothing. She was still betrothed to Kit Stratton! She lay back on her pillows and stared up at the bed-canopy. God, what a coil!

She tried not to remember that hideous interview with Papa, though she knew it would be engraven on her memory until the day she died. She had never seen him so fearfully angry, or so distant. He seemed to be immune to all thought of what his decisions were doing to his only daughter. It was almost as if he had ceased to love her. Not only was she to marry Kit Stratton, but Papa was adamant that the marriage would take place within the week. Emma had not been permitted to protest. In that totally one-sided interview, she had not even been permitted to speak. Papa had become a man she no longer knew, a man who could wrap her up like an unwanted parcel and despatch her without further thought.

Emma felt bereft and hollow inside. For all her life, the bond with her papa had been so close, so loving—but one instant of madness had ripped it all away. An inner voice whispered that Papa had never stopped loving her, never would stop loving her, that, in his shock and disappointment at his daughter's wanton behaviour, he had allowed his justifiable fury to chase away every softer emotion. Perhaps, if she went to him today, he might relent a little, postpone the wedding? But then, what would be the point? If she was to be forcibly married off to Kit Stratton, 'twere well it were done quickly. It would be better for her to have less time to brood over the prospect of being a wife—wife to an irredeemable rake.

Emma turned her thoughts to the ordeal she was about to face. For all that Mrs Mayhew had announced her intention of leaving first thing in the morning, Emma knew that she would be in the house until ten o'clock at least, for Mrs Mayhew, besides being a poisonous gossip, was also a very late riser. She would take breakfast in her room, Emma supposed, but she would then muster her little coterie of débutantes and ensure she departed in style.

Emma knew that she must not hide away. That would only give the dreadful woman even more food for gossip. No, Emma must appear and act the part of the gracious hostess saying farewell to her honoured guests. Her papa would be bound to announce her engagement at the first opportunity and he would ensure that Mrs Mayhew was left in no doubt about the match. The woman might gossip as much as she liked—afterwards. The festering boil would have been lanced. Emma had a sudden picture of herself standing in the hallway to bid farewell to the guests and receiving their hypocritical congratulations without betraying, by so much as the flicker of an eyelid, the turbulent emotions underneath. She could do it. She must.

She pulled the bell. She must not remain in bed any longer. Now would be an excellent opportunity to warn the Dowager, and Jamie too, of what had happened. She threw a wrapper over her lawn nightdress and made for the door, but hesitated when her hand touched the cool brass handle. What was she going to say to the Dowager? She would find out the bones of the affair soon enough. The servants' quarters must be fairly buzzing with it by now.

Emma shook her head despairingly. No, she must not see either the Dowager or Jamie before the Mayhew party left. She was braced for her father's anger and the disdain of the other guests. She was determined that she would maintain her dignity in front of them. But the Dowager, who had known her from a child, was like to enfold her like a mother with a tumbled child, to soothe, and pet, and surround with sympathetic love. If that happened, all Emma's hardwon armour would crack and crumble. And with Jamie, it might be even worse. Emma must not see either of them.

Emma had barely given a thought to the two gentlemen at the heart of her troubles. Kit, by all accounts, had behaved most honourably in his interview with Papa. He had not sought to excuse his behaviour or to avoid its consequences—or so Papa had said. And Hugo? Hugo must know that he was about to become her brother-in-law. It was almost amusing, given that he had spent so much effort of late in trying to avoid her. That would become much more difficult when she was his sister. But he must detest her even more now, after the insults she had heaped upon him in the garden. She had impugned his honour. Was it only a few hours ago? It felt like years. It felt like part of her distant past, a past that was enshrouded in misty dreams and fading fast.

Hugo must certainly hate her. He would meet her with cold politeness and bitter feelings in his heart. There was nothing she could say to him. Apology was quite impossible, since she must avoid all future mention of that encounter in the garden. Her wicked words would lie between them like a great black chasm. It was better so, she decided hopelessly. It would give him reason to avoid his brother's company in the future. The less they were thrown together, the easier it would be for her to suppress her feelings. She would become the perfect picture of a perfect wife, no matter how Kit behaved towards her and no matter how much she might weep inside. She had learned, once, to become the perfect débutante and now, when that façade had slipped so tragically, she must learn another role—this time, for life.

Emma's abigail came in to deliver her mistress's morning chocolate. She took one look at Emma's face and clamped her thin lips together. Normally, Sawyer was full of merry gossip about the doings of the household but, today, she clearly knew better.

Sitting on the edge of the bed, Emma sipped her

chocolate pensively. The maid was laying out a dark blue cambric gown. 'No, Sawyer,' said Emma, 'not the dark blue. It is much too sombre for such a joyous occasion. Let it be something bright and sunny—the jonquil.' Sawyer gave her a very strange sideways look but obediently fetched the jonquil muslin gown and held it up to her mistress. 'Yes, that will do very well,' Emma said. 'Now I must hurry. I know that Mrs Mayhew and her party are to leave early and it would be most remiss in a hostess to fail to bid them farewell. Make haste with my hair, Sawyer.'

Sawyer did as she was bid, but in unaccustomed silence until she was putting the last few pins into Emma's golden curls. 'Miss Emma—' Sawyer stopped. She looked uncomfortable. 'Miss Emma... Major Stratton asked me to give you a message. He begs for the favour of an urgent interview with you. He said he would be waiting in the library.'

'*Major* Stratton?' said Emma, horrified. 'Surely you mean *Mr* Stratton?'

'No, Miss Emma, no. 'Twas the Major himself. Mr Stratton is still abed—at least, his valet has not been summoned. The Major, now, was up and about uncommon early. He called for his shaving water almost before the range was lit. Had the kitchen staff in quite a panic. And then, he went out walking in the grounds. Must have been out there for hours. He has only just come in.'

'I see.' For a second, Emma did not know what to say. She would have accepted a summons from Kit who, in a few days, would be her lawful husband and entitled to command her obedience.

But Hugo? What could Hugo want at this hour? 'An urgent word', he had said. Perhaps he planned to berate her for entrapping his brother and insulting himself? Well, let him try. Let him try. Emma was no shrinking miss to be taken to task by Major Stratton like some erring ensign under his command. Not she. She would give just as good as she got. And if Major Stratton uttered one word out of line, she would tell him precisely what she thought of him and of his rake of a brother.

It was only then that Emma admitted to herself that she had already decided to face Hugo—and Hugo's wrath. There were many charges to be brought against Emma Fitzwilliam, but lack of courage would not figure among them.

Emma gave a tiny curtsy as she entered the library, leaving the door ajar in her wake. Major Stratton was standing with his back against the desk, idly gazing out of the window, but as soon as she appeared, he straightened. He strode to the door with surprising agility and closed it very deliberately.

'How dare you, sir?' she cried angrily, looking pointedly towards the door. 'You know it is improper for us to be alone together in this way. Or do you perhaps think that, since one Stratton brother has already compromised me, the other can continue the process, with my good will?'

Hugo said nothing, although she thought a shadow of guilt passed across his face. He simply moved back to the door and opened it a trifle. Without looking directly at Emma, he said, 'Will that content you,

ma'am?' His voice was low and cold, almost sinister
in its total lack of feeling.

Emma wondered what was to come. By losing her
temper, she had given him the advantage of her—and
she had promised herself she would not yield to him
in any way. She moved towards the window, to be
as far as possible from Hugo Stratton's looming figure.

Hugo made no attempt to approach her. He went
back to stand by the desk at the far side of the room.
'Now that the door is open, ma'am, it would be best
if we moderated our voices.'

This time, Emma refused to rise to the bait. Nor
did she turn towards him. She simply nodded towards
the windows and the garden beyond. Let him inter-
pret her signal as he would.

The silence lengthened. Emma began to think she
would scream if he did not speak. At last, driven to
the point of exasperation, she said, 'There is something you wished to say to me, I believe, Major? I
beg you will do so without delay, for I have many
duties to attend to this morning. Most of my guests
are leaving, you know.'

Her words seemed to provide the spur he needed.
'Yes, I do know that Mrs Mayhew and her party are
leaving,' he said quietly. 'And I know, too, the reason
for it. I am heartily sorry for the trouble my brother
has brought upon you.'

Emma only just managed to conceal a start of surprise. She had not expected an apology, especially
from the man she had so grievously insulted.

'And I know that the insult was made worse—for

you—by the fact that I myself was witness to what happened,' Hugo continued. 'Believe me, Miss Fitzwilliam, I would liefer have been anywhere but there. As it was…' His words petered out. 'As it is,' he began again, 'I am sorry, and I know that it is you who will bear the brunt of Society's censure.'

Emma was puzzled now. It seemed that Hugo Stratton had asked for this interview simply to apologise on behalf of himself and his brother. Surely that was for Kit to do? Kit—the man she would soon marry. She had not expected any understanding from Hugo Stratton. His sympathy was becoming more uncomfortable by the minute. She really ought to leave. 'Major—' she began.

'Miss Fitzwilliam,' he said quickly, 'forgive me, but I beg you will allow me to lay a proposal before you.' He waited for her brief nod and then said, 'Pardon me if I cause you pain. I must be blunt. I know you do not love my brother, nor he you. But Kit—for all his shortcomings—is a man of honour. He has promised your father that he will marry you. And he has promised *me* that he will make you a good husband. None the less, I know it is something that neither of you can really want.

'I believe there may be a solution. Let the betrothal be announced, by all means. That is surely the way to silence the gossip and to ensure that your reputation remains unsullied. But let the wedding be fixed for some months ahead…in the autumn, say, or even at Christmas. There would be nothing surprising in that. By then, this unhappy incident would be forgotten and you, Miss Fitzwilliam, could discover—

as a result of your better acquaintance with my brother—that you do not suit. You—'

'Thank you, Major,' Emma said bitterly, whirling round to face him and giving him no chance to continue with his extraordinary proposal. 'And of course there is absolutely *no* likelihood that the gossip will resurface after I have jilted your brother. None at all. It will be just as before—Emma Fitzwilliam with her pristine reputation.' Emma's hands were shaking. She gripped them together in an effort to moderate the signs of her fury. She did not dare to look him in the eye. He believed he was offering the solution to all her problems. If he uttered one more word on the subject, she would probably explode. But she must not give him the satisfaction of seeing her lose even more of her self-control. 'Thank you, but I have no desire to be branded a jilt as well as a wanton. You have little understanding of the ways of Society if you think that your plan would succeed in saving my reputation. It would save your brother, certainly. But it would ruin me.'

He made to protest but Emma would not permit him to speak. 'Oh, I acquit you of the charge of duplicity in this. You have been too long abroad, I believe, to appreciate just how malicious London gossips can be. It will not do. After last night's episode, I *must* marry. And it seems to me that the sooner it is done, the safer I shall be. Your brother acted— shall we say—unwisely? The penalty, I fear, is a life sentence.'

Hugo began to pace up and down before the desk. There was almost no trace of a limp. His recovery was clearly proceeding apace. Lucky Major Stratton, Emma concluded acidly.

'Will you not reconsider, ma'am?' Hugo said at last. He sounded weary. By now, he must be regretting that he had ever asked for this interview.

'How can I?' Emma burst out. 'In the circumstances, I *must* marry and your brother is the only available candidate. There is no choice for either of us.'

Hugo's face had twisted into something that was half-smile, half-grimace. That enigmatic look infuriated Emma beyond anything she could have imagined. It was so easy for men. They took the pleasure and the women endured the pain.

She glared at Hugo. 'There is *one* option, Major,' she said in a clipped, scornful voice. 'If you wish to save your brother, you could always offer *yourself* in his place.' There. That should put an end to this ludicrous interview, once and for all. He could have nothing more to say to her now.

Hugo's tortured smile became even more marked. An odd light flickered in his eyes for a brief moment. He raised his chin and—for the first time—looked directly into her eyes. Slowly, he closed the distance between them and extended his hand.

'If that is what it takes, Miss Fitzwilliam, I do most willingly ask you to accept of my hand in marriage.'

Chapter Thirteen

'**N**o!' Emma's despairing cry seemed to be torn from her. Hugo felt it like a sword slash. Did she really hate him so much? Or was it that the thought of him repelled her?

He held her wide-eyed gaze until embarrassment overcame her and she looked away. In a voice that was so low as to be barely audible, she said, 'You mock me, sir. That is not the act of a gentleman.'

Hugo took a deep breath and sighed it out again. He had not withdrawn his outstretched hand. 'I have never been more serious in my life, ma'am,' he said softly. 'I beg you to believe that—even if you are not now minded to accept my proposal. I do truly desire to make you my wife.'

Emma raised her eyes to his once more. Astonishment was written in her gaze but not—Hugo was sure—any trace of hatred or revulsion. Perhaps she might yet be won over, if he could but find the means…for this was surely the right solution. It had come to him even as he spoke the words. Wounded and scarred though he was, he, Hugo, would make a better husband for Emma than Kit could ever be. Kit was too young and much too devoted to his own pleasures to care for Emma's bruised spirit. But Hugo understood what it was to be shunned by Society. And if the solution to Emma's dilemma should also bring Hugo a prize that he had believed beyond his reach…well, he would not refuse it.

He took a step towards Emma, clasping her hands strongly in both of his own. Her fingers shook, but she did not pull away. Her gaze seemed to be fixed on his cravat.

He chafed her hands gently, trying to warm her. 'Trust me, Emma,' he said in a low voice, willing her to look up at him. 'I am older—and, I believe, wiser—than Kit. *My* offer is made of my own free will, not under any duress. I have not Kit's looks, but I promise you I am well able to support a wife…and I do not often frequent the gaming tables, either.' He found himself smiling a little when he referred to Kit's obvious defects. She must not be allowed to think he was a strait-laced martinet who would blight her life. 'Emma, look at me.' He waited until she did so and then continued, trying to emphasise the importance of his words by the sustained pressure of his hands, 'I am convinced we could learn to deal very comfortably together. Will you at least consider my proposal?'

She took a deep breath. 'What time is it, sir?' she said crisply.

'I beg your pardon, ma'am?'

The tiniest hint of a smile twisted one side of her mouth. 'I asked you what time it was, sir. My father will wish to announce my betrothal as soon as the guests appear this morning. It would be…unfortunate if he were to name the wrong brother.'

Hugo took a gasp of air and held it, staring down into her clear blue eyes. Then he let the air out slowly and gently, making no sound in the sudden silence that surrounded them. 'You accept?' he asked bluntly, and then immediately wished the stark words unsaid. Emma needed gentler handling than this.

'I accept, Major,' she said, with remarkable self-possession. 'And I would urge you to inform my father of our agreement at the earliest opportunity. It would not do for me to have two fiancés in the same morning.'

To cover his astonishment, Hugo raised Emma's hand to his lips. His kiss was just as chaste as a duenna would have wished. Now was certainly not the time for passion.

'You have made me a very happy man, my dear,' he said. 'And, mindful of your wise words, I shall go at once to your father. I only hope that he is as open to the power of my arguments as you have been.'

Emma smiled then, but it was not the smile of a happy woman. There was an edge of brittle pain there…and her eyes were troubled once more. 'You may tell Papa that, if he continues to insist that I marry your brother, he will have the pleasure of watching me jilt him at the altar.'

'But I do not understand, Emma,' said Jamie. The whole affair was thoroughly perplexing. 'It was Kit that you met in the garden and it is Kit that you are to marry…or so Richard told me.'

Emma shook her head, smiling brightly. 'Richard has misled you, Jamie. Husbands do, I believe.'

Jamie still felt bewildered.

'It is true that I was in the garden last night and that Kit was there, too,' Emma said. 'But I promise you there was no assignation. Kit is very handsome, I admit, but not the sort of man who… Oh dear—' Emma bit her lip, but she was smiling still 'I must learn not to cast aspersions on my future brother-in-law. What *would* the Major say?'

Jamie was forced to laugh. 'Emma, you wretch! You do it deliberately, I declare, to keep me in suspense. Shame on you!'

This time, Emma laughed aloud, though, to Jamie's ears, it sounded a little more high-pitched than normal. 'Oh, I am sorry, Jamie. I will try to do better, I promise. It was just… Well—as I said, I was in the garden. That silly little Mayhew chit had been pursuing Kit all evening. She even followed him into the garden and so, unfortunately, she saw Kit kissing me. She then announced to all the world that Kit and I were lovers, and behaving in the most licentious fashion, to boot. There was uproar, naturally, especially as neither you nor your mama was there to curb Mrs Mayhew's malicious tongue. Not unnaturally, Papa was furious and insisted that Kit marry me, giving neither of us any choice in the matter. Papa was determined that we be married within the week…to stop the scandalmongering, you understand.'

Jamie nodded. 'But—'

Emma's smile broadened. 'And then the Major intervened. He said that Kit and I should not suit—which is perfectly true—and that I had better marry him instead. So I said I would. There. Now you have it all.'

Jamie shook her head in exasperation at this bald narrative. It was so unlike Emma. She had always shared her thoughts and feelings with Jamie. 'Emma, you know very well that you have told me nothing, nothing at all. Why was Kit kissing you in the garden, if there was no assignation? Why did Major Stratton offer to take his place? Do not pretend that he sacrifices himself out of brotherly love and duty, for that makes no sense at all. And why on earth did *you* decide to accept him? That is the greatest puzzle of all and I beg you will explain it to me. Kit is a better prospect, surely? He is young and handsome, whereas the Major is—'

Emma laid a hand on Jamie's arm. 'Hugo is the man I will marry, Jamie. I will not go back on my word.'

Jamie was not prepared to give in so easily. 'And what does he think of what passed between you and his brother in the garden? That might not bode well for your future together. Husbands do not take kindly to other men making free with their wives, you know…or even to the thought that they might do so.'

'He knows exactly what happened. He has no reason to be jealous of Kit. Believe me, Jamie, there will be no trouble over that, at least.'

'At least?'

Emma coloured a little, but she did not attempt to

cover up her obvious slip. She rose from her seat, looking down at Jamie with eyes totally devoid of expression. 'Wish us happy, Jamie,' she said simply.

'I do, Emma. I do, most sincerely.'

Emma nodded politely and made for the door, excusing herself on the grounds of her duties to her other guests.

Jamie was far from satisfied, but there was nothing more to be gleaned from questioning Emma. She was taking refuge in her best company manners and treating Jamie like the merest acquaintance. It was all very strange.

Jamie hurried away to find her husband. He must, surely, be back from his morning ride by now?

Richard was in his dressing room, changing out of his riding clothes. He took one look at his wife's face and dismissed his valet.

'Richard,' she began, 'I do not understand what is going on. Last night Emma was to marry Kit. Today Emma tells me she will marry Major Stratton. Oh, I know that he is a fine man, but he is so much older than Emma…and dreadfully wounded, besides. He—'

Richard grinned wickedly. 'Hugo is younger than me, I'll have you know, *madame*, so that cock won't fight. Is that the best you can do?'

Jamie was not to be diverted. 'And what of Kit? How does he feel about being summarily rejected in favour of his older brother? Surely he feels the insult keenly?'

'Kit? I must tell you, my love, that Kit feels the insult so keenly that he has already left for Epsom.

Now that he is no longer an engaged man, he will not be forced to miss the Oaks. Had you forgotten the race was today? Kit had not, I can tell you. He plans to put all his blunt on the second favourite—and then go back to London to gamble away his winnings.'

'Oh, Richard, how can you?' Jamie tried to keep from smiling back at him. It was very difficult when he looked down at her in just that way. 'But is this true?' she said at last.

He nodded. 'Kit would have made an appalling husband for Emma...for any woman, in my opinion. He's not half the man that Hugo is. Hugo understands people. Kit thinks only of himself...and his extremely expensive pleasures. He's far too handsome for his own good, too. Give him a few more years on the town, and he might improve, I dare say, but only if he discovers that women will not always fall at his feet. A good dose of rejection would be the best possible medicine for Kit. Whereas Hugo has had trials a-plenty...'

He caught Jamie to him and started to nuzzle her neck. 'My love, I believe that this match will be better than any of us imagine. They will be good for each other. As we were, remember?' He began to kiss her greedily.

Jamie smiled into his kiss and wound her arms about his neck. There was nothing more to be said.

Emma was exhausted by the time she tumbled into bed. It was all her own doing, too, so she had no cause for complaint. She had kept herself busy all day, often to no purpose at all. So why could she not sleep?

She decided to focus on practical things—the journey home to Longacres, the arrangements for the ceremony, reorganising the apartments in the house so that Hugo could have a study separate from her father's. Surely she had enough control over her own thoughts to stop her unruly emotions from intruding? She had spent all day playing the part of the happy young woman celebrating her engagement. Why was it that the mask always cracked, the moment she was alone?

From a child, she had always had whatever she wanted. She had decided she wanted Hugo…and now she was to have him. Why, then, was she—?

She forced herself to abandon that train of thought. The ceremony…that was better. Richard had kindly offered the use of his private chapel. In the circumstances, it was preferable to the parish church where all the villagers would come to gawp. A special licence would be needed, of course, but Richard had plans for that, too. He had joked that he was certainly up to snuff, having done the same for his own marriage. On this occasion, however, some delay was inevitable. He and Hugo could post up to London on the morrow, but would have to cool their heels during the Sabbath. All being well, they would return to Harding by Monday evening. And Richard's chaplain would then perform the ceremony on Tuesday.

In four days, she would be Hugo Stratton's wife.

Why on earth had he done it? It could not be due to any degree of feeling for Emma herself, for—apart from that one, furious kiss—he had never shown her anything more than common politeness. Could it be that his kiss meant—? Emma stopped that fanciful thought before it was fully formed. He must have done it to save his brother, she decided firmly. Kit still had all his life before him. And Kit had all the advantages of looks and charm. He might make a brilliant match, one day.

But would any man sacrifice himself to save his brother?

Perhaps it was her money that had proved the deciding factor? How demeaning to think that Hugo was no different from all the money-grabbing fortune hunters who had pursued her over the years. But surely, he would have started courting her before, if that had been his aim? He had never courted her at all, though there had been opportunities at Harding…

Perhaps he had not courted her because of his wounds, believing she would never accept a disfigured husband…whereas now she had a stark choice between one of the Stratton brothers and disgrace. Had he seized on his only real chance of securing a fortune?

No, it could not be so. Hugo was neither devious, nor base. He was Richard's oldest friend…and Richard vouched for his integrity. Emma knew that Hugo was an honourable man. She had always known. He had asked her to trust him and she had found that she did, instinctively.

Besides, Hugo had wealth of his own. He had made that clear. So…his reasons must have been quite unselfish, after all. He was marrying Emma to save his brother. And what kind of basis for marriage was that?

That was a question Emma did not want to explore. She concentrated, instead, on solving the problem of her hot, sticky pillow. She sat up, turned it and smoothed it out before lying down again. That was better…cooler.

And she must coolly decide how she was going to behave. Hugo had been scrupulously polite, but distant, since the moment he proposed. Why had he not kissed her then? He had desired her once…and she had given him the right. She had been yearning for the touch of his lips, but he had behaved as distantly as if they had just been introduced—distant, and cold. And, since then, he had avoided being alone with her or discussing anything beyond the merest commonplace. She found she was relieved that he had to go to London for the licence—she would not see him again until the wedding—for his presence still tended to make her thoughts tumble and her limbs heat, even though he hardly ever touched her. During the whole day—the day when they had become betrothed—he had twice kissed her hand and that was all. The second time, he had simply bade her a cool goodnight— no mention of what would happen when they met again, no concern about her well-being in the meantime, nothing. He must be regretting his sacrifice already.

It really did not matter if he did, Emma concluded brutally. Nothing could now be altered, for either of them. Only the future mattered, and there, she would have control. In fact, her life would change very little and she was glad of it. She would continue to be mistress of her father's household, where her husband would also live. She would minister to the needs of two gentlemen instead of one. Hugo would learn about running the estate that would one day be his, while Emma would make sure that he recovered fully from his injuries. He was much too thin, for a start. She would order nourishing food for him so that he would fill out once more. And she would ensure he learned to ride and shoot again. His scars would fade but, until he regained those vital skills, he would be unable to fulfil the proper role of a country gentleman. It might take Emma a little time, but eventually Major and Mrs Stratton would take their rightful place in Society.

As soon as she arrived home tomorrow, she would set about the question of her makeshift trousseau. With the addition of some lace, her newest evening gown could be turned into a more than adequate wedding dress… It was fortunate she had chosen white silk… She would need flowers, too…

As she finally drifted into sleep, an unbidden thought floated through her mind. When Hugo had thought she would marry Kit, he had made Kit promise to be a good husband to her. How very strange…

Chapter Fourteen

'Emma, my dear child, you look ravishing.' Aunt Augusta was tweaking Emma's bridal skirts for at least the twentieth time. If only she would not fuss so much…

'Oh, look, your hem is ruffled.' Aunt Augusta knelt quickly to smooth the offending wrinkle. She seemed to take a remarkably long time over such a minor blemish. Then, in a strained and surprisingly quiet voice, she said, 'Emma, was there anything you wished to know? About…about being a wife.' She was still looking at Emma's skirt but she hurried on, 'If your mother had been here, it would have fallen to her, of course, but…' She took a deep breath. 'It is up to me to ensure you are prepared for what is to come.'

How ominous that sounded. Was there something that she should be concerned about? Emma racked her brains. She had worked so hard over these last few days—and slept so badly—that she could not think clearly any more. What could she have forgot-

ten? And why should Aunt Augusta wait until now
to remind her?

Emma reverted to the calm politeness that she had
relied on since the day of Hugo's proposal. 'I am
always very grateful for your advice, Aunt.'

Mrs Warenne looked up sharply, frowning. Then
she rose and walked over to the window where she
stood for several moments, gazing out. She cleared
her throat more than once before she spoke. And she
did not look at Emma.

'My dear…my dear, you are young…and innocent. Marriage is… There are aspects to marriage
which you may not… Oh, dear, this is all so difficult.
If only your mother were here.'

She coughed again. 'Emma, your duties to your
husband will include a degree of…of closeness. It
can be…a little upsetting for a new bride, but you
must simply accept it. You will soon become accustomed. We all do. And it is necessary, in any case,
if you are to have children. You want children, naturally. All women want children. They will be the
focus of your life.' Aunt Augusta had begun to sound
a little more like her usual self. 'And a husband's
attentions do lessen later, especially when his wife
is…especially when he has other distractions.' Aunt
Augusta cleared her throat yet again. She turned at
last, though she still did not seek to meet Emma's
eye. 'Forgive me, Emma, but I am afraid we do not
know how badly your husband was wounded.'

Emma was by now totally bemused. What was her
aunt talking about? Nothing made any sense at all.

Her aunt hurried on. 'When you retire to your

chamber, you will find it best to greet your husband in the dark, my dear. Make sure the shutters and the bed-curtains are closed so that you do not have to look upon his wounds. And if, by any chance, his injuries have impaired his ability to…perform his duties, the darkness will hide his…his embarrassment. Major Stratton is a true gentleman, my dear, and will understand that you are too shy to receive him in the light. Do not be afraid to ask. I am sure he will grant you that one request.'

Emma nodded dumbly. Darkness. Yes. She would try to remember. Darkness was important.

Aunt Augusta seemed relieved. 'Good. That is done. I have prepared you as I am sure your dear mother would have wished. And now—look at the time. We must hurry. The carriages will be at the door. A bride must be late, but not so late that her groom wonders whether she will appear at all.'

Emma took her seat in the carriage beside her father's comforting bulk. He squeezed her hand once, but said nothing. Emma was grateful. It was so peaceful now that her aunt had finally gone ahead to join the little congregation at Richard's chapel. Aunt Augusta had done nothing but talk since the moment she arrived in Emma's chamber to help her dress, besides fussing over the silliest details. Emma was too pale—should she not wear rouge? Emma's posy of flowers was too small—it was not too late to send for more. Emma's veil would look better if she wore it with an aigret…or at least a circlet. Although Emma had dumbly acquiesced to every suggestion,

it had not helped to stem Aunt Augusta's flow.
Emma's head had begun to ache well before she was
fully dressed. And from then on, it had become worse
and worse.

She promised herself that everything would soon
be over. She would simply concentrate on taking one
step at a time. That way, she would be able to remain
in control, for she was determined to appear resolute.
She must thank the servants who had come to see
her off. She must remember to hold her head up as
she arrived at the chapel. She must not allow her
knees to shake as she walked up the aisle. She
must—

One step at a time. Concentrate on the carriage
journey first. Smile farewell to the servants. Above
all things, smile, always smile.

The drive to Harding seemed to be shorter than
usual. Emma could not remember passing through
the lodge gates. Had she smiled to the lodge-keeper?
She supposed she must have done.

Papa—dear, dear Papa—held her hand firmly as
he helped her down and led her to the door of the
chapel. Jamie was there, apparently waiting for
Emma. Should she not be inside? Ah, no, Jamie had
offered to act as matron of honour. Someone had to
be there at the altar to receive Emma's flowers.

Jamie straightened Emma's lace veil. 'You look
lovely, Emma,' she said.

Papa patted Emma's hand. 'If you are ready, my
dear child?'

Emma straightened her back. One step at a time.

Walk slowly down the aisle. Keep your head up. Smile. Always smile.

'I am ready, Papa.'

They walked together through the doorway and started down the aisle, Jamie following a little way behind.

One step at a time. Keep your eyes on the altar. Smile.

After the sunshine outside, it was difficult to see clearly. The chapel was almost empty—a few hazy figures on the left, the white robes of the chaplain in the centre and, on the right, two tall dark men, standing shoulder to shoulder, waiting. Why was there no music to break this awful silence? The only sound seemed to be Emma's own footsteps.

One step at a time. Smile.

'Dearly beloved, we are gathered here…'

The familiar words were soothing, almost soporific. It would be over soon.

One step at a time. Her hand must not shake when it was given to Hugo.

'Who giveth this woman…'

One step at a time. Her vows must be strongly spoken.

'Do you, Emma Frances, take this man…?'

One step at a time. Smile.

'I now pronounce you man and wife. You may kiss the bride.'

Smile.

Hugo looked down at her. Her husband, now. What was he thinking? Should he not be smiling, too?

He lifted her hand to his lips. Then he bent to place a soft kiss on her cheek. Nothing more.

Smile.

Hugo turned, offering Emma his arm. Now they must walk back down the aisle, together.

One step at a time.

The sunshine beyond the open doorway was blindingly bright. Everything inside the chapel became dim in contrast. Emma walked slowly towards the light. Out there was her new life.

Dear God, what had she done? She was married. And to a man she barely knew. Had she really spoken those vows? She must have done.

For days, she had been wandering through a dream, a dream she had willingly created for herself. But this was no dream. She was walking out into the light of day on the arm of her husband.

She lifted her chin and focused her eyes on the bright light ahead of her. She was moving into a different world, now. She must live with the choice she had made.

Hugo Stratton was her husband. He had the right to command her obedience…in everything. He owned her, and everything about her, as surely as he owned the shirt on his back. She, whose slightest wish had always been granted, must bow to the whims of the dark, silent man at her side.

Hugo placed his hand over hers as they reached the door.

Emma did not need to look at him to understand the meaning of that casual gesture. It was a sign of possession.

* * *

'Jamie, what on earth has happened to Emma?' The Dowager had taken Jamie aside as soon as they returned to the main house. She sounded very concerned. 'She looked as if she were on a tumbrel, being taken to the guillotine. And what possessed her to wear rouge? It makes her look like a cheap painted doll.'

Jamie was just as concerned as Richard's mama. 'It was her aunt's doing, I am sure. As matron of honour, I should have been there to help her dress, but Mrs Warenne insisted on taking my place. She could see that I cannot bend, or kneel…at least, not very well. But now I wish I had not agreed. I am convinced Emma has the headache. And it is small wonder. The woman never stops fussing.'

'I will do my best to keep her away from Emma for the rest of the day,' said the Dowager firmly. 'Thank heavens we insisted on having the wedding breakfast here. At Longacres, she would have been impossible. Meanwhile, you must look to Emma herself. Help her to—' She stopped very suddenly. Then she looked down at the floor. 'Oh, dear. It occurs to me that… Jamie, Emma has no mother to prepare her. I wonder if her aunt…' She did not continue. Jamie could see that she was blushing.

'Whatever the problem, I promise I will help her, Mama,' Jamie said solemnly. 'You may rely on me.' In an attempt to relieve the Dowager's obvious embarrassment, she added, 'Provided, of course, that I can rely on *you* to deal with the impossible aunt.'

The Dowager's lip curled in scorn. 'In that, my dear daughter, you may certainly rely on me.' She moved purposefully towards Emma's aunt, who had just entered the room on her brother's arm.

Good. The gabblemongering aunt would now create no more trouble. But as for Emma… Jamie frowned, scanning the room. Emma was standing between Hugo and Richard. All three appeared to be conversing amicably enough, but the patches of red on Emma's cheeks had begun to look like fever spots. At this rate, she would collapse before the day was half over.

Emma would have to sit through the wedding breakfast, but with such a small gathering—even with the chaplain, they were only eight—it could be kept quite informal. Jamie should be able to ensure that it did not last too long for Emma's comfort. She had given orders for a suite of rooms to be prepared in the guest wing, since there had been no time for Hugo to make honeymoon arrangements. Hugo had been quite apologetic about that, when he and Richard had finally arrived back from London, dog-tired, but he had accepted with good grace when Richard invited them both to remain at Harding for a few days. In a house as large as this, their privacy could be guaranteed.

The problem, Jamie realised, would be the interminable evening. Somehow she must create an opportunity to speak to Emma alone without arousing the suspicions of her father or her aunt—and, before that, she must work out exactly what she was going to say…

Jamie glanced back towards Emma once more. Good grief, she looked as if she were about to faint.

She must be rescued—now—before ever the wedding breakfast began. There was no time for finesse. It must be a frontal attack.

In spite of her awkward bulk, Jamie reached Emma's side in a few quick strides and began to steer her away from her husband. 'Major Stratton,' she said archly, 'I do declare you have much to learn about the duties of a husband. Your poor wife is worn out with all the preparations and much in need of a little respite. You will allow me to take her upstairs for a few minutes?'

Hugo made to bow his agreement, but Jamie did not wait. She was halfway to the door when she heard her husband's laughing voice say, 'I suppose it's a little late to warn you against managing females, Hugo.'

'May we have a private word, Richard?' Hugo drew his best man away from the other guests in the drawing room. 'I ought to tell you that I've received word today from Lake Manor. Apparently the house will be ready to receive us by the end of the week, so we shall not be trespassing on your hospitality for more than a few days. I must say I'm amazed that everything has been done so quickly. The steward must have excelled himself.'

'I can understand your desire to have Emma to yourself, but are you sure the house will be habitable? I thought you said no one had lived in it since your mother died?'

'That's true, but John has been very good. He installed an excellent steward while I was abroad and visited occasionally to ensure that no essential repairs were neglected. He paid for some of them, too. I couldn't have wished for a better brother, you know.'

A slight smile quirked a corner of Richard's mouth but he said nothing. Hugo could read that smile—Richard was thinking about the unpredictable Kit, and wondering why Hugo's two brothers had so little in common.

'The land will need a great deal of work, admittedly,' Hugo continued, remembering the report he had received that very day, 'but I am glad of that. I know I have much to learn about estate management—I was not brought up to it as you were—and I would much rather do that well away from my father-in-law's watchful eye. Oh, don't mistake me, I have nothing but admiration for the way Sir Edward runs Longacres. In fact, that's the problem. There would be nothing for me to do here, nothing to change. I need to make my own mistakes, I think.'

'Knowing you, I doubt there will be many,' Richard said with a short laugh.

'You may laugh, but it's one of the most important things I learned in the army. You only do things wrong once.'

'What does Emma say about moving so far away from her father? They have always been very close, you know.'

'I haven't told her yet.' Hugo frowned at the sight of Richard's raised eyebrow. 'You know as well as I do that there has been no opportunity to speak to her about that, or anything else. However, I am sure she will be pleased to be away from the gossips for a while…and, with a new household to manage, and a whole new set of tenants, she won't have time to worry about what Society thinks of us. I'm sure it's for the best.'

'You won't be going to London?'

'Not while Kit's there. Not this year, at least. It could be awkward for Emma.'

Richard nodded. 'But won't Emma be bored? Lake Manor is pretty remote.'

Hugo was sure that remoteness was one of the main advantages of the small estate he had inherited from his mother. There would be no gossip…and precious little social intercourse at all. They would have time to become accustomed to marriage. And one day, there might even be a child, a sturdy little fellow like Richard's Dickon…

Richard cleared his throat rather too obviously.

Hugo hauled himself back to the present. 'I am not planning to keep my wife in isolation, you know,' he said. 'We shall come here often, to visit her father. And you, too, of course.'

'I'm glad to hear it,' Richard said with a wry smile. 'Otherwise Jamie would never forgive either of us. Still, at least you'll both be here tomorrow for Dickon's birthday. Jamie is planning a party on the lawn and Emma, as godmother, will have an important role to play…especially as neither of Dickon's godfathers will be making an appearance. Perhaps you'd like to deputise for them?'

Hugo bowed, smiling. 'I should be honoured.' Richard was much to be envied, having been blessed with a son so early in his marriage. In the wider Strat-

ton family, there were many childless couples.
Hugo's elder brother had no children at all, which
was a source of much sadness to them all. Hugo fer-
vently hoped that he was not destined for the same
fate.

He glanced out at the sky. 'Lady Hardinge's
wishes may be thwarted by the weather, though. I
rather think we're about to have a storm.'

As he spoke, thunder rumbled ominously in the
distance. The sky had become dark and threatening
in the space of a very few minutes, but the air was
still hot and sultry, even with the windows open.
Emma's father and aunt would be bound to leave
early if the weather did not improve. That would be
a pity. And Dickon's birthday tomorrow might well
be spoilt, too.

It occurred to Hugo that he should mention the fact
that he and little Dickon shared a birthday—but, after
a moment's thought, he decided against. After all
these years apart, Richard had clearly forgotten the
date. He would be mortally embarrassed to be reminded of it now. Hugo would say nothing. Today
had been his day—and Emma's. Tomorrow should
be for the child alone.

He would not allow himself to think about the
night between.

Chapter Fifteen

Emma straightened the sheet yet again, tucking it under her body as far as it would go. It was really too hot for so many covers, especially with the bed-curtains drawn and the shutters closed, but, even in the dark, she felt a need to cover up the lacy night-gown that Aunt Augusta had insisted she wear. Emma was not sure what kind of a woman would wear such a confection but it was certainly not a garment for a lady.

Another rumble of thunder shook the house. It seemed to have been going on for hours, yet still it did not rain.

Emma had given up trying to fathom out her aunt's advice. First Aunt Augusta had told her to say she was shy, and then she had given her a nightgown that was fit only for a...

He would be here soon. How was she to put Aunt Augusta's advice into words? What was she going to say to him? All the words she tested sounded stilted, or stupid, even to her own ears. What's more, she did not even know how to address him. He had called her by her given name at least twice now, but he had never invited her to do the same.

Her restless fingers twitched at the sheet. It seemed to be sticking to her skin. If only the storm would break.

He would never believe her shy if she used his given name. Better to avoid any name at all. It was important to receive him in the dark, she remembered that, but she could not remember why. Aunt Augusta had said something about Hugo's wounds, but Jamie had made no mention of those. In fact, Jamie's advice had made even less sense that Aunt Augusta's. Jamie had said that love between husband and wife could be wonderful. She had said a great many other things, too, but Emma had understood none of them. She had felt too ill and too tired to try. And by the time the tisane had finally cleared her throbbing headache, she had been back among the wedding party, playing the part of the happy bride.

He would be here soon.

Hugo leant back against the oak and drew deeply on his half-smoked cigar. Its tiny glow seemed much brighter than usual. The thunder had passed over at last, but it had left darkness behind. Pity that it had not rained, to break the oppressive heat.

He pulled out his watch but could not see the hands. It must be very late by now. There were almost no lights to be seen in the house—and none at all in the guest wing. Emma must be there, in the dark, waiting.

Emma Stratton. His wife.

His wife had behaved like an automaton through-out her wedding day. She had looked like a painted doll. And she had acted like one—stiff limbs, wide eyes, fixed smile. The woman he had kissed in the chapel had been as cold as marble…and she had looked at him in horror. If she found him so repellent, why had she agreed to this marriage in the first place?

His simplest attempts at reassurance had been re-buffed. She had bristled with hostility at the slightest touch of his hand.

Hugo swore roundly at the oak above him, using words that the meanest of his soldiers might have used. It solved nothing. His wife had married him because she had no choice. His wife despised him. Had she not told him so?

He had done everything he could think of to make this day less of an ordeal for her, but not even Rich-ard had succeeded in making her laugh…and he had certainly tried. The wedding breakfast had been a trial for them all. Emma had been polite—so polite that he had wanted to slap her. It had been a blessing when her father and her aunt had left. They had blamed the approaching storm, but Hugo had not be-lieved them. Even the Dowager had seemed relieved to say her farewells.

And now Emma would have retired. She might even be in bed by now, waiting for him to come to her. Would she welcome him? He doubted it very much. She had no feelings of love, or even liking, for her new husband, as far as he could tell. And if she truly detested him, she would be as unyielding as the oak at his back.

Dear God, this was no way to think about his wife. He ought to be able to make her first experience of love a pleasure...but he was not sure that he knew how to begin. Emma was a lady, and a virgin besides. And Hugo had experience of neither. There had been plenty of women willing to become the mistress of a handsome young British officer, but not one of them had been a lady...and they had been anything but innocent. When he had first arrived in the Peninsula, still young but far from green, the dark-eyed Spanish women had been happy to teach him everything they knew about the arts of love. They had taught him to give pleasure as well as take it, and shown him that physical love could bring unbounded joy to man and woman alike.

But that had been aeons ago.

That was long before those last hectic weeks with Wellington's army, before Waterloo, before the noise and the stench and the gore...before all those hours that he had lain on the battlefield, soaked in his own blood and unable to move, staring up at the smoke-streaked sky. That was long before those months of lying on a filthy bed, trying to remember who he was and wondering if he would survive to see the next sunrise.

He had been forced to be celibate for a long, long time. Tonight he would find out whether it was too long. That knowledge could not be put off any longer.

Hugo threw away the remains of his cigar. He watched it arc through the darkness and disappear into the night, and then he strode back to the house and up the side stairs to the guest wing.

As instructed, his valet was nowhere to be seen, but everything was ready. His blue silk dressing-gown lay across the chair by the empty grate. Beside it, on a small table, was a decanter of brandy and a single glass.

Hugo pulled off his cravat and poured brandy into his glass. Then he thought better of it. He could not go to her reeking of strong drink. He owed her that, at least.

He methodically removed the rest of his clothing and donned his dressing gown. He would not take a candle. Its light, so close to his scarred face, would horrify her even more. He would trust to the light from the night sky.

Quietly, he opened the door to Emma's room. It was pitch dark. The shutters were closed and locked. And the curtains were drawn tight round the huge bed.

It was as hot as Hades, and as dark as a tomb.

At the sound of the opening door, Emma plucked convulsively at the damp sheet, trying to ensure that every last vestige of the nightgown was hidden. She still did not know what she would say to him.

In a moment he would slip between the bed-curtains and—

The crash of opening shutters echoed like thunder through the room. Hugo was pulling them back with incredible force…as if he hated them. And he was throwing open the windows too.

Emma felt the merest breath of cooler air through the tightly drawn bed-curtains. It was still dark, but she could sense the lightening beyond. She drew the sheet more tightly around her body, trying to make herself as small as possible.

Hugo's footsteps were not loud, but she knew he was standing beyond the curtain, between the bed and the open window. She saw two strong hands appear through the dark velvet. Then, in a single powerful gesture, the curtains were thrown open. Silhouetted against the dim light from the window was Hugo's tall figure, its arms still raised, forcing the curtains apart.

Without a thought, she shrank away from him. She could not prevent herself. His outline looked so huge, so dark, so menacing. If he wanted to humiliate her, to provide the final proof of his ownership, he could not have chosen a better way than this.

His hands dropped to his sides. Still she could not see his face. She closed her eyes, tightly.

'Emma?'

Keeping her eyes closed against the light, she said, 'I am sorry about the shutters. I…I thought that, in the dark, it would be easier to…easier for…' She could not go on. The words would not come.

She did not move. She could feel that he was looking down at her, thinking. For a long time, he did not move. She could not even hear him breathe.

At last she heard a tiny rustle of silk and then the edge of the sheet was lifted. The cool air touched her body. She shivered. It felt as if a hand had hovered a hair's breadth over her naked skin. Then the bed

dipped as he lay down beside her and drew the sheet
back over them both. Now, she could feel the waves
of heat from his body reaching out to encircle her
like a comforting arm. She opened her eyes in surprise. She could see now, just a little. Hugo was
watching her, but his expression was unreadable.

He reached out a hand to touch her cheek.
'Emma—'

Dear God, he was naked! She closed her eyes in
panic at the realisation. What on earth was going to
happen now?

The scrape of curtain rings provided her answer.
She opened her eyes to find that Hugo had closed the
bed-curtains once more, offering her the gift of
blessed darkness.

She screwed up her eyes again, not to shut out the
light—for that was gone—but to stop the tears that
threatened. She had not expected kindness, not from
this man who had been so cold and forbidding. But
she would not allow herself to weep. No matter what
this night might bring, she would not weep.

Hugo lay awake, staring up at the canopy. Beside
him, his wife was asleep at last, curled up like a child,
with her back towards him. Had she wept? He did
not know—and, in the dark, he could not see her
face.

Surreptitiously, he pulled open the curtain on his
side of the bed. The cooler air was sweet and refresh-
ing but he did not dare to move. He might wake her
if he rose. And then she would see the naked body
that repelled her.

Was it always to be like this? He had always hated making love in the dark. He wanted to make her respond to him, to see her face come alight with passion, to run his fingers over her silky skin and watch it glow…

But none of that had happened. Even in the darkness she craved, she had not yielded to him. She had not even said his name. This was not the soft responsive woman he had kissed in the conservatory. This was still the woman in the chapel, who received his kisses as if she were made of cold white marble. Nor was she the dreamer, beautiful as the flowers around her, who had sat in the garden looking as if she longed to melt into a lover's arms. Here, in the dark, he had felt the tension of her skin and the tightening of her muscles wherever he touched her. She was capable of responding—he knew she was—but he must have frightened her into silence and revulsion with the strength of his own passions and the sight of his shattered body.

If only he had been more careful, gone more slowly…

It was too late. It was done…and badly done. Would she ever learn to forgive him? For the first time in his life, he cursed all those years with the army, fighting for his country while other men learned how to move among the *ton* and to woo and win Society ladies. He had promised they could be comfortable together, but there was nothing comfortable about this. He did not know how to make love to a lady, even when she was his wife. His overwhelming physical desire—the desire he feared he had lost—had driven him to lose control as he had never done before. With other women—before—he had been sometimes passionate, sometimes playful, but always in control. With Emma…

It must be the effect of being celibate for so long, surely? Next time, he would not let his passions overcome his reason. Next time, he would be caressing, loving—

He was not sure that he could.

The sight of Emma lying there had roused him to a height of desire he had not imagined. He must not let it happen again, not like that. And there was only one way to prevent it. They must not share a bed again until they were safely installed at Lake Manor and had learned to be more…comfortable together. As he had promised.

He looked back at her sleeping form. Her breathing was slow now, and measured. He could leave without disturbing her.

Very gently, he eased himself from the bed and closed the curtains around her. Then he retrieved his robe and made his way back to his own room and his decanter of brandy.

When his wife woke up to the light of day, she would at least be spared the sight of her husband, naked, beside her.

Chapter Sixteen

Emma awoke feeling cold. The windows must have been open all night. For several moments, she lay staring at the bed-curtains, trying to muster the courage to turn and look her husband in the face.

It could no longer be avoided. She took a deep breath and rolled on to her back.

She was alone in the huge bed. No wonder she had felt cold. She should have realised that Hugo's comforting warmth was gone from her side.

And she was naked!

She felt herself blushing as she remembered. Hugo had had no patience with the filmy silk and lace. He would have no barriers between them, he had said. In no time at all, the nightgown had been thrown to the floor.

And then...

And then Hugo had made her his wife. This time, he *had* kissed her, fiercely and possessively. It had been frightening at first—a little—but the fear had passed as soon as her body had begun to heat. This time, there had been no risk of their being disturbed.

She had felt free to glory in the way he made her feel, hoping that, if she lay completely still, the sensations he created would go on for ever.

But they had not. One moment he was almost devouring her with his drugging kisses, murmuring her name as if it were the only word he knew; the next he had taken her body under his own and... She remembered only the streak of pain and the sudden weight of his body on hers. Everything else was hazy—except that he was soon gone from her, silent, rolling on to his back and closing his eyes. He had not touched her again.

Emma understood none of it. First, those amazing feelings, as if something magical were about to happen, and then—nothing. It could not be right. Not like this. Jamie had said it could be wonderful. Was this what she meant? Surely not. Emma had felt as tense as a coiled spring—which was far from wonderful—and then she had felt...bereft.

Perhaps Jamie would explain, now that Emma was truly a wife?

Perhaps she would, if only Emma could find the courage to ask. She felt herself blushing even more. She could not possibly talk of this night, not to anyone.

Emma pulled the sheet round her body and reached out through the curtains for her nightgown. She would be mortified if her abigail found her naked. And what if Hugo came in? She hastily donned the robe. She was not sure whether a husband would think it necessary to knock.

She had so much to learn about being a wife, much

more than she had ever imagined. She could run a household, or host a dinner for royalty, without the slightest qualm. It was as easy as riding a horse. But she did not know what to say to her husband when they were alone, or whether she might touch him, or how to show him that she loved him.

For she did. In spite of everything, she did.

She had been stunned by Hugo's cold reaction to her acceptance of his proposal. It was as if he had slapped her. It seemed that he would not forgive her those wounding insults, that he was offering to marry a woman he despised, only because he wanted to save his younger brother. But by then it was too late—her words could not be unsaid. She had spent four whole days trying to shut out the thought of what she had done by accepting him, and the prospect of spending the rest of her life with such a calculating, cold-blooded man.

But there was nothing cold-blooded about the man who came to her bed. He might despise her—though she was no longer sure of that—but he was certainly not cold-blooded. His passionate kisses, the way his hands skimmed her body, learning its contours in the darkness, the anguish in his voice as he spoke her name, over and over... He had lit a flame in her, *certes*, but he, too, had been burning.

Throwing back the bed-curtains, she rose and donned a heavy silk wrapper. Its concealing folds helped restore much of her normal strength of mind. Today was her godson's birthday and she must make ready to face the world.

She had been a fool these last four days, allowing

her fears to rule her. There was no need. She was Hugo's wife and she could make him proud of her.

An unbidden thought arose. Perhaps one day he might even value her enough to care for her, a little? Perhaps then she would not feel so desolate?

She must try. She would prove to him that she was the perfect wife. Such a woman would care for her husband and look to his slightest needs without being asked. A husband would never have cause to find fault with such a paragon of wifely virtues. It could not be so difficult, surely?

Emma straightened her back and lifted her chin. It would be a role, like all the others she had played in her life. She would play it to perfection.

'You made all these arrangements without saying a word to me?' Emma's voice had not risen appreciably, but she was white with fury.

Hugo took his wife by the arm and steered her away from the rest of the guests on the lawn. Little Dickon was the centre of everyone's attention, chortling happily as he played with his new toys and was petted by first one, then another, of the admiring adults. No one would notice their departure.

When they were hidden by the broad trunk of the ancestral oak, Hugo loosed his hold on her arm. She stared at him, accusingly, rubbing her flesh as if it were bruised.

'There is no need for all this outrage, Emma,' he said, frowning. As a soldier, he had prided himself on his coolness in the face of provocation, but today he was having great difficulty in keeping a rein on his temper. She had no right to challenge him, especially in public.

'How dare—'

'I am your husband,' Hugo said as calmly as he could. 'Such decisions are mine to make. We leave for Lake Manor on Friday, and that is where we shall live, for the rest of this year, at least.' At the sight of the sudden hurt in her eyes, he tried to soften his tone. 'Trust me, Emma, it is for the best.'

It took her a long time to reply. Hugo thought she was weighing her words.

'What about my father?'

Hugo was tempted to remind her of her wedding vows, to forsake all others and cleave only to him, but that would have been too cruel. He ought to have prepared her for being uprooted from her home. He put his hand on her arm, gently this time. 'Your father knows precisely what I plan, Emma. And he is in full agreement. He knows we have to make our own life together, my dear. Living in your father's house is no way to do that.'

'You discussed all this with my father?' she said. She sounded shocked. She threw him a swift, angry glare and then fixed her gaze on the grass beneath her feet.

Hugo was not prepared to argue the point. 'Of course. He naturally wished to know how I planned to support his daughter and the kind of life I could offer her. He was relieved to learn that a man of means, rather than a fortune hunter, was about to become his son-in-law.'

Emma said nothing. She still did not look at him.

'And now, I think we should return to Dickon's party, do not you? It is the child's day and we should not spoil it with petty quarrels. Come, Emma.' He held out his hand.

For a moment she did not move. Then she nodded. 'You are right. A godmother must be gay on her godson's birthday.' Ignoring his outstretched hand, she walked out from behind the oak and rejoined the group around the child.

Hugo gritted his teeth and followed. She had started talking to the Rector as if nothing had happened. And she was laughing.

Emma watched Hugo out of the corner of her eye. She still wanted to hit him, though she had managed to restrain herself…just. That would have been a public humiliation for them both.

He was unfair. He was a tyrant. He was forcing her to live on his run-down estate, miles from anywhere, so that he could have her all to himself, so that she would be cut off from her father and her friends and all the places she had known since childhood. And she had no choice but to go with him. No one—not even her father—would take her part against her lawful husband.

She had been wrong about marriage. She had been wrong about Hugo. She could not begin to be the quiet, conformable wife she had pictured in her mind. She was not sure how she had ever thought to love a man who treated her with so little consideration.

She watched her husband throw little Dickon high into the air, catching him easily when he tumbled,

squealing, back to earth. Hugo had regained his physical strength much faster than she would have
thought possible. He would have no need of her min-
istrations. He was self-sufficient to an extent that was
almost frightening.

Emma began to feel hollow inside. How many
more of her ambitions would be brought to naught
by this man she had married? Did he need her at all?
How naïve she had been, earlier, to think that she
could turn herself into the perfect submissive wife.
Hugo might welcome it—judging by his attitude today, he took her submission for granted—but Emma
had learned she was incapable of it.

Hugo and Dickon were down on the grass now,
playing with a pair of wooden horses. But Dickon
clearly wanted a real live horse—so Hugo obligingly
went down on all fours and allowed the child to ride
on his back. Emma watched, suddenly envious. Her
husband was more understanding of the needs of
Richard's child than he was of his wife's.

Richard came at last to retrieve his son, ignoring
Dickon's protests. Hugo yielded with good grace, but
there was something in his face that Emma recognised, even though it was gone in a moment. She had
seen that expression before, the very first time she
had seen Hugo on the lawn with Dickon. In a flash
of insight, she understood the hunger behind that
look. Hugo loved children. And Hugo had been convinced he would never have a family of his own. Did
he think so still?

Emma could not continue to watch from a distance. She was beginning to realise that her husband

was a very complex man. It was too easy to brand him a tyrant, on the grounds of a few sharp words. And, in truth, she had given him little choice by challenging him as she had. Having made his decision to take her to Lake Manor, he could not be expected to change it—in public—at the first sign of opposition from his wife.

She must try again…not to be submissive and unquestioning, for that would be beyond her, but to understand him better. Hugo might be more difficult than the other men she knew, but there must be a way to reach him. She had always been able to bend every other man to her will.

She would begin by apologising for her outburst. That would surely disarm him.

Emma made her way to her husband's side, but her good intentions were frustrated by the arrival of Richard's butler, in search of Hugo. 'May I have a word, sir?' Digby said quietly. That was all Emma heard. The rest of the butler's words were for Hugo alone.

Hugo raised an eyebrow but said nothing. Then, with a slight shrug of his shoulders, he followed the butler across the lawn to the house.

'Kit! What the devil—?' Kit was the last person Hugo had expected to see in Richard's bookroom. Digby had told him only that a gentleman was come, on urgent business.

Kit looked more embarrassed than Hugo had ever seen him. 'I'm sorry, Hugo,' he said. 'Believe me, I would never have intruded on your honeymoon if I'd had any choice. Emma…Mrs Stratton doesn't know I'm here, does she?'

'No. Digby was very discreet. But what on earth possessed you to come here? The gossips will have a field day with this.'

'I had no choice, Hugo. I am in real trouble.'

'Oh, God. What now?'

'Money,' Kit said in a hollow voice. 'I lost five thousand pounds to Lady Luce—and she's demanding immediate payment.'

First Emma, and now Kit. Hugo's fraying temper snapped. 'Have you *no* sense of honour? You played with money you do not have. Worse, you did so against a lady. You're a disgrace to the name you bear.'

Kit stood ramrod straight, taking Hugo's angry words as if they were blows.

Hugo's voice rose even more. 'I take it you *don't* have the money to pay her?'

Kit did not move, though he coloured a little.

'Well, do you?'

'No. But I—'

'Don't give me your lame excuses, Kit. We'll finish this bout with the buttons off. You lost a fortune at the tables and now you have a debt of honour that you can't pay. Well? What do you intend to do about it?'

Kit looked his brother straight in the eye. 'I did think to blow my brains out, but I have already brought you trouble enough.'

The intent expression in Kit's face shocked Hugo. He meant it. All Hugo's anger drained from him at the thought of what his rash young fool of a brother might have done. Hugo gripped the back of the chair for support, his mind racing. 'Good of you to think about the rest of the family. I'm sure John will be suitably grateful,' he said with heavy sarcasm. 'Pity you didn't think of us before you set about losing money you don't have.'

Kit still stood rigidly to attention. 'You are furious, Hugo,' he said at last. 'I suppose you have every right to be. I own it was a stupid thing to do. If it hadn't been for Forster—'

'Forster?' Hugo thundered. 'Forster was there?'

At last, Kit hung his head a little. 'Yes. I know I should have left as soon as he joined the table, but I didn't want anyone to think I was afraid to face him.'

Hugo nodded. He knew Forster's ways only too well.

'So I stayed,' Kit continued, 'and played. And when Lady Luce started winning so heavily, he said…he implied that I wasn't man enough to stick at the table when I was losing. After that, I couldn't leave, could I?'

Hugo nodded a little reluctantly. He fancied he would have done the same in his brother's place.

'I was sure I would win eventually. You know I've always been lucky with the cards and the bones. Thought it was just a matter of time. Lady Luce's luck would turn, I would recoup my losses, and no-body would be any the wiser. Especially Forster.'

'But your luck didn't turn,' Hugo said flatly.

'The grasping old witch gave me no chance. I swear I'll have my revenge on her yet. She'd take the last farthing from a beggar. She must have been keeping count. The moment my losses reached five thousand, she announced that she had had enough for the night and would retire. Said she expected me to call on her within the week.'

Hugo found he was still gripping the chair. He deliberately relaxed his hands, one at a time, while he thought through Kit's story so far. There must be more. He knew that. He waited in silence for Kit to resume.

'She refused point blank to give me any chance of recouping my losses. Said she wouldn't be playing for more than chicken-stakes for a while.'

'That doesn't sound like Lady Luce at all,' Hugo said, surprised.

'Transpires that she needs the money to cover her own losses. For once, her son is refusing to pay—word is he can't lay his hands on the blunt—so she is desperate. She would still be received, given her pedigree…but no one in his right mind would ever allow her to play again.'

Hugo made to speak but Kit forestalled him.

'You don't need to say it, Hugo. I know I was mad to play. And for such stakes. Do you think I would have chosen to come cap in hand to you if I could have found another way? Believe me, I tried every other avenue I could think of.'

Hugo went over to the desk and leaned against it, breathing heavily. 'And you think I might just happen to have five thousand pounds about me? Kit, you really must be mad.'

This time, Kit refused to meet Hugo's eyes. His

neck was very red above his snowy cravat. 'I thought...I knew John could never raise so much. You were my last hope. I knew you had Emma's dowry.'

'*What?*'

As Hugo's shout of fury echoed around the wooden panels, the door opened.

'Excuse me, I did knock, but—' At the sight of Kit, Emma stopped dead, eyes wide and face suddenly ashen.

Hugo crossed the room in a few strides, taking her arm in a fierce grip and turning her back towards the open door. 'You have no business here, Emma,' he said angrily. 'You will have the goodness to leave us. At once.'

She gasped in protest, but Hugo took no notice. He propelled her into the corridor and shut the door firmly at her back.

Chapter Seventeen

Emma's hand came up to her mouth, trying to stop the cry of anguish that had risen in her throat. Hugo's furious words seemed to be echoing inside her head. No man had ever spoken to her in such a fashion. And this man was her husband.

She could still hear Hugo's angry voice from the other side of the door. This time, he must be berating his brother. The heavy wood muffled most of the sound, but the word 'dowry' was unmistakable…as was the venom with which it was spoken.

Emma fled before she could hear any more.

She found herself in Jamie's conservatory. How had she come there? She did not know. Only that she had been desperate to escape from the sound of Hugo's anger.

She threaded her way through the lush greenery and sank down on to the stone bench. It was shaded, though uncomfortably humid. That was a blessing, she decided. No one would think to look for her here, on such a hot day. She would have time to gather her thoughts, to decide what to do.

A drip of water fell on to her face from one of the huge leaves.

Emma started to laugh. It might as well have been a bucketful, for it had brought her back to reality. *She* could not decide what to do, for Hugo had made all the decisions for her. It did not matter what she thought, or what she wished. Her husband did not see a need to consult her in any way. It seemed he did not even wish to talk to her.

Emma bowed her head. She felt very close to despair. Why did it have to be like this?

The leaf dripped again.

Emma edged along the stone bench to avoid the next drip. The stone was cool under her hand. It reminded her of the seat in the garden at Epsom where this nightmare had begun. And it reminded her of the moment when she had understood that she loved Hugo Stratton.

Did she still? Could she love a man who treated her so abominably?

No.

Yes.

She did not know. Everything was so confused. In this very spot she had seen Hugo kissing Jamie…but she had been mistaken. On the other side of those plants, she had accused Hugo of the vilest conduct imaginable and he had lost his temper. His hard grey eyes had narrowed to furious slits. He had been about to strike her. But he had kissed her instead.

That kiss was the cause of everything.

Hugo was standing by the desk, drumming his fingers on the polished wood. Kit had not moved. He looked like a man about to face his execution.

Hugo glanced towards the door. Emma must be long gone. What had he said to her? He could not remember, but he was sure it had been insulting. He had never known such black rage.

He ran his free hand through his hair and stared distractedly at the wood beneath his fingers. This would not do. Hot words achieved nothing. He needed a cool head to deal with Kit. And then there was Emma…

Hugo trod slowly across to the window. Thank goodness it was not open. It was bad enough that Emma had walked in on them, but if Richard and the others had heard too…

First things first. He forced his thoughts back to his impossible brother. Kit had been right to come to him. Courageous, too. He must have known that Hugo would be furiously angry, but he had not flinched once.

Kit's losses were enormous, a fortune, but it was not his fault, not totally. A more experienced man would have found a way to side-step Forster's malicious insinuations, but Kit, at twenty-two, could not have encountered many of Forster's stamp. Kit's magnificent figure and dashing ways made it too easy to forget just how young he was.

Kit had stayed—and played—to protect the family's good name.

Hugo turned on his heel to face his brother. His mind was made up. Now that he had regained control of his temper, he could clearly see the way ahead.

'You have been a fool, Kit,' he said, without heat,

'but I can understand why you acted so rashly. And, believe me, I *am* glad that you decided not to blow your brains out. Think of the mess it would have left for the servants.'

Kit started, looked searchingly at Hugo, and then laughed in relief. 'Hugo—'

'Don't think you'll get off scot-free, though, for you won't. I'll pay your debts, but there are conditions.'

Kit raised his head a fraction and narrowed his eyes.

'First,' Hugo continued implacably, 'you will give me your solemn promise never again to play for more than you can afford to lose. Not even against Lady Luce.' Hugo stopped, glaring sternly at his brother, but Kit met his challenge, and nodded briefly. 'And second, you will take yourself off abroad for a year or two so that all this madness may be forgotten.'

This time, Kit's nod took a little longer to come. He had gained quite a following among the young bloods of London Society. It was not surprising that he should be loath to relinquish his position there.

'Go to Paris. Or—better still—Vienna. Make yourself useful. I've quite a few friends in both places who would be glad of another pair of hands.'

Kit grimaced.

'I should tell you, I suppose,' said Hugo, trying not to smile, 'that there are…er…other attractions in Vienna, too. It's not as glittering as it was during the Congress, but I believe the social round is quite as hectic as London's.'

'I would go in any case, Hugo, and you know it,' Kit said seriously. Then he grinned. 'But you have just made my penance sound a great deal more attractive.'

They both laughed.

Hugo went back to the desk. He must start to organise the money to pay Kit's debts. And it would have to be taken from Emma's dowry. Kit had been right about that. There was no time to do anything else before Lady Luce's deadline. Hugo drew a sheet of paper towards him and dipped his pen in the standish.

'Hugo, what are we going to do about Forster? He's clearly determined to do you mischief now that he knows you're back in England.'

Hugo felt the black rage beginning to rise again. He forced himself to remain calm. 'The man is a blackguard. And a coward. A great many men died because of him, Kit, and he didn't give a rap. This time, I *shall* find a way to stop him.'

'Careful, Hugo, he's got friends in high places.'

'So have I. Don't forget it was Wellington himself who gave me my majority. And he had the measure of Forster almost from the start. Sent him back to Horse Guards at the first opportunity. Knew he was bound to toady up to the Duke of York, but in London, at least, he couldn't be responsible for any more disastrous sallies like the one at Ciudad Rodrigo. I swore then that Forster would pay, one day, and I don't intend to break my oath. Langley and the others died because Forster sent us to take that impregnable ridge—'

'Against your advice,' interposed Kit.

'Yes, against my advice. But that doesn't make me blameless, Kit. I was experienced enough to know that the attack was unnecessary—and that it would be a disaster. But I wasn't nearly wise enough to hide my contempt for Forster when I warned him not to issue the order. He was furious that a young whippersnapper like me should dare to question his judgement. Almost had an apoplexy on the spot. God, I wish he had. It would have saved all those lives. As it was, the attack went ahead, and more than a hundred good men died, needlessly. Only a handful of us came back. If I had been less concerned about showing Forster that I was the better soldier, I might have made him listen to me. As it was—'

'As it was, it cost you your career. And, if it hadn't been for Wellington's intervention, it would have cost you your good name, too, once Forster started telling the world that you were a coward as well as insubordinate. He wanted you dishonoured, Hugo. I am sure he still does.'

'I didn't *feel* honourable after seeing all my friends die for nothing, knowing I could have stopped it.'

'But you can't *know* that,' Kit protested. 'Forster would never have heeded your advice, even if you'd offered it on your knees. It was his responsibility, not yours, Hugo. He accused you of cowardice just to cover up his own incompetence. He's the coward, not you. He'd run a mile if his own life were in danger. I've a mind to call him out. I could easily find an excuse—'

'No! For God's sake, haven't you caused enough

trouble already, you young hothead? Society already holds you convicted of seduction and gambling away the Stratton family fortune. Would you add murder to the list?'

Kit grinned like a mischievous schoolboy. 'I might miss, you know.'

Hugo snorted in disbelief. 'If you did, it would be the first time.' Hugo had been a first-class shot before his injury, but Kit was even better, and they both knew it. 'Be serious, Kit. Think of the damage you might do—to the whole family—and try to rein in that impetuous spirit of yours.'

'It's no worse than yours, brother.'

'But I have learnt—since Rodrigo—to temper mine, lest it harm the innocent. You must learn to do the same. Look where it almost got you this time.'

'Oh, very well, but—'

'Leave Forster to me, Kit. I will deal with him in my own way and in my own time. I believe I have the right.'

Kit looked mutinous for a moment, but then nodded.

'And, in the meantime, you must pay your debts to Lady Luce and make ready to go on your travels. Come, sit down and have a glass of madeira, while I compose a letter to my bankers. They will be surprised to learn that I am coming up to London... especially as I wrote to them only the other day about what I wanted them to do.'

Kit choked a little on his wine. But then, irrepressible as always, he favoured Hugo with a rueful grin that made him look handsomer than ever. Raising his glass in salute, he said, 'Happy birthday, big brother.'

'Heaven help the ladies of Vienna,' Hugo said under his breath.

Hugo was at first surprised to find that Emma had not returned to Dickon's party in the garden, but then he recalled just how brusquely he had expelled her from the bookroom. He had not given her a single word of explanation for Kit's arrival. And he had not listened to a single word she had to say.

She would be furious. Again. And—this time—she had cause.

He must find her before he left and try to explain. But what could he say?

He made his way back into the guest wing and climbed the stairs to their suite. He could not race up the stairs two at a time, as he had when he was younger, but his self-imposed exercise programme was certainly working—stairs were nothing like the ordeal they had been. He had been looking forward to the move to Lake Manor so that he could start to ride again—in secret. He did not want anyone to see him on a horse until he was sure he could control his mount...and stay on its back. Emma was a remarkably fine horsewoman, and she would have even more cause to despise him if she found he could not stay in the saddle. He would not dare to invite her to ride out with him until he was very, very sure.

His own bedchamber was empty, of course, but it provided the best route to Emma's. If he went in from the corridor, the servants might well see how she received him. They always seemed to be hovering about the guest wing, watching. He had no desire to provide any more food for backstairs gossip.

He hesitated at the door into Emma's room. Was it only a few hours since he had left her there, curled up on the other side of that great bed, as far a possible from her new husband? The very presence of that bed was going to make this interview even more difficult.

But it had to be faced.

He knocked sharply and opened the door, without waiting for an invitation.

The chamber was empty.

The shutters and the windows were open, just as he had left them, but the bed had been made and the curtains drawn back. A heavy wrapper lay across the end of the bed. There was no sign of a nightgown.

Hugo remembered the feel of it—thin, slippery, with long panels of lace at front and back. He wished he had seen how she looked in it, but he had been in too much of a hurry for that. He had needed to feel her naked skin against his own. Had he ripped it? It was possible. It had been such a fragile thing…just like his wife.

This would not do. Nothing could be changed, no matter how guilty he felt. They had to go forward from where they were. He could not apologise for last night—Emma would probably be mortified if he made the slightest reference to that hasty and brutal coupling—but he could certainly apologise for his behaviour in the library.

After a moment's thought, his tactics were decided. It was easy enough to determine what not to say. He could not tell her about Forster. And he would not tell her about Kit's debts. He would simply tell her that he was going to London with Kit; that she was to go to Lake Manor alone. She would probably welcome the time away from him. So would he. While he was not with her, he would not be tempted to break his resolve to stay away from her bed. For that—if only she knew of it—she should be grateful.

Glancing out of the window, Hugo saw that Richard and his guests had remained on the lawn. But Emma was still missing. She must be in the house somewhere—alone.

Time was pressing, but Hugo began a methodical search of all the rooms where she might be found. All were empty. Where on earth had she got to? If she were outside, she would have returned to the party on the lawn. She *must* be in the house. But where?

When the answer came to him, eventually, he groaned. She must be in Lady Hardinge's conservatory, the place where he had attacked her that first time. She had been bristling with outrage then, and she would be so again.

He made his way back downstairs and along the corridor. He looked through the glass panel. There was no sign of her.

He opened the door, not trying to conceal the noise of his arrival. The last thing he wanted was to creep up on her unawares. 'Emma?' he said in a low voice. There was no response. Perhaps he had spoken too softly? 'Emma,' he said again, his voice a little louder.

There was a movement behind the cluster of exotic plants. They were pushed apart by a petite blonde figure in a pale muslin gown. Against the deep greens around her, Emma looked almost ethereally beautiful. Hugo caught his breath.

She looked at him unwaveringly. Her eyes were as blue as the Spanish sky.

'I am here, Major,' she said.

Chapter Eighteen

That was the last response Hugo had expected. What on earth was the matter with her? Why did she not use his given name? They were husband and wife.

He stood staring at her motionless figure, trying to recall all their exchanges since she had become his wife. She had called him by name at the altar—repeating the words of the chaplain—but he could not remember a single instance when she had done so since they walked together down the aisle. In fact, he could not remember that she had called him anything at all.

Until now.

But that was about to change. Immediately.

'For heaven's sake, Emma. You are my wife, not my lackey. My name is Hugo.'

She nodded coolly in the face of his hot words. 'As you wish.' She did not move.

Hugo forced himself to remain where he was, to keep a distance between them. He moved only far enough to close the door behind him.

'I have had to change my plans, Emma. As a result of urgent…family business, I must go up to London with Kit. We leave immediately.'

Emma's face brightened. Was she so delighted to be rid of him?

'I will join you at Lake Manor as soon as I can,' Hugo said, trying not to look at her. 'I should not be more than a few days behind you.'

'But I know no one at Lake Manor,' she cried, 'and nothing about the estate. You cannot expect me to go there alone.' Before he could say a word in response, she went on, 'Oh. I see. You are ashamed to have me appear in London, so hard on the heels of the scandal at Epsom. So your solution is to banish me.'

'Nothing of the sort,' Hugo snapped. 'What kind of man do you think I am?'

Her expression gave him his answer. She was hurt; and she thought he was cruel.

'Emma, I cannot take you to London because Kit and I…because Kit and I have business to attend to. And I have no house in London fit for you. I shall be sharing Kit's rooms while I am there.'

Emma sighed. It sounded like exasperation. The expression in her eyes had not softened. 'My father has a London house. He would open it for us if we asked. My Aunt Augusta, too, is always delighted to welcome her family to her London home. And she left for London first thing this morning.'

Hugo waited for her to continue. She was surely about to ask if they might both stay with her aunt. But she said nothing more. In the silence, Hugo realised she was too proud to ask for favours that she

feared would be denied. She just looked at him, with
hurt in her eyes.

She thought he was ashamed of her. How could he
be? She was everything he had ever dreamed of in a
wife. A tiny inner voice reminded him that one qual-
ity was lacking—she did not love him. He refused to
heed it.

'Emma, I promise you I had no thought of banish-
ing you. I merely sought—' He shook his head in
annoyance. Excuses would not do here. 'I do not expect to be in London for more than a few days, but
if you wish to accompany me—and if suitable ac-
commodation is available with your aunt—I should
be more than happy to have you there.'

Emma gave a curt little nod of agreement.

'Then that is settled. Kit and I must drive on today
as we planned, but you may follow us as soon as you
wish. Will that content you?'

'I will be ready to leave first thing in the morning,'
she said promptly. 'May I ask...?' She sounded hesitant. And she was looking at the floor. 'Forgive me,
but may I ask about this urgent business? Does it
concern me?'

It was the first time she had ventured a question
of any kind. Hugo wondered how much she might
have heard. Nothing about Forster, surely? She had
been long gone before the discussion turned to that
blackguard. Kit, then? Possibly. What could he tell
her? He could not betray his brother's follies. But
neither could he lie to his wife. He had done her harm
enough already.

'Kit is going abroad for a time, Emma, and funds

must be arranged before he goes. John is in Scotland, as you know, and so it falls to me, as the next brother, to see to matters.'

Emma blushed fierily. 'A sudden departure, I collect?'

Hugo winced. She thought it was because of her, because of the scandal. He was tying himself in knots, tighter and tighter. And his poor wife, whom he had treated cruelly since their wedding, was being humiliated in the process. She was beginning to look distraught.

Hugo could not stand to see her so. In two strides he was beside her and had taken her in his arms. His resolutions could go hang. 'Emma, it is not what you think. Trust me,' he said in a low voice. He cupped his fingers under her chin and forced her to look up at him. 'Kit's departure has nothing to do with what happened between you. Please believe that. I cannot tell you more without betraying a confidence. I only ask you to trust me.' He gazed into her eyes for a long time, willing her to yield to him. 'Will you do that?' he said at last.

'Of course I trust you, Hugo,' she said immediately, making his heart begin to race. Then she spoiled the moment by adding, 'I am your wife.'

It was too much. He crushed her to him and began to devour her luscious mouth. It was their wedding night, all over again. But, this time, her tiny whimper of protest reached him, damping down the madness that seemed to overtake him whenever he touched her. He dragged his lips from hers and, with an effort, put her from him.

'Forgive me, Emma. That was…uncalled for.'

'As you say. But then—' she stopped, looking up at him through her dark lashes '—I am your wife.'

And this time, she smiled.

Hugo and Kit were together on the step when Emma appeared in the doorway to bid them farewell. She was fully in control now, she was sure of that.

Kit, clearly, was not. The moment Emma appeared, he bowed awkwardly to her and retreated, striding across the gravel to climb into the chaise. Emma did not give him another thought. She was much more concerned about her husband. How would he take his leave of her? He had left the conservatory without another word. He had asked her to trust him—again—but he had explained nothing. And her lips were still burning from his searing, passionate kisses. He desired her still, but he seemed to be fighting desperately to resist his feelings. He did not want to want her. It was all so demeaning.

They would be together again in London. There, they would have a chance to right matters. Or would they? Staying with Mrs Warenne would make life difficult, to say the least. Aunt Augusta was kind, and well-meaning, but she never stopped talking and fussing. She would surely drive Hugo mad. And then there was Kit, too. Would she have to entertain him? If the brothers had such important business to transact, they would certainly be together a great deal. Emma began to think that London was not the solution after all. Lake Manor, for all its remoteness, might have more attractions than she had imagined.

Hugo barely glanced at Kit when his brother strode across to the chaise. Hugo was looking at Emma, and his look seemed very serious indeed. Emma thought his eyes had grown very dark, more black than grey. What was it he saw when he looked at her? If only she knew.

Hugo stepped forward to take Emma's hands in his. He kissed one, then the other, and held them both in his own for a long time, looking deeply into her eyes. Then he leant forward and placed a chaste kiss on her cheek.

'I shall look to find you at your aunt's, in a day or two.'

Emma nodded, but she was still anxious. 'You will join me there, I hope?'

'Of course,' Hugo said calmly. The strong clasp of his hands was reassuring. 'I have no intention of providing any more food for the gossips, you may be sure of that. Take care not to overtax yourself on the journey, my dear. There is no need to rush, you know.'

Something told Emma that there was every need to rush to her husband's side, but it was only a vague feeling. He had told her nothing about the reasons for his haste. That story about arranging money for Kit was not the truth, of that she was sure. Not the whole truth, at any rate.

Hugo was still holding her hands. It felt comforting, and comfortable. She wished he would stay a little longer, so that they might travel together. She was a little afraid of what might happen, though she could not begin to understand why.

The moment lengthened. There seemed to be nothing but Hugo's eyes gazing into hers, and the touch of his hands.

The restless horses broke the spell.

'Goodbye, Emma,' Hugo said softly, with just the suggestion of a smile in his eyes. Then he bent his head and kissed her hands once more, lingering a little over each one. He seemed reluctant to relinquish them.

When he turned to join his brother in the post-chaise, Emma felt as if the pressure of his fingers was still on hers. He had run his thumbs across her palms, leaving an imprint behind like a finger running across velvet. It tingled strangely.

Emma thrust her hands into her skirts. She thought that, if she looked at them, there would be marks.

The chaise started to move. In a few seconds, the horses were speeding down the avenue towards the gates. Soon they would be out of sight.

Emma picked up her skirts and dashed into the house. If she ran, she would be able to catch sight of the chaise from the upstairs window before it turned out of the estate. She was gasping for breath by the time she gained her bedchamber, but she was not disappointed. The chaise was still in sight. Hugo's arm was resting on the frame of the open window, his ungloved hand just visible against the dark wood. And then the chaise was lost to view behind the trees.

She could still feel the warm trail of his fingers across her palm.

Emma opened the connecting door into Hugo's room, hesitating on the threshold. There was no reason not to go in. It was her husband's room. Nevertheless, she felt like an intruder, somehow. This was Hugo's domain. They had never shared it, not in any way. It was a purely masculine room. Even the scents were male—shaving soap, tobacco, a hint of cologne. She crossed to the bed and sat on the very edge, hardly daring to touch. This was where her husband had slept after he left her. If only he had stayed. If he had been there when she woke, things would have been easier between them, surely?

She reached out a hand to smooth Hugo's pillow. Soon, the maids would come to take the bedlinen to be laundered. It would no longer be Hugo's pillow, with Hugo's scent. It would be fresh, and clean, and totally anonymous. He would be gone from her.

Emma lay down on the bed and put her cheek on the pillow, feeling its softness. She could smell the faintest lingering trace of his cologne. She closed her eyes, breathing deeply. For a moment, she would imagine that he was still here, that he was about to come to join her, there on his bed, that he would take her in his arms…that he would tell her he loved her. It was a dream, Emma knew, but such a wonderful dream…

'Emma? Oh, there you are.' It was Jamie's soft voice, sounding a little concerned.

Emma opened her eyes to see her friend's rounded figure standing in the open doorway that led to her own room. She sat up hurriedly, trying to assume a nonchalant pose. What on earth must Jamie think, finding Emma lying on Hugo's bed, eyes closed, fingers stroking the pillow? She would surely think she was run mad.

'I came to ask whether you needed any help. I understand that you plan to leave for London tomorrow.' Jamie sounded neither surprised, nor curious. She was just her usual matter-of-fact self.

'Bless you,' Emma said, and meant it. She did not deserve such a staunch friend. 'I expect we shall be in London for only a few days, and so I shall not need much by way of baggage. If I have Sawyer pack up the rest, perhaps you would be so good as to send it on to Lake Manor?' She rose and followed Jamie back into the other bedroom.

'Certainly I will. But are you sure you may not stay longer in London? Your aunt is bound to press you to remain, especially as the Season is in full swing. I fancy she will wish to parade her newly married niece before the world.'

Emma grimaced. 'I doubt that Hugo would take kindly to that,' she said. 'And what use is a newly married niece if her husband refuses to be paraded at her side?'

Jamie laughed. 'You are quite right. Major Stratton detests being the object of vulgar curiosity, especially now… He is a very private man, I think.'

Emma nodded, but said nothing.

'Emma, will you allow me to give you a word of advice?'

Emma could not look at her friend. She was too embarrassed at the thought of what Jamie might wish to say. But she managed to nod. Jamie was wise, and she had Emma's interests at heart. Her advice would be worth hearing.

Jamie paused, preparing her words. 'I said that your husband is a very private man, Emma. He is proud, too. I think that he is very conscious of his scars and of the weakness caused by his wounds. Richard says Hugo used to be a very active man, never still, always riding out, or shooting, or following some sport or other. It must gall him to be less than the man he was. And it galls him even more—of this I am sure—to think that others might pity him. Especially you, Emma. I think he is afraid that you think him less than a whole man.'

Emma swallowed hard. She could not speak. She nodded to Jamie to continue.

'One of the things I have learned in my own marriage, Emma, is that sometimes it is necessary to take risks.'

Emma looked up in surprise.

Jamie smiled slightly. 'That sounds strange, does it not? I do not mean risks of the physical kind, but risks with your own...your own self-esteem. A proud man will find it difficult, perhaps impossible, to allow his new wife to see his weaknesses, lest she use them to wound him. And if the wife feels the same, then the barriers will never be removed. They will never really be able to talk, or trust, or—'

'But what can I do?' Emma burst out. Jamie's uncanny ability to describe Emma's relationship with Hugo had wiped away any thought of reserve. Jamie knew what was wrong between them. Jamie knew what could be done.

Jamie continued in the same soft, measured voice. 'If the wife is brave enough to expose her own weaknesses first, her husband may learn to trust her enough to do the same. Especially if he loves her.'

Emma shook her head. Hugo did not love her. Jamie was wrong there. He despised her. And she had given him cause. She shook her head again.

Jamie did not pursue the point. 'There is one other thing I must say to you, Emma, though it will worry you, I fear. There is something in your husband's past, relating to his time in the Peninsula. I cannot give you details. Even Richard does not know what happened. I only know that it happened many years ago—and that it worries him still.'

So there *was* something. And it had to do with Colonel Forster, of that she was sure. She thought back to that extraordinary exchange between the Colonel and Kit at the Derby. The animosity had been almost palpable, barely covered by a veneer of politeness. If Richard or Jamie had seen it, there would have been no doubt in their minds about the origins of Hugo's concern.

But they had not seen. They did not know. And it was not Emma's place to tell them. If Hugo wished to share his past with Richard, he would do so, in his own time.

Would he, one day, trust Emma enough to share it with her?

Chapter Nineteen

'Well, my dear, I am delighted to see you. And so soon after your wedding, too.'

Emma nodded politely. Aunt Augusta was at her worst when one had just arrived. The only solution was to allow her to talk herself out.

'I am surprised that the Major permitted you to travel such a way alone, however. Most unseemly.'

Emma could not allow criticism of Hugo, not from anyone. 'But I was by no means alone, Aunt. My abigail was with me and two stout grooms besides. Indeed, I travelled in exactly the same style when I came to you a few weeks ago.'

'Hmph.' Aunt Augusta did not like to be proved wrong. 'When can we expect your husband? I do hope he does not neglect you, now you are both in London, Emma. People are bound to remark on it, if he does not join you here.'

Emma hoped her expression did not betray her. Her aunt had given voice to the thing she most feared. She forced a smile. 'My husband plans to join me here, naturally, but said he would not trouble you until I had arrived,' she lied. 'No doubt he will make an appearance in the course of the day. I have sent word to Kit's lodgings.'

'So that's where he is,' said Aunt Augusta with satisfaction. 'I only hope his presence will serve to curb that wild young man's excesses.'

Emma gritted her teeth, wishing her aunt could be a little less forthright. She did not need to be reminded of the scandal that she and Kit had created.

'Oh, I did not mean you, my dear child,' said Aunt Augusta, stretching across to pat Emma's hand. 'No, indeed. Your brother-in-law's indiscretion at Epsom is all but forgotten now. Have you not heard? He lost five thousand pounds to Lady Luce the very next day.'

Emma gasped. Five thousand pounds was a fortune.

'And Colonel Forster was playing, too, I believe, though his losses were nowhere near as bad as Kit's. I find I cannot like that man, Emma, for all that he is one of the Duke of York's friends. By all accounts, he made very sure that the news of Kit's losses was all over London before breakfast. There is no love lost there, I fancy.'

Emma was well aware of that. She had seen the animosity with her own eyes. But what had possessed Kit to play so high? It was madness. And, of course, he had had to come to Hugo for help. No wonder her husband had been so blazingly angry. He was going to have to use Emma's dowry to pay his wastrel brother's gaming debts.

Was that why Kit was to be sent abroad? And what

of Colonel Forster? What was his role in all this?
Emma had instinctively mistrusted the Colonel's mo-
tives. He had struck her, on that one short encounter,
as a vindictive man—and no true gentleman. She was
sure he was not to be trusted, not in any way.

Emma forced herself to pay attention to her aunt's
interminable gossip.

'And so Sally Jersey was silenced. I swear it was
for the first time in her life.'

'Indeed,' Emma said, wishing that someone would
do the same for her aunt.

Her prayer was answered by the arrival of her
aunt's butler. He was an old man, slow and rather
stooped, but he was still very conscious of his important position in the household. 'Major Stratton has
arrived, ma'am,' he began in a pompous voice. 'Shall
I—'

'Show him up, man, show him up,' snapped Aunt
Augusta. 'There is no need to stand on ceremony
with the Major. He is a guest in the house, remember.'

The butler bowed and made his stately way out of
the room.

Emma giggled nervously.

'Yes, I know, my dear, but he has been with me
for ever. I could not turn him off, no matter how
preposterous he has become. It would break his
heart.'

Emma nodded. She had not been thinking about
the butler. Hugo was downstairs and would appear at
any moment. She smoothed her silken skirts and put
her hands to her hair.

'You look very well indeed, my dear,' said Aunt Augusta kindly. 'He will find no fault with your appearance.'

The door was thrown open with exaggerated ceremony. 'Major Stratton to see you, ma'am,' the butler intoned, completely ignoring his mistress's instructions.

Emma thought her aunt muttered irritably under her breath as she rose to greet her guest. Emma rose, too, thankful that her legs were fairly steady beneath her. Her insides had turned over at the sight of him. He was wearing a new blue coat which fitted him much better than those he had worn at Harding. He no longer looked thin. Indeed, he had greater breadth of shoulder than she had remembered. He looked almost normal—tall, straight and strong, the epitome of a gentleman of the *ton*. The only outward sign of his wounds was the scar on his face. Even that was fading. Soon it would be only a thin silvery line.

Hugo bowed elegantly over Mrs Warenne's hand. 'Good afternoon to you, ma'am. I hope I find you well?'

When he moved past Mrs Warenne to greet Emma, she found she was holding her breath. He bowed over her hand, too, but at the last moment, he turned it to place a kiss on her palm. Emma let out her breath in a gasp of surprise.

Hugo looked up into her face and smiled at what he saw there. Then he straightened and placed a chaste kiss on Emma's cheek. 'Good day to you, too, my dear wife,' he said. 'I need not ask if I find you well. It is obvious that you are blooming, in spite of your long and arduous journey up to London.'

'You have a very poor opinion of me, sir, if you think I would find such a journey arduous,' she said, returning his smile.

'Touché, madame,' he replied, running his thumb over her palm before finally relinquishing her hand. 'I see that you are as tough as the doughtiest of my soldiers, and that not even the most difficult journey would hold any terrors for you. Beware. I may yet put your mettle to the test.'

Emma's smile widened a little. There was so much warmth in his eyes when he looked at her, and a wicked glint, too, when he teased her. She wished he had not let go of her hand.

Behind them, Aunt Augusta coughed. She was not used to being ignored, especially in her own house. 'I have had a suite of rooms prepared for you,' she said briskly. 'I hope you will both be comfortable.'

Emma knew she had not imagined that slight emphasis on the word 'both'. 'Thank you, Aunt,' she said politely. 'I am sure we shall.'

Aunt Augusta had started talking again, as volubly as before. 'And what of that scapegrace brother of yours, Major? Is he still in London?'

Hugo frowned. Mrs Warenne might be family now, but he did not take kindly to such strictures on Kit, even though he himself was wont to use much harsher language. 'He is well, ma'am, I thank you.'

Aunt Augusta clearly expected him to say more, but his lips were set in the firm line that Emma had already learned to recognise. 'I think perhaps I should like to lie down for a while, after all, Aunt,' she said, rising. 'Especially as we are bidden to Lady Duns-more's musical soirée this evening. I would not disgrace you by falling asleep during the arias.'

Hugo, too, had risen. Listening to his wife's blatant lies had brought a touch of a smile to the corner of his firm mouth.

Aunt Augusta was not deceived either. 'Get along with you, you little minx,' she said, smiling indulgently. 'And take that husband of yours with you. Show him the rest of the house. He needs to know his way about, now that he's joined the family.'

Hugo bowed and moved to open the door for Emma. No sooner had it closed behind them than he whispered, 'How many days shall we be forced to remain here, Emma? I'd liefer face a French cavalry charge, I think.'

Emma tried not to smile. 'It all depends upon you, sir. I can be ready to leave for Lake Manor as soon as you give the word. Or for anywhere else you should choose.'

'You tempt me, Emma, you tempt me greatly. I should dearly like to carry you off to Paris, or Rome. Never mind. Lake Manor it shall be.' He glanced back at the door with obvious distaste. 'And our deliverance shall not be long delayed, I promise.'

The attractions of Lake Manor were growing by the minute.

Emma had no intention of dragging Hugo all over the house. He would find his way perfectly well by himself. It was only when they arrived at the door to her room that she realised where they were. Heavens, she had brought him straight to her bedchamber. With a quick change of direction, she led him a little further along the corridor and opened the door to a small sitting room. 'Aunt has been most generous, as you see. We have this private sitting room as well as the two bedchambers. Mine is through that door.' She pointed. 'And yours is over there.'

'Splendid,' Hugo said, surveying the comfortable room. When Emma moved towards her own bedchamber, he strode across to open the door for her. Then, without a word, he went to the sofa and threw himself down on it, closing his eyes and stretching out his long legs with a sigh of relief. Emma watched from the doorway. She fancied she had seen a hint of a limp when he was climbing the stairs. He was tired, clearly. Rest would do him good. She wondered what he had been doing since his arrival in London— apart from dragging Kit out of a very expensive hole. She paused, her hand on the doorknob. 'Would you like some tea? I can send for some if you would like.'

He rose to his feet immediately. 'Forgive me for my rudeness, Emma. I thought you had gone through to lie down.'

'Oh, no,' she replied airily. 'That was only for Aunt Augusta's benefit. I am not in the least tired, as I told you.' It was clear from the tone of her voice that she thought her husband was the one in need of rest.

'You wretch, Emma,' he said with a rueful grin. 'Your face betrays you, you know. Yes, I am tired, but I shall survive, never fear. A cup of tea would revive me wonderfully, I am sure—always provided you remain to share it with me.'

Emma did not attempt to engage in a battle of wits. Hugo was too tired—and she was too unsure of how a wife should behave, especially when they were alone like this…

She crossed to pull the bell and then sat in the chair by the fireplace, so that Hugo would feel able to resume his place on the sofa. Neither spoke again until the tea had been ordered.

'Do you—?'

'Shall I—?'

Both stopped in mid-sentence, laughing awkwardly. From his lazy position on the sofa, Hugo waved an indulgent hand. 'After you, *madame*.'

Emma resisted the urge to repeat the gesture to him. The young man she had known all those years ago had dearly loved a jest, even at his own expense, but the man she had married was not the same. His experiences—whatever they had been—had changed him greatly. She said simply, 'Do you accompany us to the soirée this evening?'

'I fear not, Emma. I am…engaged to Kit. Our business is not yet completed.'

It was a strange sort of business that took place in the hours of darkness, in Emma's opinion, but she refrained from saying so.

'As I said, your face betrays you, my dear,' Hugo said with a wry smile. 'But, truly, I must be with Kit this evening. It cannot be avoided. Our engagement is for later, however, so I could certainly escort you to Lady Dunsmore's and stay for an aria or two. That should silence the wagging tongues. And when I leave, you may tell the tabbies that your husband has absolutely no ear for music and takes to his heels at the first opportunity. A sad case, indeed.'

The arrival of the tea tray intervened to save Emma's blushes. She was sure she would never say anything so insulting, even in jest.

She made to pour but stopped, the silver pot poised over his cup. 'I'm afraid I do not remember how you take your tea.'

Hugo made a face. 'Good grief! What kind of a wife have I saddled myself with?'

This time she was prepared to respond in kind. 'One who will put five spoons of sugar in your tea, if you do not speedily enlighten her.'

'Aargh!' he cried, falling back on the sofa with his hands to his throat. 'My wife has poisoned me!'

Emma threw him a speaking look, replaced the pot and picked up the sugar basin. 'One,' she said menacingly, dropping a spoonful into his cup.

'Spare me!' he cried, grinning like the madcap boy he had once been. 'Save me, fair princess, from the hands of the wife who would murder me!'

'I collect that means only one sugar, Major,' Emma said demurely, pursing her lips to stop herself from responding to his infectious grin. She finished pouring his tea and rose to take it to him.

He was on his feet in an instant. She had not known he could move so fast. If there had been a limp earlier, it certainly did not prevent him from moving his limbs as much and as fast as he wished.

'Emma…' The laughter was gone from his voice.

He sounded serious, almost angry. What could be wrong?

'Is something the matter, Hugo?'

He smiled, satisfied. 'Not now,' he said, taking his cup from her. 'Not any more.'

Emma returned to her seat to pour tea for herself. Now was the time. He seemed to have relaxed with her. 'Hugo, will you tell me about your time in Spain?'

'No, my dear, I think not.'

'But you used to write such wonderful letters— Oh! Now I remember.' Emma puzzled over her disjointed recollections for a second. The memory of Hugo's letters had been dancing round at the back of her mind since the day she had first seen him again, but until now it had refused to be caught. Now she grasped it, firmly. 'Those wonderful letters you used to send to Richard every month or so, telling him all about your adventures. When you described your arrival in Portugal, the colours, the noise—I could almost taste it.'

'Richard let you read my letters?' Hugo was troubled to think of it. He could not remember how much he might have said. He was sure they had not been fit for a lady's ears.

'No. But he used to read them aloud to me. Well…parts of them.' Emma smiled at the recollection. 'It all sounded so magical, so different from our humdrum life here in England. I think Richard envied you.'

Hugo grimaced.

'And then the letters stopped.' Emma looked questioningly at her husband. He seemed bleak and distant. 'Richard said you must be too busy to write. Responsibilities and so on. But it wasn't that, was it?'

'No,' Hugo said, refusing to elaborate.

Sensing his withdrawal, Emma did not press him further. She reverted to her gay, light-hearted Society mode. 'And then I went to stay with Aunt Augusta—to be finished, you understand—and I saw Richard much less often. He said you did write—occasionally—but he never read your letters to me any more. I missed them. I thought I knew you so well, and then, suddenly, you weren't there any more.' She blushed. 'Oh dear, how childish that must sound. I—'

'It sounds much kinder than I deserve, Emma,' Hugo said wonderingly, 'and I thank you for it. I suppose I should have known that Richard was sharing my letters with you. He spoke of you so often in his own.'

Emma was blushing even more now.

'I used to laugh at his tales of your antics. That was all before your aunt turned you into a fine lady, naturally.'

Seeing Hugo's indulgent smile, Emma longed to ask why he had stopped writing, but decided against. It was clearly a very sensitive subject. She had no wish to undermine their new-found rapport. 'Perhaps it is as well that you both stopped writing regularly. You would have been thoroughly bored by anything Richard said of me after I came to live with Aunt Augusta. It was all very tame and insipid, I fear.' She smiled teasingly at him. Would he respond?

Hugo smiled too. 'I take leave to doubt that, my dear.'

'I declare, you seek to insult me, sir,' Emma said in mock outrage, throwing him a wicked look from under her lashes.

It was too much. He went to her and pulled her roughly into his arms. 'Now that, my dear wife, is something I would never do,' he said huskily, bending his head to touch her lips with his own.

It was a gentle, teasing, tantalising kiss, quite unlike anything he had done before. Emma's whole body responded. Her belly turned to hot, churning liquid, the warmth spreading rapidly up into her breast and down into her thighs. This time she could not remain passive; the feelings were too strong. She leant into him, sliding her arms around his neck, and responding to his lips and his tongue, first shyly, then passionately. Hugo's response was immediate. He pulled her body hard against his own, one hand behind her head, the other gliding down her back. The kiss went on and on. It was terrifying how he made her feel.

It was magical how he made her feel.

At last, Hugo pulled away from her, breathing rapidly. Emma herself was gasping for breath, gazing at him wide-eyed. She did not begin to understand what had happened to her, but she knew she had behaved like a wanton. What would he think of her? She could feel the flush rising on her neck. She turned to flee to her room, but Hugo was before her.

Taking her hand gently, he said, 'Emma, there is nothing to fear.' He raised the hand to his lips, kissing it with exquisite courtesy. 'I have upset you. I apologise. But pray believe that I would never hurt you. You have no need to run from me.'

Emma turned away. She was afraid of what she might see in his eyes. And she knew his words did not excuse her appalling behaviour.

'I will go,' Hugo said quietly. He sounded strained. 'I had hoped you would come to accept me, but I can understand how difficult it must be for a beautiful young woman like you, forcibly married to such a wreck of a husband. Perhaps, in time—'

Guilt engulfed Emma. Her eyes filled with tears that threatened to well over at any moment. She did not want him to see—but she must not let him leave like this. She steeled herself to reply. 'You are wrong, Hugo,' she said in a low voice. 'I am not afraid of you. And you are not—' Her hands were shaking now. She clasped them together in an attempt to hide her emotions from him. In a whisper she continued, 'But I *am* afraid of the way you make me feel.'

Chapter Twenty

In the sudden silence, Emma swallowed hard. What had she said? She must get away from him; she must be alone. Head bowed, she made for the door.

Hugo reached the door in a few strides and pulled it closed. Then he leant back against it, looking intently at her. His arms hung loosely by his sides. He made no move to touch her. A great surge of anger had coursed through him at the thought that he had hurt her, but now, seeing her tears, and hearing her words, he felt only joy. She must be made to believe him now. 'You have no need to be afraid of anything, my dear one,' he said softly, willing her to look at him. He opened his arms to her. 'Come,' he said. 'Let me show you it is true.'

Emma looked up at him then and walked into his embrace without pause for thought. He held her tenderly for a long time, not attempting to kiss her again. She felt warm and protected.

At last, Hugo bent to kiss her tear-streaked face. 'Do not weep, Emma. I promise you there is no need.' He held her gently, hesitating. The moment

was too special to be spoilt by allowing his passions
to rule him. He desperately wanted to make love to
her, but she must be willing, totally and completely
willing. He would not repeat the brutality of their
wedding night.

He could not find the words to ask her. Instead he
began to plant tiny kisses on her eyelids, her cheeks,
the corners of her mouth, the side of her neck. When
he began to nuzzle her earlobe, she groaned, tightening her arms around him.

'Emma, my dearest, I want you so much,' he said
huskily, 'but I am afraid to frighten you with my
desire. If you want me to, I will stop. You have but
to say the word.' In truth, he was not sure whether
he could, especially if she continued to respond to
him like this.

'I…' Emma's voice was barely audible. She tried
again. 'I am not afraid, Hugo. I do want you to…'
She could not say the words, but her blushes told
him everything.

'Oh, my beauty,' he said, awe in his voice. 'My
sweet, wonderful wife.'

She was blushing so much that she looked to be
on fire. This would not do. He must help her through
her embarrassment.

He turned to the door that led to her bedchamber,
the bedchamber they would share. 'Emma, my dear,
I believe I have been remiss in my duty.' Good. Now
curiosity was overcoming her embarrassment. 'Is it
not a fact that a husband should carry his new wife
over the threshold into their new life? And have I not
failed?'

'But you cannot,' she said at once. 'Your wounds…your weak arm… Hugo, I am no lightweight, in spite of my lack of inches. Do not attempt it, I beg of you.'

'Am I to understand that my wife has no faith in her husband's ability to perform his duties, ma'am?' he said, trying to assume the kind of voice he used to lacerate an incompetent subaltern. 'You try my patience, wife, indeed you do.'

Clearly, he was not as good an actor as he thought, for his wife was laughing up at him. 'You, sir,' she said archly, 'are a fraud. But, none the less, I beg you will not attempt it.'

'Coward,' he said, laughing with her now. 'Why should I not? For who is there to see, apart from my faithful wife? And she, I know, will not betray me if I should fail, even though she has my permission to upbraid me roundly if I should drop her on the floor.'

Emma shook her head in wonderment, laughing still. It was such a little thing, but the thought that Hugo would trust her to see his weakness was a prize to be cherished. 'Since you are determined, husband, I must obey you. Did I not take a vow to do so?'

Hugo kissed her soundly to seal their bargain. Then he opened the door to her bedchamber and took his stance by the threshold. 'Put your arms around my neck, Emma,' he said crisply, 'and do not let go, whatever happens. This will be something of an experiment…'

Emma did as she was bid. Hugo put his weaker arm around her waist, then bent and slipped his strong right arm under her knees. With a sharp intake of breath, he lifted her from the floor and stepped through the doorway into the bedchamber. He had done it. But it was not enough. It was but a few more steps to the bed—and that was where he should deposit his lovely burden.

After two more steps his hold was weakening.

'Hugo, put me down,' Emma cried.

He took one more step and catapulted them both on to the huge bed in a tangle of arms and legs. Emma lay almost crushed beneath him.

'You did it,' she said, as soon as she had caught her breath. She tightened her arms around his neck. 'And see what an obedient wife I am become—I did not let you go for even a second.'

It was true. And she was laughing up at him, her eyes like huge pools filled with summer sky. She was beautiful. And she was his laughing, willing wife. He lowered his lips to hers, to begin the long, slow, and infinitely delicious task of arousing her passions.

The first knock barely registered with Hugo. But the second knock was louder, more insistent. He raised his head and glanced towards the open door to their sitting room. There was no one there.

The knock came a third time. Someone was in the corridor, and knocking urgently at the door to his own bedchamber. Damn! Damn! Damn! He pushed himself up and swung his body round to put his feet to the floor.

Emma opened wide, unseeing eyes. 'Hugo?'

Again that strident knocking.

She had heard it now. And she clearly expected that someone would walk in on them at any moment.

Hugo took her hand and squeezed it. 'It is nothing, my sweet,' he said reassuringly. 'Someone is a little impatient to find me, that is all. Give me a moment, and I will send him away with a flea in his ear.' He looked down at her. She was so desirable that his whole body ached for her. 'Stay there,' he whispered. 'I shall be but a moment.' He made for the door, mechanically straightening his cravat.

In his own bedchamber, the knocking had continued. Hugo wrenched open the door. 'What the devil is the meaning of all this noise?' he cried angrily, and then stopped in surprise.

Trouble.

'Oh, God,' Hugo said wearily, 'what is it this time?'

Kit said nothing, merely glancing warily up and down the corridor.

'I suppose you'd better come in,' Hugo said, turning away and leaving his brother to shut the door behind him. Hugo himself was more concerned to ensure that the door to the sitting room was securely closed. It would not do for Emma to hear anything that was said.

Emma kept her eyes closed and desperately tried not to think. Thinking would get in the way of feeling—and feeling was blissful. He wanted her. When he touched her, she burned. When he kissed her, she longed to melt into him, to become part of him. In a moment, he would return, and he would start to kiss her again…

She felt her limbs sinking weakly into the soft bed.

It was a kind of lethargy—and yet every fibre of her body was tingling in expectation of a resumption of his touch. He had the ability to bring her alive, as she had never been. She let out a long, contented sigh and snuggled deeper still. Time together—alone— was the answer to their problems. She was more than ready to let him see her weaknesses, if only he would show her that he did not despise her. And surely he could not? Not now. Not the way he had touched her.

She began to relive the last few minutes, the kisses, the laughing words, the joy of being carried in his arms. She would keep those pictures in her heart for ever, she told herself, trying hard to remember exactly how his brow had furrowed with the exertion of carrying her across the threshold. He was much, much stronger than she had thought. Much, much stronger…

The effort of focusing her mind was becoming increasingly difficult. She had forgotten how tiring a long carriage journey could be. Perhaps Aunt Augusta had been right. It would not matter if she took just a little nap. Hugo would be sure to wake her when he returned…

'No, ma'am,' said the abigail, white-faced, 'that is exactly what the Major said. He made me repeat it twice before he left with the other gentleman.'

Emma rose from her chair and began to pace. It could not be true. He had promised. 'Tell me again, Sawyer,' she said sharply.

'The Major said to tell you as how he had been called away on urgent business. He would try to return to escort you to Lady Dunsmore's, ma'am, but you were not to delay on his account if he did not arrive in time.'

'I see,' Emma said unhappily. What could be so urgent, so important, that he could walk out on her without a word? That was not the act of a caring husband. She felt an overwhelming urge to throw something, but she managed to resist. The ornaments in this room belonged to her aunt.

'Oh, and he said to give you his apologies, ma'am. I forgot that the first time.'

'Thank you,' said Emma quietly. That was some small consolation, though hardly enough to make up for her shattered dreams. She was desirable, but her attractions appeared to rank well below a casual summons from one of his male friends. She was clearly insignificant in Major Hugo Stratton's world. He had paused only to change his dress, and then left without a word.

It would not do to let him see how much his neglect had hurt her. She had shown him weaknesses enough already. Tonight, she would show him the practised lady of the *ton*, at home in the most exalted company. He would not be *allowed* to despise her. She would show him...

But would he condescend to appear at all? Emma swallowed a very unladylike curse.

'You had better make a start on my hair, Sawyer,' she said, moving calmly to sit down at the dressing-table. 'Something fairly plain, please. Tonight I shall leave the froth and feathers to the singers, I think.'

* * *

Hugo arrived back at Mrs Warenne's house just as the ladies were on the point of leaving. The carriage stood at the open door. He could see shining silks and flashing jewels in the hallway beyond.

He took the steps two at a time, something he had not even dared to try until now. But there was no time to savour the moment. Emma was standing a little way behind her aunt—and looking daggers at him. Her anger only served to enhance her golden beauty. She was wearing a simple low-necked gown of old gold silk and her shining hair was severely dressed in a knot on top of her head. Her only jewellery was a pair of topaz earrings and the plain gold wedding band he had put on her finger.

He was still relishing the sight of her when her aunt interrupted, tapping him on the arm with her folded fan. The purple feather on her elaborate turban wobbled precariously with every movement. 'We had all but given you up, Major.'

'My apologies, ma'am,' he said immediately, with a polite bow. 'It was not my intention to have you wait.'

'No,' said Mrs Warenne sharply, 'but you knew very well that we were agreed it would be best for you and your wife to arrive together.'

Hugo nodded. There was nothing he could say. Out of the corner of his eye, he could see that Emma was enjoying his discomfiture. That did not bode well for the rest of the evening.

'I can see that there is no time to be lost, ma'am,' he said with a grim smile, offering his arm to Emma's aunt. 'May I escort you to your carriage?'

Mrs Warenne looked suspiciously at him, but apparently saw nothing amiss. She allowed him to help her down the steps and into the carriage. Emma followed, unescorted. When Hugo turned to help her down the steps, he found that she was already beside him on the flagway. He held out his hand to help her into the carriage.

'Thank you,' she said, in a cold, polite voice. He might as well have been a servant, for she did not look at him. The pressure of her hand on his was so fleeting that he could not be sure she actually touched him. She took her seat beside her aunt and started to make conversation as if he did not exist.

And with all three of them in the carriage, it would be useless to attempt any kind of explanation. Hugo swallowed his burgeoning anger and took his place in the carriage opposite the ladies, allowing them to monopolise the conversation throughout the short journey to Lady Dunsmore's.

'Ah, here we are at last,' said Mrs Warenne, for all the world as if they had been travelling for hours. She looked at her niece sitting rigidly alongside her. 'I think it would be for the best if you were to go in on the Major's arm, Emma,' she said decidedly. 'No need to wait for me. The footman will help me down.'

'As you wish, Aunt,' Emma said in a colourless voice.

Hugo wanted to shake her. She was behaving like a spoilt child. Just give him a moment alone with her…

He alighted first and reached up to offer his hand

to his wife. She fixed her gaze on a point over the top of his head when she put her hand in his. Hugo caught her fingers and squeezed sharply, surprising her into looking directly at him. 'Emma,' he said in a warning whisper, 'remember how important this is.'

Her eyes widened. She gave the tiniest nod.

Hugo gave a sigh of relief, tucking her gloved fingers under his arm while he led her up to the entrance. With his free hand, he gave her an encouraging pat. 'Smile,' he said softly.

Smile.

Emma groaned inwardly. She was to be put on show, as she had been on her wedding day. The slightest chink in her armour, and the tabbies' claws would reach in to tear her flesh. She straightened her back even more. It would not be allowed to happen.

One step at a time.

Smile.

Chapter Twenty-One

The interminable aria was followed by warm applause—much too warm, in Hugo's opinion. The tenor had definitely been straining a great deal to reach his top notes, and at least one of them was decidedly flat. Hugo would be glad to leave.

He looked down at Emma at his side, engrossed in polite conversation with her other neighbour. He would not be glad to leave her like this. She was still bristling with anger. He could almost feel it sparking out across the gap between their bodies. The laughing, willing wife who had lain in his arms had been supplanted by a hissing cat, ready to scratch his eyes out the moment he said a word to her. It was almost impossible to believe that these were two aspects of the same woman. She was desirable, delightful—and utterly exasperating. She made him furious. She made him ache for her. She was driving him mad.

He did not see what else he could have done. There had been barely time enough to change into evening dress—and certainly no time to write a note to her. There would have been time—just—for a kiss and a few words, but when he saw her so peacefully asleep, her cheek pillowed on her hand, he could not bring himself to wake her. He had even resisted the temptation to stroke the peach-like bloom of her cheek.

And in the end it had been for nothing. They had not found Forster, or any useful evidence against him. Kit's supposedly infallible source of information was as unreliable as all the others. So far, they were making no headway at all. Their carefully crafted plans for dealing quietly with the blackguard colonel might have to give way to more direct action, unless they could find an opening very soon. Forster's rumours were beginning to be repeated in the clubs; they had to be scotched. Perhaps tonight they would find the lever they needed? At least they knew that Forster could not fail to appear this time, since he himself had issued the challenge to the assembled hazard players. Everyone had agreed to return to the table to give Forster a chance to recoup his losses.

In the interval between the arias, Hugo rose and extended his hand to Emma. 'My dear,' he said politely, 'I have to leave now, as you know. Will you walk with me to the door?'

Emma looked first at Hugo and then at his outstretched hand. She had no choice. She could not possibly refuse her husband's request in front of all these witnesses. He obviously knew it, too.

'Of course,' she said, rising. 'Excuse me for a few moments, Mrs Gray. I hope to return before the music restarts. It would be a pity to miss such splendid entertainment, do you not think?'

Emma's neighbour nodded her agreement. Hugo

took her hand in his and led her out into the hallway where he bent and whispered in her ear, 'Emma, you lie with such conviction, you should have been on the stage. You would have made a fortune.'

'Thank you, sir,' Emma said bitterly. She should have known he would wish to take her to task. He was the one in the wrong, but he would surely put the blame on her. 'I take it there was something more you wished to say to me?'

Hugo straightened as if he had been stung. 'Indeed there was,' he said sharply. 'It was this. Whatever may be wrong between us is a private matter. It is not to be spread around London as a result of your childish behaviour.'

Emma gasped.

'Think, Emma. Think of the impression you are creating and the gossip you are giving rise to. You are supposed to be a new—and happy—bride, but you have spoken hardly a word to your husband all evening. You hold yourself aloof in the most obvious way. You smile—I grant you that—but a painted smile would be more natural than yours. You look, for all the world, like a martyr going to the stake.'

'Have you quite finished?' Emma hissed. She was having difficulty controlling her temper.

'For the moment,' Hugo said crisply, beckoning to the footman to bring his hat and cane. 'We will discuss this in the morning, Emma, when we have both cooled a little. And, in the meantime, I would strongly counsel you to have a care how you act. A lady's reputation, once lost, cannot be regained.'

Emma bit back the words that rose to her lips. The

servant was watching them with barely concealed curiosity. She could not afford to insult Hugo in public, however much satisfaction it might give her.

Hugo bent over her gloved hand for a moment, before leaning forward and gently kissing her cheek. 'Goodnight, my dear,' he said, loudly enough for the servants to hear. 'Forgive me for deserting you but, as you know, I have an engagement that cannot be broken. Do not wait up for me. I may be very late.' He smiled at her. It was a crooked smile. And, as he smiled, the steely hardness melted from his eyes. He leant forward once more. 'Sleep well, my dear wife,' he whispered. Then he was gone.

Emma stood for several moments staring at the door. Her face was beginning to ache from the effort of maintaining that fixed smile. She allowed her muscles to relax. No one would think it surprising if she ceased to smile, having bade farewell to her husband.

She needed to be alone. She needed to think.

She strolled back along the hallway, bypassing the door to the music room in favour of a small, empty saloon with a bay window. She pushed her way behind the drawn curtains and looked out into the street, trying to catch a glimpse of Hugo's tall figure. Too late. He had gone to keep his engagement, whatever it was. He had left her here to mend her reputation as best she might.

She stroked the plush velvet with the back of one hand. How very soft and sensuous it felt, to be sure. It reminded her of the way Hugo had stroked her skin—with a touch so light and gentle that it was as if a butterfly had settled there.

She continued to stroke the pile in a long sweeping motion. It was almost hypnotic. She wanted to close her eyes and sink into strong, loving arms—Hugo's arms. It was no use trying to stoke her anger. It would serve only to make things worse between them, when—if she were to admit the truth—she wanted things to be as they were before that cursed knock on the door. She wanted—

Footsteps on the wooden floor interrupted her thoughts. She shrank back against the wall, hoping that her presence would not be noticed. How could she explain herself, if she were found hiding behind the curtains in an empty room? It would have the appearance of an assignation, and with Hugo now gone— It did not bear thinking about. She held her breath.

'Thank goodness for a little peace,' said an elderly female voice. 'What on earth persuaded Amelia Dunsmore to hire that man? He must be the worst tenor in London.'

'She doesn't know the difference,' drawled a younger voice. 'Never did have the least ear for music, y'know. Thinks musical evenings will enhance her standing.' She gave a very unladylike snort.

'I was surprised to see the Strattons here,' said the older woman. 'Were not you? She always was a pert little madam, I thought, but to walk in here on her husband's arm, as though it was the most natural thing in the world... I didn't think even *she* would have the gall to do that. Still, I suppose we should be grateful she didn't arrive with the brother in tow as well.'

The younger woman laughed nastily. 'Kit is to be sent abroad, by all accounts. Major Stratton apparently made that the price of clearing the young man's debts. And, of course, it will also ensure that Kit is kept well away from the new Mrs Stratton. He's no fool, the Major.'

'He may be no fool, but…' The voice was lowered to a conspiratorial whisper. 'The latest *on dit* is that he's nothing like the hero he purports to be. Had you not heard? When he was in the Peninsula, he was all but cashiered for insubordination and cowardice.'

'*No!* Surely not? We would all have known, long before this.'

'Apparently it was hushed up. Wellington himself did not want it known. He must have some distant link with the Stratton family, or something of the kind. It was all put down to a misunderstanding. The officers were transferred.'

'Then Emma Fitzwilliam is well served,' hissed the younger voice. 'She deserves it, after queening it in Society for so long, and tempting all the eligible young men away from young ladies of much better pedigree.'

'You are probably right, my dear. And I am sure your daughter will receive several eligible offers this Season. She looks remarkably well, especially now that you are dressing her at Célestine's.'

A male voice intervened. 'Excuse me, ladies. Lady Dunsmore asked me to tell you that refreshments are about to be served. Will you come this way?'

Slippered footsteps retreated. There was the sound of a closing door.

Behind the curtain, Emma sagged against the wall, her clenched fist hard against her quivering lips.

It was not true!

She wanted to throw open the curtains and scream the words after those wicked women. It was not true! Hugo Stratton was no coward. He had almost died at Waterloo, while Forster—his accuser, without a doubt—had sat snugly in Horse Guards, resting on the patronage of his royal crony.

She would have to tell Hugo what she had heard. He had to know what was being said of him. But how could she? He was already furious with her for behaving like a spoilt child. And he was right. She had done exactly that. If only she had known...

She must make amends. She must help Hugo.

Pulling aside the curtain, she went back into the room and made for the door. There would be no more eavesdropping. She must do what she could to retrieve the situation, here and now. She could not defend Hugo's honour against his malign accusers, not yet at least, but she would show those harpies that she was happy—aye, and proud—to be Hugo Stratton's wife.

'I still can't understand what possessed you to do such a thing, Hugo. We could have found another way, surely?'

'Keep your voice down, Kit. It's after four in the morning. Do you want to wake the whole household?'

Kit gave his brother an exasperated look, but allowed his voice to sink to a whisper. 'If only you had told me what you meant to do. Why couldn't you let *me* challenge him? I am younger and fitter than you are, and a better shot, besides.'

'And you have no real cause. He would have refused to fight you, you know. He's so much older than you are that it would have seemed perfectly proper. Against me, on the other hand, he had no such excuse. Some of those around the table were well aware of the vile rumours Forster has been spreading. He had no honourable way of avoiding my challenge. He would have been ruined, and branded a coward himself. That might have been justice, but he was not fool enough to do it. No, Kit, I had to be the one. I am the target of his lying tongue. And I am the one who has comrades to avenge.'

Kit shook his head despairingly.

'You can procure another second today, I take it?' Hugo asked. 'I could send to Richard, or one of my other friends, but it would only lead to delay. We must have this speedily resolved, before even worse rumours start. Emma has suffered enough. She would be totally humiliated if Forster's rumours were added to the gossip over our marriage. I could not let that happen, Kit. Let it be tomorrow morning, and early.' He laughed wryly. 'I would happily let Forster sweat, but I don't want him to have too much time for sword practice.'

'Good God, Hugo, surely not swords? He would truly have you at a disadvantage then. When was the last time you used a sword?'

'I'm not as weak as you imagine, Kit, though I'll own I'm not in practice. If he chooses swords, I'll have to rely on remembering all my old skills and hoping my body will respond to the challenge. My sword arm is still strong enough, I think.' He paused to look assessingly at his brother's worried face. 'But, on reflection, I fancy Forster will choose pistols. He's not man enough for cold steel. Too protracted. Too many chances that I might kill him. And he'd have to be prepared to look me in the eye, which isn't his style at all. With pistols, we keep our distance. And I have only one shot.'

'You won't miss?'

'No. I won't miss. Langley and the others will be avenged.'

'Good. Though a quick death is better than he deserves.'

'You're too bloodthirsty, Kit. I shan't kill him. I would have—before—but not now.'

Kit looked hard at his brother. 'But—' he began. He stopped, frowning. 'No. It is not for me to say. You will do as you think fit.'

Hugo smiled. Kit was learning, at last.

Kit cleared his throat. 'Forster will kill *you*, if he has the chance, Hugo, whether it's swords or pistols.'

'I know that. And he's not above a trick or two, either, if he thinks it might help his cause. I look to you to watch my back. Believe me, I have every intention of coming off with a whole skin. I've wasted enough time playing the wounded soldier. I have better things to do, now.'

Kit grinned knowingly but said nothing.

'I need to change—and wash away the smell of Forster.' Hugo grimaced. 'I will join you at your lodgings as soon as I can. You can give me an early breakfast, before you go to settle matters with Forster's seconds. And then you can give me a little practice, if Forster does decide for swords. We'd have to find a quiet spot, I suppose, since it's Sunday?'

'I think I can find somewhere suitable, brother, though I am sure it won't be needed. Leave everything to me.' With a breezy wave, Kit left to roust out a fellow second.

Hugo sighed at the closing door. He had not planned for this at all, though Kit seemed to believe that he had. He had known at once, from the reactions of the players round the hazard table, that Forster's ready tongue had already begun to accuse him of unspeakable things. The gentlemen were clearly chary about being seen in the company of a man who had been branded a coward by his own commanding officer. When Hugo had reached for the dice, the gentleman on his left had pulled his hand away as if he had been burnt. Hugo had known—then—that he had no choice but to force a challenge on Forster—even if he died as a result. That was certainly possible. For all his show of confidence to Kit, Hugo knew that Forster was likely to choose swords. If he did, Hugo would be at a severe disadvantage. Unless he could bring the duel to a very speedy conclusion, he was bound to lose, for he was not strong enough to endure a lengthy contest.

His sweet Emma would be a widow before she had really become a wife.

Chapter Twenty-Two

Emma lay on her side, staring out through the open curtains towards the garden. The sun was up long ago, but her husband had not returned. Surely she would have heard something if he had? She had deliberately left open the door to their sitting-room, in hopes that he would see and come to her. There were so many things she needed to say to him—that she believed in him, that she loved him…that she was sorry for her appalling behaviour.

She had lain awake, waiting, but he had not come.

The sound of distant bells reminded her that it was Sunday. She rose and went to the window. It was a beautiful day. And they must go to church. Would Hugo return in time to accompany them? He had said he would speak to her this morning when his temper had cooled—and hers, too. He had known perfectly well that she was furious with him. Had he known why? Possibly not. In any case, her reasons were petty and insignificant now, in the light of Forster's nefarious accusations. She shuddered at the thought of what the man might yet do, for he was clearly out to ruin Hugo.

Emma told herself sternly to stop thinking about Forster. Spinning ever more fantastic possibilities would only serve to heighten her own fears. She must concentrate on what she could do. She could outface the gossips, just as she had done at Lady Dunsmore's last night, and she could show Hugo that she believed in him and would do her utmost to help him...if he would let her.

Oh, if only he would come home.

Tightening the belt of her heavy wrapper, she crossed into the little sitting-room and put her ear to the door of Hugo's bedchamber. No sound at all. If he was there, he must be asleep.

She put her hand on the doorknob. The polished brass was cool and slippery to the touch. It needed a firm grip but her palm was damp. She rubbed it vigorously on the side of her wrapper, grasped the handle firmly, and opened the door.

The room was empty.

All the curtains were open. The bed had not been slept in. Emma wandered slowly into the room, touching first the table by the bed, then the hangings, then the bedpost. If only he would come home to her.

She sank on to the bed, listlessly surveying the rest of the room. Hugo's valet was clearly not up to his work, for he had left some of his master's clothes draped over the back of a chair in thoroughly haphazard fashion.

Evening clothes.

Emma flew across the chamber. She had to be sure.

There was no room for doubt. These were the clothes Hugo had been wearing at Lady Dunsmore's last evening. He must have returned at some time during the night, changed his dress without even calling for his valet, and left again. Without a word to his wife.

She ran her fingers over his crumpled cravat. Where was he? What was going on? An involuntary shiver shook her frame. It was Forster. The business that Hugo and Kit had to attend to so urgently—it was Forster.

And it was very, very dangerous.

Hugo had now spent at least half an hour pacing up and down in Kit's rooms. What the devil was keeping them? It was only a simple matter of agreeing the hour and the place—and the weapons. There was no point in wasting their breath over attempts at conciliation. That was impossible.

Hugo had hoped to be in time to escort Emma to church. He knew she would need his support.

Emma. His wife—who might soon become a widow, especially if Forster chose swords, as he was surely bound to do. Hugo must write a letter to leave behind for Emma. And now was as good a time as any. She was amply provided for—his will had been made at the time of their marriage—but he could not desert her with no word of explanation. That would be unspeakably cruel.

He sat down at Kit's untidy writing table, eventually finding the materials he needed. What could he say? The ink dried on his pen as he gazed at the blank wall. How could he tell his wife of less than a week that she was become a widow because of something that had happened all those years ago, because of men who were long dead and buried? Was he to tell her that he loved her, but that love alone was not enough to prevent the duel? No. He could never tell her that, though it pained him deeply to know that she was bound to think it. Would she ever believe that he had cared for her at all?

There was no way out of that impasse. He must simply stick to the bare facts.

Swiftly, he wrote an account of what Forster had done—and might still do. God willing, she would understand that he had had no choice.

'I go to avenge their honour, and my own,' he wrote, concluding his recital of Forster's iniquities. 'I ask you to forgive me for my failure to return to you. To do so was my greatest wish. Your loving husband, Hugo.'

Kit came in just as Hugo was putting the sealed letter safely in an inner pocket. It was as well that he knew nothing of it, Hugo thought. With the confidence of youth, Kit was certain his elder brother could not lose. Hugo—older, and much more experienced in the ways of men—was not so sure.

Hugo rose, grateful to find that his heartbeat was as steady as ever. His fears were for Emma, not for himself, but for her those fears were very real. If he should die, his widow would be at the mercy of Forster and his cronies, who would do their best to ruin her, too. That thought terrified him. It must not be allowed to happen.

In two strides he was at Kit's side and had laid a hand on his shoulder. 'Kit,' he said urgently, 'if I should fall, *you* must protect Emma from Forster. You must give me your word on it, Kit.'

Kit grinned. 'You have it, Hugo, but there is no need. It is pistols.'

Hugo's jaw clenched. Surely not?

'Why do you look so surprised?' said Kit. 'You yourself predicted it. The man has not the stomach for a long drawn-out fight. Indeed, I am not convinced he has the stomach for any fight at all. We did not see the man himself, of course, but his seconds seemed decidedly uncomfortable about something.'

'That is of no moment. Come. Tell me what you have agreed. Is it for tomorrow?'

'Yes. At five o'clock,' Kit said, and then proceeded to detail the rest of the arrangements. 'Now it only remains for me to ensure we have a surgeon on hand. I shall do that this morning.'

'Good,' said Hugo curtly. 'Now, I must go. I am already late. You will have the carriage at Mrs Warenne's in good time tomorrow?'

Kit nodded. 'You may rely on me.'

'I know that,' Hugo said sincerely. He gripped his brother's hand fiercely for a moment. 'And I thank you.'

It took too long to find a hackney and too long for it to thread its way through the traffic. All the inhabitants of London seemed to be out upon the streets on this Sunday morning.

He was too late. Emma and her aunt were long gone.

Hugo made his way impatiently to the church, but the service was well under way. He could not interrupt by arriving so late. That would cause even more scandal, more trouble for Emma. He would wait until she came out and then join her as if it were the most natural thing in the world.

He paced up and down St George Street for what seemed like hours. Why was it that, on this day of all days, the service had to go on so long? The sermonising should have been over hours ago. He paused to gaze at the grand doorway of St George's, willing the service to end. His gloved hand gripped the railing ever more tightly, as if he were trying to snap it to relieve his frustrations. They had so little time left. They needed to be together.

The congregation began to emerge at last, most of them stopping for a few words with the vicar. Where was Emma? He scanned the crowd for her petite blonde figure. Perhaps she was not here at all? Perhaps her abigail had mistaken the church?

This would not do. He marched across the street and up the steps, forcing his way through the chattering worshippers. Emma and her aunt were just emerging from the gloom, hidden behind two elderly ladies who were so large that they almost overflowed the aisle.

Emma's face lit up when she spied him. She was not yet close enough to speak, but she smiled, a wonderfully tender smile such as she had never before

granted him. She was surely telling him he was for-
given—and more, too, perhaps?

Hugo held out his hand and waited for her to come
to him. She did so without a word, smiling still as
he tucked her hand under his arm and possessively
placed his gloved fingers over hers. He gazed down
at her glowing face. There was nothing to say. It was
enough to have her touching him, looking up at him
with that soft gleam in her azure eyes.

'You are late, Major.'

Confound it! The impossible aunt! For a moment,
it had seemed as if he and Emma stood alone on the
step. But that was an illusion. Reality had intruded,
like a blow, in the shape of Mrs Warenne.

'Good morning, ma'am,' Hugo said, bowing
quickly so that she would not offer her hand. He had
no intention of letting go of his wife for even a second. 'I am afraid I was unavoidably detained. Pray
accept my apologies.'

Mrs Warenne nodded an acknowledgement and
launched into a description—in excruciating detail—
of the glories of the service he had missed.

Hugo closed his eyes for a second and took a deep
breath in an attempt to control his urge to strangle
the woman. He wanted…he needed to be alone with
his wife, but her aunt seemed determined to prevent
it. Now she had finished talking about the sermon
and was laying out plans for the rest of their day.
Had she no understanding at all?

It seemed not.

'Ah, here is the carriage at last,' she said. 'Where
was I? Ah, yes. I had thought that, since we have no

engagements this evening, we might dine quite informally and have a little music afterwards. Emma may sing for us. She has such a beautiful voice. Do you know, Major, that, until she came to me at sixteen, she had had hardly any training at all? Most remiss of my brother. And I told him so, in no uncertain terms. However, I soon put matters to rights. It was only a question of finding the best London masters and, naturally, I knew exactly how to do that.'

Hugo felt a gentle pressure on his arm. He looked down at his wife. She was smiling politely now—her company smile—as she listened to her incorrigible aunt, but the expression in her eyes was eloquent. He could read rueful laughter and resignation…and something deeper, something almost hidden. Was it longing?

If only the blasted woman would vanish off the face of the earth. He needed to be alone with his wife. And she with him. He could read that in her eyes. It was almost as if Emma knew how little time they had left.

'At last,' said Aunt Augusta, sinking into a crimson damask chair. 'What an incredibly boring day we have had, to be sure. With no engagements, it is difficult to know how to pass the time, especially on a Sunday. Do you not agree, Emma?'

Emma acquiesced politely. What else could she do? Hugo had spent the whole day at her side but they had barely had a moment alone. Aunt Augusta had hovered around them like a persistent wasp which could not—unfortunately—be swatted.

'Will you play, Emma? I am sure the Major will not linger over his port when there is no male company.'

Emma rather fancied that Hugo might enjoy the blessed silence of a few moments alone with a glass of wine, but she was proved wrong. The door opened to admit him before she had played more than a few bars. She smiled at him, willing him to come to her. He could pretend to be turning her music, surely?

'Ah, there you are at last, Major,' said Aunt Augusta acidly. 'Do come and sit here by me, so that we can both appreciate Emma's talent.'

Emma's fingers fumbled the notes.

'Good gracious, Emma, what is the matter with you? I have just been telling your husband what a fine player you are, too. Perhaps you would like to start again.'

It was a statement, not a question. Emma was sure she must be as red as her aunt's chair. To cover her embarrassment, she busied herself with choosing a different piece, something loud enough to cover even the worst of her aunt's carrying voice.

She began to play, without bestowing so much as a glance on either of them. She did not dare. She forced herself to concentrate on the difficult phrasing of the sonata and when she reached the *fortissimo* passage, she fairly pounded the keys in her frustration. If only they were at Lake Manor, or at Harding…or anywhere else but here.

The gentle slow movement calmed her. She could

hear Hugo's deep voice talking quietly to her aunt. What could he be saying?

The final lively movement was soon over. Hugo rose from his seat, applauding, and came across to the instrument, closely followed by Aunt Augusta. 'I have prevailed upon your aunt to play for us, Emma,' he said, smiling at her in the strangest way. 'I should like to try—here, in the privacy of Mrs Warenne's drawing-room—whether I can learn to waltz again. Will you honour me, my dear?' He held out his hand.

Emma sat, frozen, staring up at him in disbelief.

'Come along, my dear,' said Aunt Augusta sharply. 'If you do not give up your place, I shall dance with the Major myself, you know.'

Hugo bent down and took Emma's hand from her lap, gently raising her from the stool. 'You do not object?' he said very softly.

Emma closed her eyes and shook her head.

'Good,' he whispered and pulled her into his arms. He turned towards the instrument. 'When you are ready, ma'am?'

Aunt Augusta began to play a waltz, marking the time rather too strongly. Emma wanted to focus on helping Hugo, but her feet seemed to be weighted with lead. His hand was burning its way through the back of her gown, and that familiar heat was starting to uncoil in her belly.

Hugo bent his head so that his lips were close to her ear. 'I know I am much in need of practice, my sweet wife, but I begin to think that you are no better.' Emma could hear the thread of laughter in his voice. 'Shall I dance with your aunt instead?'

His light-hearted mockery almost made her laugh. She steadied herself. She must try to ignore his touch. She must mind her steps.

She tried to concentrate on his cravat. That seemed to work rather better than looking up into his face. Hugo's grey eyes, full of teasing mischief, were like to be her undoing.

He had begun a little stiffly, but now he was starting to move with much greater ease, guiding her deftly into turns and reverses. He had obviously been a very good dancer, before. With a little more practice, he would be the equal of any of her cavaliers.

When the music ended, Hugo let her go, bowing formally. Emma automatically sank into a curtsy.

Before Aunt Augusta could say a word, Hugo smiled generously at her and said, 'That was splendid, ma'am. You play quite delightfully. But one waltz has simply proved how much I am in need of practice, as you, with your unerring eye, will certainly have seen. I should disgrace you by daring to step on to a dance floor as I am. Might I prevail upon you to play just one more waltz?' Aunt Augusta was so flustered by his compliments that she nodded without speaking. Emma was astonished.

Hugo held out his hand to Emma once more. His face wore a look of studied innocence. His eyes were laughing.

They had barely begun this second waltz when he whispered, 'After this, I think we should retire to our suite, do not you?'

Emma stumbled, but his strong arm steadied her.

He grinned wickedly at her. 'I am minded to continue our practice upstairs—alone.'

Chapter Twenty-Three

'Will you honour me, *madame*?' Hugo held out his hand.

Emma stared at his fingers in amazement. She could not move another inch. It had taken all her courage to accept his invitation to accompany him upstairs at such an early hour. Hugo had delivered his proposal with every appearance of innocence, but Aunt Augusta had not been deceived. Emma could still see the look of distaste on her aunt's face, as if she had just been confronted by a bad smell.

Hugo closed the space between them, took Emma's right hand in his left, and pulled her towards him.

Emma felt suddenly very shy. 'Wh-what are you doing?' she stammered.

'Exactly what I said I should do. Practising the waltz,' he said with maddening simplicity.

Emma gasped, but it was too late. Her husband had started to dance her round their little sitting room, steering expertly between the chairs and tables and humming a waltz all the while. It was absurd. It was childish. It was heaven. She had been longing to be held in his arms and to be alone with him. Now, at last, it was happening. A bubble of laughter rose in her throat, demanding to be liberated. This was what she had ached for since the moment he had stretched out his hand to her on the step of the church. She let her laughter peal out, joyous as Easter bells.

Hugo stopped humming long enough to say, 'I hope you are not making mock of my singing, wife. I know I am not your equal, not by any means, but I believe I can hold a tune.' He did not wait for a response. Waltzing required music. He resumed his humming.

He really had a very fine voice, Emma decided, a baritone as rich and as warm as thick, dark chocolate. Without quite knowing when she had begun, she found herself humming in harmony with him, blending her voice with his. To Emma, it sounded as if they had been made to sing duets together.

When Hugo put his lips on the topmost curve of her ear, Emma's humming stopped abruptly; she gasped in response to his warm breath on her face. The feeling was amazingly seductive, even though he was barely touching her. It felt as if his humming was vibrating every inch of her skin. A shiver ran down her spine. The tiny hairs on her arms prickled in response to his nearness. Hugo seemed to sense the change in her, for he pulled her even closer, holding her so that their bodies touched from breast to thigh. She could feel the hardness of him against her belly and his chest crushing her breasts into her ribs. Her heart was beating very fast, knocking so strongly that he must surely be able to hear it. Could he not see what he was doing to her?

Hugo continued to waltz, supporting Emma with his strength, pulling her ever closer. And he continued to hum until her whole body was quivering like the strings of a harp, plucked by a master's hand.

Slowly, delicately, he began to undo the buttons on the back of her gown. She felt his fingers moving on her. She knew he was timing each move with the steps of the dance. She found she was waiting eagerly for every touch, for it was taking them closer to something she knew she desired, perhaps as much as he.

Hugo continued to hum and to guide her through their sensuous waltz until every button had been undone. A little pressure on the neckline of her gown and it would fall to her feet. Emma closed her eyes, leaning in to him. She felt such love and longing. She wanted to look into his eyes, to see her own emotions mirrored there, but she did not dare. She could not bear to think that they might be absent. Hugo's humming moved down the curve of her ear to her earlobe and thence to the line of her jaw. And still he continued to waltz. She no longer knew where she was—except that she was floating.

When at last his lips touched hers, she let out a little groan. Now the music must stop. Now he would stop waltzing and kiss her properly. Her lips parted of their own accord.

But she was wrong. Even as his tongue slipped teasingly between her lips, the music continued from somewhere in his throat. And he was still whirling her round and round. She had to stop him. She would go mad with frustration if she did not stop him.

With a cry of protest, she wrested her hand free and flung her arms around his neck, returning his gentle kiss with a passion so fierce that it frightened her. She did not know what she was doing or why, only that she must find a way of showing him what she felt, even at the risk of repelling him with her behaviour.

The answering moan, deep in his throat, was eloquent, as was the way his hand skimmed down her back to press her hard against him. He drew his lips away from hers to whisper, in a voice so husky that she barely recognised it, 'Emma, you are like to drive me mad.'

So he felt it, too. Why, then, had he stopped kissing her?

She opened her eyes. They were in her bedchamber. She did not know how they had come there. And the shutters were closed. For a moment, she was blind in the sudden gloom. She could barely see his face, though she knew instinctively that his eyes were gazing into hers. As her eyes became accustomed to the dark, she had a fleeting fancy that he was studying her face, as if trying to carry away her picture, but then he smiled down at her and she forgot everything but the joy of being in his arms at last.

When he put his hands on her shoulders, pushing the neckline of her gown aside, she held his gaze bravely. There was nothing to blush for. Not now. Obedient to his touch, she let her arms slide down to her sides. With the softness of a lover's hand, the gown whispered over her skin to pool at her feet.

Hugo stood transfixed, looking at her as if he had never seen anything so beautiful. Then he crushed her fiercely to him, kissing her with such desperation that she thought she was about to be consumed. She tried to speak, but it was impossible. His mouth was too strong, too insistent. Without another thought, she gave herself up to him.

The noise of her chemise tearing seemed to come from a long way off. She barely noticed it. All her being was focused on returning his passion, kiss for kiss, and pushing aside his clothing so that she could put her hands on his naked body, and make him share the tremors that were beginning to torment her. 'Hugo,' she groaned into his mouth. 'Hugo, I love you.'

He stopped kissing her. He stopped breathing altogether. Then he swung her naked body into his arms and on to the bed as if she weighed no more than thistledown. She cried out at the loss of his touch, but in seconds, it seemed, he was beside her again, and as naked as she.

He put his hand on her cheek, turning her to face him. 'Emma, my darling wife,' he began throatily.

It was too much. She did not care what was to come. She would endure any amount of pain to have his kisses, his touch. She needed them now. 'Kiss me, Hugo,' she said desperately. 'Please.'

He could not resist the longing in her voice. She loved him. And she wanted him. This time, he would show her how it should be between lovers. This time, it would be for her alone.

He began to kiss her delectable mouth, not frantically now, but with controlled passion, fierce and tender by turns until she was moaning with desire. His own cravings he ruthlessly suppressed, even while the glories of her body under his questing hands painted pictures of wild abandon in his mind. He would not give in to their call, not until his wife— the woman he loved—was mindless with need.

Emma's hands were roaming over his body, stroking his hair when he took her proud nipple into his mouth, scoring her nails down his back when he pulled her beneath him at long last, cupping his buttocks to urge him on. This time, she did not flinch when he entered her, but welcomed him with a deep sigh of longing fulfilled. It seemed to echo through his whole being. He held himself very still, in wonderment.

'Don't stop!' she cried. 'Please!'

Hugo's hard-won control was snapped by that single word. He began to move within her, urged on by the passion of her responses. He needed to give her the fulfilment she sought but he was losing control, he could not hold back, he had to—

Emma gasped for breath as the shudders began to rack her body.

Hugo let go at last. And, as he reached his own climax, he heard a strangled voice which sounded somehow like his own. It was surely inside his head. And it was saying hoarsely, over and over, 'I love you.'

* * *

Hugo stood looking down at his sleeping wife, trying to absorb every detail of her beauty. If he was to die this day, he wanted her face to be the last picture in his mind, and her name to be the last word on his lips. He closed his eyes for a second. Yes, he could still see her image, her golden curls spread over the pillow in disarray, her lips a fraction open as if in invitation of his kisses, her breast rising and falling with each slow breath. In his mind, her eyes were open and filled with love—eyes as blue as the Spanish skies.

He must leave.

He took one last look at Emma. She slept peacefully, a picture of innocent yet seductive womanhood against the tumbled evidence of their passion. He would not have believed that she could respond to him as she had. Under her chaste exterior, he had uncovered a woman as sensuous and as bewitching as the goddess of love herself. He could not leave without one more touch.

He dared not kiss her lips, lest she wake. Instead, he leant across the bed to place a tiny kiss on her cheek. She moved a little in her sleep, making a faint sound in her throat. It was like an echo of the cries of pleasure that his love-making had drawn from her last night.

'I love you, Emma,' he said in a low voice, willing her to understand even though she slept. 'I love you. Forgive me.'

He went out quickly then and regained his own bedchamber before the sight of her could break his resolve. He had been on the point of taking her in his arms and kissing her until they were both lost in passion all over again.

He closed his door firmly but he could not bring himself to turn the key in the lock. He could not shut her out, even today.

His valet had already brought his shaving water and was laying out his clothes—dark, unostentatious garments to make him less of a target in the early light. 'Thank you,' Hugo said quietly. 'I shall not need you now. Go downstairs and watch for my brother's arrival. Make sure he does not wake the house.'

The valet nodded grimly and left.

Hugo began the methodical business of readying himself for what might be his last day on earth. He was not afraid. His resolve was unshakeable. He was determined that Forster would suffer for what he had done, but he would not kill the man, much though he deserved it. Emma could not be married to a murderer. No. Forster would be scarred, and preferably for life. And he? That would depend on Forster's nerve, and Forster's skill with a pistol.

Hugo straightened his dark coat and sat down at the little table by the window where he had placed his letter to Emma. The black ink of the superscription stood out starkly against the white paper—*To my wife, to be opened only in the event of my death*. He took it in his hand, remembering the words he had written. He could not leave her like that.

A soft knock was followed by the return of his valet. 'Sir,' he said, 'your brother is waiting for you.

I am to tell you to hurry, he says. If you do not leave now, you will be late.'

Hugo waved him away with an impatient hand. 'Tell him I will be there presently.'

He opened the letter and reread what he had written. It was just as cold and stiff as he had thought. He should write another. But there was no time.

He hunted around for a usable pen and dipped it in the ink. There was no time to compose fine words. He must write what he felt and hope she would understand.

'PS I do not have time to write again. This short postscript must suffice. Emma, my love, my darling wife, it grieves me not to be able to look into your eyes as I say this farewell. I love you. Believe that, whatever else you may not believe. Your love goes with me, my most cherished possession. I beg you to try to forgive me for deserting you. It was not for want of love. God bless you, always. H.S.'

The door opened again just as he finished those few lines. 'For God's sake, Hugo,' hissed Kit. 'You must come now!'

'Yes,' said Hugo, rising, and trying to refold the letter into its existing creases. Where were the wafers? He cursed. The more he tried to hurry, the clumsier he seemed to become.

At last he propped the letter on the table where she would find it—if he did not return. Kit was standing in the open doorway, beckoning urgently to him. With a final glance in the direction of the sitting room and his sleeping wife, Hugo hastened out.

But he closed the door too hastily. The sudden draught caught the letter and carried it to the floor where it lay, face down, concealed by the shadow of the chair.

Chapter Twenty-Four

It was a strange morning, its atmosphere almost uncanny. Hugo could not decide why he felt so detached from everyday reality. For a man who was going to face death, he knew himself to be unnaturally calm.

He looked out across the expanse of the park as they drove by. There was something peculiar about the way the early morning mist hugged the ground, obscuring all but the tallest trees. The treetops seemed to be floating, disembodied, beneath the bloody orb of the sun. Was it an omen? He refused to believe that it could be. Forster, too, must be seeing the same baleful image. Its message could as easily be for him.

It was a long time since Hugo had been about so early. In Spain, there had been many a day when he had risen at first light, but the dawn chorus was never like this. He found it hard to believe that London could be home to so many songbirds, even in early summer. Like the mist, the sound seemed magical. Was it just his own heightened senses drinking in the beauty of his surroundings for, possibly, the last time?

He smiled to himself. No. It was not any morbid fascination with his last day on earth. It was joy: joy that his wife, his Emma, was in love with him; joy that she had found fulfilment in his arms; joy that they had been able to share their passion at last, even though for only one night.

But there would be other nights. He was almost sure of that, now. Emma's love made him feel armoured, almost invincible. He must survive to return to her.

At his side, Kit was silent, giving all his attention to his horses. There was little traffic at such an early hour, but it was vital not to be late. Blessing Kit for his understanding, Hugo leant back against the soft leather and closed his eyes. He would allow himself a few moments to dream of Emma. And then he would bury every vestige of emotion deep within himself, to prepare for this meeting with his mortal enemy. He was determined to be cold and implacable. Forster had as good as murdered Hugo's comrades. Such a man deserved no mercy at all.

By the time they reached Paddington Green, the sun would have begun to burn off the mist. There was yet time. By five o'clock, they would surely face each other in bright, dazzling daylight.

Emma stretched contentedly but did not wake. She was not dreaming. Waking or sleeping, she now knew that she had no need of dreams, for the man she yearned for was the man she had married. He loved her, and he had spent the night teaching her the joys of love between husband and wife. He had shown her that physical love could carry her to a place of wonder and ecstasy. And he had let her see that she had more power over him than she could ever have imagined. When she touched him, his body responded, just as hers responded to him. He was powerless to control his hunger for her. And he was proud of his own weakness, confessing it to her between kisses that drugged her senses. She had conquered him, he told her, and he was more than willing to yield.

She moaned a little, remembering. Soon she would wake and turn to him. He would be waiting for her. And he would respond.

Hugo paced up and down, impatiently slapping his thigh with his gloves. His seconds were here. The surgeon was here, standing apart in his rusty black coat. But there was no sign of Forster.

Kit made his way to his brother's side and put a hand on his arm. 'It still wants five minutes to the hour, Hugo. He is bound to appear. He would be branded a coward, else.'

Hugo was in no mood to be placated. He shrugged off Kit's hand and resumed his pacing without a word.

Kit merely shook his head and walked back to consult with his fellow second.

The bell of St Mary's began to chime the hour. Hugo looked up, listening. One. Two. Still no sign of Forster. Three. The distant sound of galloping horses broke the stillness.

On the fifth stroke, a closed carriage appeared through the trees, drawn by steaming horses. Forster had arrived.

Hugo nodded towards his seconds and resumed his pacing. There was nothing for him to do until they had examined the weapons and marked out the ground. Kit would come for him when all was ready. Hugo strode away from the little group. Twenty-five paces, he thought, counting. Then he would turn and take twenty-five paces back. It seemed appropriate. They would face each other at just such a distance.

He turned, still counting. One, two… What on earth was going on? The seconds were conferring in considerable agitation. There was still no sign of Forster. Hugo supposed he must still be in the carriage. Stupid man. His muscles would be cramped from sitting. Not the best preparation for a duel, even if it was not to be swords. Eleven, twelve…

The seconds had begun to pace out the ground at last, taking care to ensure that neither protagonist would have the morning sun in his eyes. The bloody orb was gone now, as was the mist. A slight, fresh breeze had arisen, stirring the trees like a whispering voice. The sky was as blue as Emma's eyes and the sun was as gold, as dazzling, as her hair. Hugo swallowed hard and banished her image. Not now. He dare not think of her now. Later. When it was over.

Kit came to meet him and lead him to his place. Forster had still not emerged from the carriage. Kit touched Hugo on the arm. 'Forster's second will drop the handkerchief,' he said. 'I will—' He broke off. Forster was climbing down from the carriage at last. 'Good God!' Kit exclaimed. 'I'm not having that!' He strode off towards the other seconds, indignation clear in the set of his shoulders.

Forster was dressed, like Hugo, in a plain dark coat. But, while Hugo's head was bare, Forster had covered his with a close-fitting black cap, such as might be worn by an elderly invalid, crouching by the fire to keep warm.

Hugo could hear Kit's angry voice though he could not make out the words. There was no need. Kit would certainly be accusing Forster of ungentlemanly conduct, covering his head to make himself less of a target. The exchange would not last long. Hugo smiled grimly. He had complete faith in his brother's ability to carry his point.

He was right. Forster's seconds had begun to remonstrate with their principal even as he chose his pistol. And Kit was walking across the grass, carrying the remaining pistol by its barrel.

Hugo took it, checking it mechanically. It was primed and cocked. He let his arm hang by his side, pointing the pistol at the ground, feeling the weight of it. Not long now.

Kit gave him one long, meaningful look and walked calmly back to his place.

Hugo took his stance, his right shoulder and arm towards his opponent, his body sideways to make the smallest possible target. He looked towards Forster. The man had his pistol in his hand now, but had still not uncovered his head. He was arguing with one of his seconds in a low angry voice. The second seemed to lose patience. He reached up and pulled off the cap.

Forster's cry of anger echoed round the green. His brown hair was white.

No one moved. Everyone was staring at Forster. It was impossible, surely? Except... Hugo smiled grimly to himself. Fear was the answer, of course. Forster's seconds had obviously had to drag their man to this meeting. He was such an abject coward that his hair had turned white overnight at the prospect of facing Hugo along the barrel of a pistol. No wonder he had tried to conceal his hair. It was the badge of his shame. And now, all London would know it.

'Get on with it.' Forster's angry shout, and the accompanying curse, carried clearly across the field.

The seconds moved to their places. The doctor turned his back. The handkerchief was raised.

Hugo fixed his gaze on his target. The pistol hung heavy in his hand. In a moment, the handkerchief would fall, he would raise his pistol and—

The ball reached him almost before he heard the sound of the shot.

Forster had fired before the signal!

Hugo was stunned. He could hardly believe it, even of a man like Forster. He stood motionless, watching the shocked reactions of the others as if they were actors on a distant stage. The turf between them now seemed to stretch for miles. The seconds at the far end were closing on Forster, shouting in angry voices. Kit looked ready to kill the man with his bare hands.

But the second with the handkerchief was rock steady, as if such perfidy was an everyday occurrence. 'Stand back, gentlemen,' he called loudly, looking sternly first at Forster and then at Hugo. 'I am about to begin.'

Silence.

The handkerchief fluttered to the ground, swirling a little in the breeze.

Very slowly, Hugo raised his arm and levelled his pistol. Forster had not dared to move from his place. His shaking was clearly visible at twenty-five yards. His white head shone like a beacon.

A fly settled on Hugo's forehead and started to crawl down towards his eye. Hugo cursed silently and reached up to brush it away with his free hand. But there was no fly. It was blood, trickling down his face. Blood! He must have been hit. And yet he had felt nothing but the wind when the ball sped past him.

He narrowed his eyes and took a bead on Forster's white head. The man seemed to be trying to cower away now. It would be so easy to kill him, to rid the earth of a proven coward.

But he had promised not to make Emma the wife of a murderer.

He gradually lowered his aim, pausing at Forster's belly. No, that too would probably kill him…though gratifyingly slowly. His legs, then? A shattered knee would leave him crippled. Hugo knew exactly how it felt to be pitied and despised as less than a whole man. Forster, coward and blackguard, had never been a whole man. It would be simple justice to let the world see it at a glance.

His finger was almost on the hair-trigger. It would take only the slightest pressure. Hugo took one last look up at the sun and the sky, and fired.

Emma sat up in bed with a start. She had been dreaming, and—

She was alone.

No! Not again! He could not have left her again!

She sprang out of bed, forgetting her nakedness until forcibly reminded by the cool morning air on her skin. She dragged her wrapper around her body, fumbling with the fastenings.

She needed to be able to see. This gloom was almost oppressive.

She flung back the shutters. Sunlight streamed in, temporarily blinding her. She found there were tears in her eyes.

She wiped them away impatiently. It was only the sudden glare. She was not crying. She would not cry.

It was a beautiful day. And he had left her.

She leant wearily against the shutter, gazing out across the empty square. Nothing moved. It was much too early. The solid wood pushed into her arm, as if trying to remind her of its presence. Mechanically she folded the shutters back into place. Someone had undone them last night, closing them so that her bedchamber would be dark when she came there…in her husband's arms. Someone knew she preferred the dark, even though her husband did not. Someone…Hugo?

She ran her hand caressingly down the smooth wood. There was no need of darkness now. If Hugo preferred the light, she would not deny him. Not now. There was nothing she could deny him now.

She had to find him.

He must have gone back to his own bedchamber, his own bed. She would find him, tell him... She took a deep breath and made for the door. Yes, she would tell him that she wanted—needed—him to be beside her when she awoke. She trusted him completely. She would tell him that, and more. She was no longer afraid.

The sound of Hugo's shot broke the stillness. He remained absolutely still, his contemptuous gaze still fixed on Forster, his arm still pointing at his target. Then he threw the pistol to the ground. 'Killing is too good for you,' he said venomously, turning to walk away.

The snarl sounded like a wounded beast, but it came from Forster's lips. Hugo continued to walk. He would not deign to look back at such a man.

Behind him, he heard the scuffling sound of several pairs of running feet on the grass and then Kit's voice, crying out in anger.

Hugo turned.

Forster was face down on the ground, only ten yards away. And Kit was on top of him, wrestling with him for possession of a small silver pistol.

Hugo strode back towards them, ignoring the fact that the pistol was meant for him. The other seconds had almost reached the pair on the ground but Hugo calmly held up a hand to stop them from interfering. He could deal with Forster without any help from anyone. He bent to wrench the pistol from Forster's grasp.

Kit leapt to his feet, automatically brushing grass and dust from his coat. His features were grimly set.

Hugo smiled down at the wicked little pistol in his hand. 'I do not think it is safe for you to carry a loaded weapon, Forster,' he said, taking aim.

A third shot rang out.

'It throws a trifle left,' Hugo said nonchalantly, dropping it.

The bullet had hit the same tree as Hugo's pistol shot, but some two inches to the left. Forster's seconds gazed at Hugo in awe. Then they looked down at their man, and their expressions changed to disgust.

'Come, Kit,' Hugo said, putting an arm round his brother's shoulder. 'We have nothing more to do here.'

Kit grinned. 'He could have killed you, you idiot,' he said.

'Oh, I doubt it,' replied Hugo. 'You seemed to be getting the better of him. I had every faith in your ability to subdue him.' He threw a quick glance over his shoulder. Forster had been dragged to his feet and was being propelled towards his coach. 'I must say that your technique leaves something to be desired, though, Kit. I'd take some boxing lessons if I were you.'

Kit choked. 'I'll have you know, brother—'

Hugo stopped in his tracks and turned to face his

brother. 'You don't have to say it,' he said quietly. 'You saved my life, and we both know it.' He gripped Kit's hand. 'And I *am* grateful.' He paused. A wicked smile tugged at the corners of his mouth. 'I suppose you expect some kind of recompense? Like calling off your banishment, perhaps?

Kit punched Hugo's shoulder with his free hand. 'Oh, you can do so if you like,' he said airily, 'but I fancy I shall go in any case. I have a notion I am going to enjoy Vienna.'

The curricle was taking much too long to get back to town. 'For God's sake, can't you go any faster?' Hugo said impatiently. 'Let me drive.'

'No,' said Kit. 'You are in no fit state to do so. And you know perfectly well that even you could go no faster, unless you were prepared to mow down all these people.' He nodded in the direction of the thronging traffic on the road, now that London was up and about its business. 'You would do better, Hugo,' Kit went on kindly, 'to do something about all that blood. Emma will have a fit if she sees you like that.'

Hugo blanched. He had not stayed to allow the doctor to tend his wound. It was only a scratch, but it was still bleeding sluggishly. He took out his hand-kerchief and rubbed it vigorously across his forehead.

'There's blood in your hair, too,' Kit said, glancing sideways at him.

'Thank you,' Hugo said politely. 'I think I can manage.' Then he laughed ruefully. Now he could feel the crease where the ball had grazed his forehead and his scalp. 'I shall probably have another scar, right alongside the sword-cut. Poor Emma. What a pitiful specimen of a husband she has taken, to be sure.'

Kit shook his head in mock despair. He was laughing, too. 'I am sure Emma knows that she had the best of the bargain,' he said. 'You will make a much better husband than I—provided that she will let you near her after this.' He gestured towards Hugo's bleeding head. 'She is bound to find out now, Hugo. What will you tell her?'

Hugo was no longer laughing. His hand stilled, holding the handkerchief over his wound. 'The truth, perhaps. Or...' He shook his head. 'I don't know. I...I'll know when I see her. For heaven's sake, Kit, can you go no faster?'

Chapter Twenty-Five

Emma was standing in Hugo's bedchamber, staring hopelessly at the empty bed. Hugo was gone. The bed had not been slept in. It was just as before.

She could not bring herself to go near it. She could not touch it. She felt hollow inside. She had given her heart into his keeping, she had trusted him, and he had left her without a word. Where had he gone?

Terrible, wicked thoughts rose in her mind. She did not have the strength to fight them off. He was leaning over the gambling table, staking her fortune on the turn of a card. He was clasped in the arms of a faceless harlot, groaning with pleasure. He was…

Her knees started to buckle. She ought to sit down. The bed was nearer but it repelled her. She stumbled towards the window, holding on to the back of the chair for support. She noted, absently, that the writing table was strewn with papers. How strange. That did not seem like Hugo at all. Her husband was a methodical man. Her husband…

Her husband had left her alone.

She needed to sit down. Just for a moment. Then

she would go back to her own room and prepare to face the day.

With shaking hands, she pulled the chair out a little way and sank gratefully on to it. She leant forward, pushing aside the jumble of papers to make room for her hands. She clasped them together, and closed her eyes. She pulled her knees together to stop them shaking.

There was something on the floor, under her bare foot.

It was a letter. And it was half open.

She bent down to pick it up. It had been clumsily folded, and the wafer had not stuck properly. She started to put it away from her. She could not read someone else's letter.

Her own name shouted up at her from the page.

With white, shaking fingers she spread the crackling paper and began to read. Hugo and Forster. Hugo branded a coward. All those men dead. She could hardly bear to read on. When she came to the end of his explanation, she was suddenly cold with fear. Hugo had gone to fight a duel with Forster. For the sake of a hundred dead men who must now be nothing more than bones. Why? Nothing could bring them back. Why must it be Hugo? The cry screamed through her head. He had gone from her. And he might never return.

She could hardly bring herself to look at the paper again, but she knew there was more. Tears were pouring down her face. She could barely make out the words.

It was difficult to decipher the last few lines. They

must have been written in a great hurry. She wiped her eyes, trying to focus. And then she saw what he had written.

A great sob rose in her throat and burst forth. She crushed the letter to her breast, holding it as if it was the most precious thing she had ever owned. Then she smoothed it out again, desperate to reread those last, loving words. He loved her. And he had gone. At any moment, some servant would knock at the door to bring her the news that he had fallen, dead of a murderer's bullet.

She looked towards the door to the corridor. Silence.

She rose, still clutching the letter, and moved across to the bed. Hugo's blue silk robe lay across it. She reached out, touched it. Then, overcome with the horror of her loss, she seized it and hugged it to her, breathing in his scent.

It was all she had left of him.

A soft knock on the door to the corridor sent a shiver of terror down her spine. She heard a voice say something, but the words did not register. She recognised that voice. It was Hugo's valet, come to tell her. She must be strong. She must not disgrace his memory.

She turned towards the opening door.

'Emma!'

This voice came from behind her, from the door to the sitting room. It sounded like Hugo's voice. But that was impossible, wasn't it?

She turned, saw, and sank to the floor in a dead faint.

Hugo rushed across to catch her, but he was too late. He knelt to take his wife in his arms. She was deathly pale. He was not sure that she was breathing.

His valet seemed to appear from nowhere. 'Sir,' he began, 'I came to see if you wanted—' He broke off at the sight of that white face. 'Shall I fetch madam's abigail?'

'Out!' Hugo cried furiously, raising his eyes from Emma's face for only a second. 'Leave us!'

The valet scuttled for the door.

Hugo pulled Emma into his arms and swung her from the floor. He felt as if he had the strength of ten as he carried her across to his bed and laid her tenderly on top of the covers. His precious wife. She must come back to him. She must forgive him.

He prised his robe from her grasp but, when he tried to take the letter, he could not. She held it fast. How cold she was. He put his hands over hers, willing the warmth from his own body into her freezing fingers. It was not enough. He pulled the covers out from the far side of the bed and wrapped them round her. She was shivering now. And her eyes were still closed.

It was not enough.

He dragged himself out of his coat and tore off the rest of his clothing, ignoring the sound of ripping cloth and popping buttons. Then he slid between the covers and took her in his arms. Still, it was not enough. He slid his hands down her silken wrapper until he found the belt. He pulled it apart and drew her naked body into his, covering her with his limbs. At last, her shivering began to wane.

He put his lips to her ear. 'Emma,' he whispered, 'Emma, my love, my darling, come back to me.' He dropped a tiny kiss on the corner of her jaw. 'Emma—'

Her eyes flickered and closed again. She pushed even closer into his warmth.

'Emma? Emma, speak to me.'

'No,' she said, whispering into his chest. 'I can't. I just want to feel you holding me, to know that you are safe.'

He could feel her tears on his skin. And the stiff paper of his letter was digging into his ribs. He eased it out and threw it on the floor, wondering how it was that she had come to read it. He would ask her. Later.

Her tears seemed to have stopped. She was feathering tiny kisses across his chest. When she reached the long scar, she continued her trail, down towards his belly. The hairs on the back of his neck were standing on end. It was too much. He groaned in dismay as his body began to heat even more. They were much too close. Now was not the time.

He made to put her from him, to leave her to recover from her swoon, but she would not let him go. The moment she felt his withdrawal, she clung to him with more strength than he would have thought possible from such a tiny frame. 'Emma, let me go,' he said gently, trying to remove her fingers from his arm. 'You need to rest now, my love. I will come back later, I promise.'

She lifted her head from his burning skin and fixed him with a stern glare. 'What I need *now*, Hugo Stratton, is you,' she said decisively. He had left her once already this day. She would not permit him to do so again. She lowered her head and began to flick her tongue over his skin, moving slowly down his body. When she reach his navel, he groaned with pleasure. She smiled against his skin and kissed his flat belly.

'Now, Hugo,' she commanded.

'Hugo, are you awake?'

'No.' He gently pulled her closer, so that her back and bottom curved into his body and she could feel his legs caressing her all the way down to her toes. It felt heavenly to be so loved. He had slept with his arm encircling her waist, but now he slid his hand idly down on to her belly. She turned into him, before he could divert her yet again. She had to tell him.

She touched her hand to his new wound. It was not serious, though there would probably be a scar. Another scar. She ran her finger down the silver line on his face, from forehead to chin, then placed her palm gently over his cheek. She had explained about the letter. That was simple. She had apologised for her hot, hurtful words when he came to her in the garden. But there was something more he had to understand, something much more important. 'Hugo, that night in the garden, I—'

'Hush. I know you did not go willingly into Kit's arms.'

'But I did.'

Hugo went very still under her hand.

'I thought it was you.'

The stillness vanished in an instant. Hugo rolled over, taking her with him, so that she lay on her back and he could look down into her beautiful eyes. They were wide and loving and honest as they gazed up into his. 'I don't understand,' he said softly, the question clear in his voice.

'I thought I was alone. I was daydreaming, I suppose. It was such a magical place in the moonlight, so still, so exotic. I was dreaming that the man I loved would appear out of the gloom and sweep me into his arms. And when Kit appeared, I opened my eyes and…it was you I saw. It sounds so strange, now, though you are quite alike, I suppose…'

Hugo stroked her cheek lovingly. 'Mmm?'

'And then he kissed me and, in that moment, I knew it was not you.'

Hugo laughed deep in his throat. 'Kit would be mightily displeased if he ever learned that. He thinks himself the most accomplished of lovers.'

'Oh,' said Emma, blushing. 'I…oh, dear…'

'Do you know, wife,' said Hugo huskily, trailing his fingers down her throat and on to her breast, 'you are quite delightful when you blush. It starts on your throat, here—' he kissed the spot '—and it rises into your cheek, here—' he kissed that spot, too '—but, at the same time, it travels down to—' He began to feather kisses down her neck and on to her breasts, both now thoroughly rosy. 'Whenever I see you blush in company, I shall know that, under your gown, you are blushing too—in places that are reserved for me alone.'

'Hugo,' said Emma in a constricted whisper, 'how can you say such a thing? I shall never dare to look at you in company if that is what you are thinking. I shall do nothing *but* blush.'

'Mmm,' he said teasingly. 'I shall look forward to that.' He eased himself between her thighs and began to kiss her breasts in earnest until she moaned in response. Lifting his head, he said, 'I shall be thinking of things much, much more exciting than mere blushes, my love. And I dare say that—eventually— you will become accustomed.'

She tried to hide her face in his shoulder, but he rolled over on to his back, never letting go of her for a second. He lay back on the pillows and laughed up at her as she tried to push herself out of his embrace. She could not look at him.

'By the bye, wife, I have received a letter—from the Duke.'

'York?' said Emma, turning back to him in horror. His Royal Highness was Forster's patron. And Hugo had just ruined the man.

'No. Wellington,' Hugo said with a grin of triumph. 'He wrote to felicitate me on my marriage. He hopes to make the acquaintance of my lady wife at an early date.'

'But he already knows me,' protested Emma 'He has met me on several occasions.'

'Ah, but he has not met Mrs Stratton, my love. You forget, perhaps, about the Duke's reputation with the ladies. You may have been safe from him when you were an innocent young débutante, but now that you are married, he will consider you fair game.'

Emma eyed him suspiciously. 'And will you challenge him to a duel, too?'

'That depends,' he said, trailing his fingers round the top of her arm and then down to rest on the underside of her delicate breast. 'Were you planning to give me cause?'

Two could play at that game, Emma decided, trying to ignore the way her breast was settling heavily into his hand. She poised the tips of her fingers around his nipple and squeezed, just a fraction, so that her fingernails tightened into his taut flesh. His intake of breath was satisfyingly sharp.

'Not immediately,' she said.

Epilogue

Jamie looked up at Emma with eyes shining with happiness, in spite of her obvious exhaustion. 'Are they not beautiful, Emma?' she said.

Emma shook her head in wonderment at the two tiny babies cradled in their mother's arms. She knew she had witnessed a miracle. She felt very close to tears. 'They are, indeed. Truly beautiful, Jamie. Richard will be so proud of you.'

At that moment, the bedroom door was thrust open to admit Richard, followed by the Dowager, and the nursemaid. Emma was decidedly *de trop*. With a softly murmured 'congratulations' to Richard, she quietly left the room and made her way downstairs to the garden.

Hugo was pacing up and down on the terrace, for all the world like the expectant father. He turned at the sound of the opening door. 'Emma! What has happened? The servant could not say.'

Emma smiled joyfully at him and saw the strain disappear from his face in a moment. 'Richard has a son. And a daughter. And Jamie is very well. I am no longer needed.'

Hugo inspected his wife for signs of fatigue. She had not left Jamie's side since labour had begun, hours and hours ago. And there was a smear of blood on the side of her gown, where the apron had failed to protect her. He put a sustaining arm around her waist and pulled her close.

'Are you very tired, my love?' he asked.

'A little, I admit, but nothing compared with Jamie. She was wonderful. So brave.' Emma remembered Jamie's hours of pain. It had been frightening at first, but Jamie had never complained. In a moment of calm, she had taken Emma's hand and told her that she did not mind the pain, for each spasm brought her nearer to the moment of birth. And now that Emma had seen that miracle with her own eyes, she had begun to understand.

'Poor Richard was wearing a track on the flags,' Hugo said. 'And he was cracking his knuckles incessantly all the while, too. I've never seen him do that before. When I mentioned it to him, he had no idea what I was talking about. He looked at me as if I were quite mad.' Hugo shook his head, laughing. 'I might have expected such a reaction in a first-time father, perhaps, but he's done it before—'

'Not with twins, Hugo. That was always going to be more difficult for Jamie. You must see that?'

Hugo led her across the terrace and down on to the lawn before he answered. 'I do not seek to make light of the matter, believe me,' he said, seriously. 'The problem is, we men feel quite helpless at times like this. I know that Richard longed for another child, but his first thought was always for Jamie. I hate to think what he would have done if—'

Emma put a finger across his lips. 'Hush,' she said softly. 'Do not say it. Everything is well.'

They strolled across the lawn in companionable silence until they reached the ancestral oak.

Emma looked up into its branches. Autumn was late. The leaves had not yet begun to turn.

'You know, when I was a child, I probably climbed this oak as often as I climbed my own. If I sat very still, the birds would sometimes start to sing again, forgetting I was there. I used to watch the sunset through the branches and conjure up a magical, musical kingdom where everyone obeyed my slightest command.'

Hugo laughed. 'You always were a little madam, or so Richard told me in his letters.' He bent and kissed her, slowly and thoroughly. When he raised his head again, her skin was pink and her eyes were glowing with love.

'That reminds me,' he said with a sly smile. 'A letter arrived this afternoon, from Kit.' He reached into his pocket and drew out the folded sheets.

'May I read it?' Emma asked, stretching out her hand.

He flung his hand high above her head, taking the letter well out of reach. 'Absolutely not,' he said, with mock severity. 'Think of how your delicate sensibilities might be outraged by what he has to say about his…er…adventures. It did not take him long to tire of the delights of Paris. He has been in Vienna these last four weeks. And it seems he is already…er…making his mark.'

Emma looked quizzically up at him.

'It appears that the ladies of the Austrian court are quite as dazzling as any to be found in London, or Paris. And—' he opened the letter to remind himself of its exact contents '—rather more amenable, according to Kit.' He refolded the letter and restored it to his pocket. 'More than that, I dare not tell you. Kit's letters shall be treated like mine to Richard— fit for a lady's ears only if savagely censored.'

Emma leant into his warm, strong body, tilting her head back against his shoulder so that she could look up into his face. He smiled down at her. The scar was a thin silver line now. It made his smile a little twisted on one side, but she had long ago decided that it was an endearing mismatch. Hugo's face was full of character when he smiled—especially when he smiled at his wife as he did now.

'What are you thinking, my love?' Hugo said quietly, starting to run his free hand delicately up and down her spine.

She shivered in response. She could see in his eyes that he was deliberately trying to arouse her. They would have to go inside soon or else—

'Mmm?' said Hugo, fixing his eyes hungrily on her mouth.

'I was thinking, sir, that though Kit is a rake and may never be redeemed, his elder brother is but little better.'

'Indeed?' Hugo was trying to sound severe, but the mischievous glint in his eyes gave him away.

'Indeed, sir. A few years abroad may do wonders for a young man like Kit, but you, at your age—I fear you are beyond redemption.'

'I see,' said Hugo, beginning to nuzzle Emma's neck. 'Well, in that case...'

Emma felt the familiar thrills running through her body, making her belly heat and her skin yearn for his touch. The months of marriage had made no difference at all to Hugo's effect on her, except perhaps to make the feelings, and the pleasure, more intense.

'Hugo, may we not go inside?'

He laughed against her skin but went on planting those tantalising little kisses on her neck, exactly where he knew they would create havoc with her senses.

'Hugo, you wretch! Think who may be watching.'

'No one, my love. They are all concentrating on the new arrivals. Nobody would notice if I took you round behind this ancient oak and—'

'Don't you dare, Hugo Stratton!' Emma exclaimed. 'I declare, you are quite as bad as that brother of yours. You take a woman in your arms, and—'

'And if that woman is my beautiful wife, I am lost.' He drew her back towards the house. 'But I admit that a feather bed is rather more comfortable than this damp lawn.'

When they reached the terrace, still walking arm in arm, a tiny wail broke the silence. 'Ah,' said Hugo, 'I hear the sound of a godchild.'

'Hugo! Has Richard asked you to stand as godfather?'

Hugo nodded. 'I think he believes I am in need of a little practice,' he said teasingly. 'He says that I was excused on the last occasion only because I was dead.'

Emma giggled. 'You, sir, are quite preposterous.' She paused. 'On the other hand...Richard is quite right. You do need the practice.'

'Emma?'

She hid her face in his waistcoat, feeling unaccountably shy. At last she said, so low that he could barely make out the words, 'You will have a few months to practise, Hugo, but only a very few, I'm afraid.'

'Emma! For heaven's sake, tell me!'

'You will be a father, too, Hugo. In the spring, I think.'

Hugo gave a soft whoop and lifted her off her feet, whirling her round and round until she was quite dizzy and breathless.

'Hugo, put me down.'

'No—why? I have you, and I mean to keep you, my darling, wonderful wife.'

Emma ran her hand over his dark shining hair. 'I have no intention of trying to escape,' she said softly, offering her lips for his kiss. 'My one, my only love.'

*   *   *   *   *

From Regency romps to mesmerizing Medievals, savor these stirring tales from Harlequin Historicals®

On sale January 2004

THE KNAVE AND THE MAIDEN by Blythe Gifford

A cynical knight's life is forever changed when he falls in love with a naive young woman while journeying to a holy shrine.

MARRYING THE MAJOR by Joanna Maitland

Can a war hero wounded in body and spirit find happiness with his childhood sweetheart, now that she has become the toast of London society?

On sale February 2004

THE CHAPERON BRIDE by Nicola Cornick

When England's most notorious rake is attracted to a proper ladies' chaperon, could it be true love?

THE WEDDING KNIGHT by Joanne Rock

A dashing knight abducts a young woman to marry his brother, but soon falls in love with her instead!

PICK UP THESE HARLEQUIN HISTORICALS AND IMMERSE YOURSELF IN THRILLING AND EMOTIONAL LOVE STORIES SET IN THE AMERICAN FRONTIER

On sale January 2004

CHEYENNE WIFE by Judith Stacy
(Colorado, 1844)

Will opposites attract when a handsome
half-Cheyenne horse trader comes to the rescue
of a proper young lady from back east?

WHIRLWIND BRIDE by Debra Cowan
(Texas, 1883)

A widowed rancher unexpectedly falls in love with
a beautiful and pregnant young woman.

On sale February 2004

COLORADO COURTSHIP by Carolyn Davidson
(Colorado, 1862)

A young widow finds a father for her unborn child—
and a man for her heart—in a loving wagon train scout.

THE LIGHTKEEPER'S WOMAN by Mary Burton
(North Carolina, 1879)

When an heiress reunites with her former fiancée,
will they rekindle their romance or say goodbye
once and for all?

Visit us at www.eHarlequin.com

HARLEQUIN HISTORICALS®

LUNA is a brand-new imprint
dedicated to bringing
readers powerful, gifted
and magical women living
in fantastical worlds.
These wonderful worlds
and spirited characters
will be written by fantasy
fiction's top authors, as well
as many new and fresh voices.

LUNA

Launch book from
fantasy legend

Mercedes
Lackey

January 2004

Available now
wherever hardcover
books are sold.

Visit www.luna-books.com.

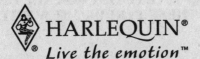

COMING NEXT MONTH FROM

HARLEQUIN HISTORICALS®

- **COLORADO COURTSHIP**
  by **Carolyn Davidson,** the second of three historicals in the *Colorado Confidential* series
  Jessica Beaumont's husband had cheated Finley Carson's brother ou
  of a land claim and killed him. Now a pregnant widow, Jessica need
  ed to marry…and her only choice was Finn!
  HH #691 ISBN# 29291-0 $5.25 U.S./$6.25 CAN.

- **THE CHAPERON BRIDE**
  by **Nicola Cornick,** author of THE EARL'S PRIZE
  Lady Annis Wycherley might have been feisty, but she was
  a chaperon and her reputation was first-class. Rakes and romance
  were strictly off-limits…especially the likes of Lord Adam Ashwick
  who seemed all too intent on seducing her.…
  HH #692 ISBN# 29292-9 $5.25 U.S./$6.25 CAN.

- **THE LIGHTKEEPER'S WOMAN**
  by **Mary Burton,** author of RAFFERTY'S BRIDE
  After her father's death, heiress Alanna Patterson sought out
  Caleb Pitt, her former fiancé, to determine if their love was still
  alive. What she found instead was a broken man who had never for-
  given her. Would they find their way back to each other or say goodbye once and for all?
  HH #693 ISBN# 29293-7 $5.25 U.S./$6.25 CAN.

- **THE WEDDING KNIGHT**
  by **Joanne Rock,** Harlequin Historical debut
  When knight Lucian Barret abducted Melissande Deverell from
  a convent, he never expected the sizzling attraction he felt for the
  woman he intended to be his younger brother's bride. But would
  a secret from Barret's past be an insurmountable obstacle to their
  love…?
  HH #694 ISBN# 29294-5 $5.25 U.S./$6.25 CAN.

KEEP AN EYE OUT FOR ALL FOUR OF THESE TERRIFIC NEW TITLES